HOOKED ON HOLLYWOOD

Big Star, Small town

MIA SUMMERS

STERLING & STONE

ONE

Olivia

THE MORNING MIST kissed my face as I made a right onto Hollyhock Drive. The passel of yipping chihuahuas and playful pugs in front of me were surprisingly compliant, even if they were also wildly jostling my arms.

When I lived in Los Angeles — back when Taylor and I were pretending to be a happy couple and he was pretending to be a faithful fiancé — I was the top-rated dog walker on HoundHub. We were supposed to settle down together. Then he told me the only settling that was happening was that he was settling for me. "Old Reliable," he called me.

Like I was a diesel truck. The vehicle he could count on when his sports car was in the shop. When I came home early from a dog walking gig and found him servicing a slender Miata with its top down, I packed my reliable butt up and left.

Now I was home.

Living in my mom's house.

Eating my mom's food.

And still walking dogs. It seemed only natural for me to

take that duty over for my mom. At least until I found something else. Unfortunately, "awesome ice cream maker" wasn't a job.

Was my original move to LA totally delusional?

Probably.

Delusional — and a mistake.

I loved Ocean Springs. Having been lucky enough to grow up in this small town, I should have known better than to expect that I could find perfection like this anywhere else.

Nestled between whispers of the sea and the embrace of towering evergreens, my neighborhood street was even more charming than the rest of town. Every street looked like another love letter from a bygone era. Victorian homes adorned with ornate gingerbread trim standing side by side, most with flourishing gardens full of blossoming flowers out front that flooded the air with a lingering perfume.

Henry started barking, and then of course Fisher instantly joined him.

"Quiet!" I yelled. If the two of them got going, then the other five dogs would chime in with their own opinions. I continued my stroll through town on the way to meet up with my best friend, Madison, and her adorable new baby, Kai. Seeing his little feet kicking with excitement and his tiny brown eyes sparkling with curiosity were yet another thing to appreciate about Ocean Springs.

Because this was the best place for me.

And yes, that was the second (third? fourth?) time I had told myself that in the last five minutes, but it was a reminder I constantly needed. Like a hug in my head reminding me that what happened in Los Angeles was a good thing, because otherwise, I would have ended up as Old Reliable to a mechanic who wanted to spend time under every sports car in a ten-mile radius. Including my best friend.

My Los Angeles best friend.

Make that former best friend. Whom I never should have trusted in the first place.

Especially not when I already had Madison. Here in Ocean Springs.

I was Rapunzel, and Ocean Springs was my tower. Only unlike actual Rapunzel, who left her tower and had a musical adventure that ended in her finding her true love (and getting a killer haircut), my journey to the outside world had shown me nothing but heartbreak. So I retreated back to my tower, and there I would stay.

My tower — Ocean Springs — was picturesque. Beyond adorable with Victorian-style homes perched on steep, wooded hillsides, with breathtaking views of the ocean. The mini burg was a bustling trading post for furs and pelts and timber before its storied past full of exploration and industry surrendered to the years. It was now a bustling waterfront lined with docks, shops, and eateries that offered a taste of the sea, with fresh seafood being a local specialty.

After living in the Los Angeles smog for the last few years, I was glad to be back near so many forests, without having to be far from the beach.

Ocean Springs, I told myself for the umpteenth time that morning, was the best possible place on the planet for me right now. The only place on the planet for me now.

And maybe forever.

"You look happy this morning," Madison said as she walked up to me, pushing Kai in her stroller. "Do we still have time to go to the boardwalk?"

"Of course we're going to the boardwalk." We always went to the boardwalk, because even though I never ate fried dough, the smell at the Donut Dock made my mouth water in the best way. The dogs liked it, too.

"Are you any further ahead in your plans to get back to LA?" Madison asked, surprising me not at all.

"You mean, your plans for my moving back to LA. I'm staying in Ocean Springs forever."

"You can't stay here forever, Olivia. You're my best friend, and I would love for you to live walking distance away from me more than anything. But we both know that this isn't where you belong."

"You do keep saying that."

"Because it's true," Madison said.

"I don't belong in Los Angeles. I never belonged there."

"You said that you were coming home to Ocean Springs because you needed a couple of months to recover—"

"The operative word being 'home.'"

"—but a couple of months has turned into—"

"Nine. I know, Madison."

"So, do you have a plan? Because you can't keep living in your childhood bedroom and working part time as a barista for the rest of your life."

Madison could be harsh, but she was also my biggest cheerleader. So I didn't take her misguided tough love personally.

"I know. But that doesn't mean that I have to move back to LA. I'm still sorting things out and saving money for my business venture."

"That will sound a lot more real if you give the idea a name, but then I guess you would need an actual idea."

"I have plenty of ideas." Not that I wanted to say any of them out loud. "I'm going to open a business, and it will be even better than the one that — what? Why are you making that face?" And then when she didn't respond, "Tell me, Madison."

"Well, speaking of your business ventures, I did see you-know-who's social media post about Book Bean—"

"Oh that. I know. I already saw it when Taylor posted this morning. Whatever. To heck with him."

"To heck with him? Really?" Madison said. "Kai is still sleeping, so you can say all the bad words if you want to."

"I'm not saying any bad words around the baby."

"Just let it out."

"No way. I will not be the person who accidentally teaches your child his first swear word."

"You have to be."

"What? Why?"

"Because if you don't teach him his first swear word, then we both know it's going to be me who slips up. And my mother-in-law would just looooove that. Every family dinner from now until the end of time she'll be all like 'did you teach him any new bad words?' It's bad enough I have to suffer through her desert-dry turkey and watery gravy. I can't stomach the condescension, too."

I paused. "Maybe you're the one who needs to say bad words this morning."

"Maybe. But we're on you right now. So... Book Bean?"

Madison waited. Because of course, more was coming.

I had no other choice, even though my best friend had heard it all before. "Book Bean was my idea — a coffee-library where you could sign out small packets of coffee beans, with flavors you weren't sure about trying and maybe didn't want to buy in a full bag..."

"I know, honey..."

"Taylor stole my idea!"

"Yes, he did." Madison nodded along with me.

"And he opened what should have been our coffee shop with my maid of honor after I caught him cheating on me! You're a lawyer. Can't you sue him or something?"

"What would I sue him for?"

"Fraud?"

Madison laughed. "No, I can't just sue him for fraud. That's not how the law works. But everything else you said is true, and we don't even have to talk about the fact that I should have been your maid of honor."

"How many times do I have to tell you that I'm sorry about that?" Every time Madison brought it up, I felt even worse about it than I had the last time, which was obviously why she kept doing it. Not because she was mean, but because she was mischievous, like a cat batting at its favorite ball of yarn.

Madison was great at the tough-love love, her way of trying to break me out of the pity parties I sometimes threw for myself. And a friendly spat sure felt safer than the fury I still felt over Taylor.

"And how many times do I have to tell you that I'm fine with it? Really and truly, the situation has been aptly explained."

"Then why bring it up all the time?" I asked.

"It's hardly all the time." She laughed. "And I was just trying to change the subject."

We passed the local theater. Giant movie-style posters were plastered all around the theater, far more than for any other production that I had ever seen in Ocean Springs.

Cops and Robbers Night, starring Ryan Jones.

The actor was tall and athletic, with striking blue eyes and a chiseled jawline. Short cropped sandy brown hair and an expression that made him look somehow both heroic and brooding.

Lydia and her merry band of theater supporters were

hoping that the subsequent silent auction would bring in enough money to pay off the theater's rather substantial and still escalating debts.

Madison pointed to an especially obnoxious poster with a mugging Ryan as they passed the theater. "You should buy a ticket."

"Why would I buy a ticket?" I knew exactly why I should buy a ticket, and where this conversation would be going.

But I wasn't fast enough to think my way out of it.

"Ryan Jones is coming!" Madison trumpeted, as if the abundance of posters had not already made that perfectly clear.

Yes, Ryan Jones.

I knew all about Ryan Jones.

He used to be my favorite actor.

We were the same age at twenty-four, but the young (and absurdly famous) thespian had lived three lifetimes, or so it seemed already, according to the multiple spreads in various magazines, most of them of which I had read, and my favorite among them being a rather flattering piece in *Entertainment Weekly* where the writer said that Ryan "displayed a rare ability to meld physicality with emotional depth."

Even only after a few years of working, his commitment to the craft was considered impressive in the industry, despite the recent kerfuffle that proved the actor was also a total jerk, and the only real reason that I ever liked him (I was pretty sure about this) was because we had once dated in fourth grade.

And by dated, I mean we attended a school-sponsored sock hop together.

These days, I had zero tolerance for the man who had clearly climbed all the way up his own butt. I would never like or respect him again, not after I saw that viral video of him yelling at a director.

It was awful. And it got worse each of the seven times I had watched it, all in a row, me liking Ryan Jones less and less and less by the viewing. Every time I heard the string of curse words coming out of Ryan's mouth, he looked more and more like the egotistical jerk I always feared Hollywood would turn him into. That poor director.

So maybe I never really even liked him at all.

Maybe it was just the sock hop and the good feeling that I had known someone famous in real life.

"You don't seem that interested," Madison opined.

The last thing I wanted to do was to explain the whole video thing.

"I'm just distracted," I said. "There's a lot going on right now, and I'm having a hard time focusing—"

Madison cut me off with a laugh. "Who do you think you're talking to? You have absolutely nothing going on in your life."

She laughed again so that my feelings wouldn't be hurt.

Not that there was any chance of that. I knew my bestie (who really should have been my maid of honor) didn't have a molecule of ill will for me inside her.

Besides, I liked that I had absolutely nothing going on right now.

So I laughed along with her. "I'm not going to this benefit. Maybe next time."

"I bet—"

Madison never got to finish her thought, because three of my seven dogs started to whine all at once, which was the number needed to get the other four going. Kai woke up and started crying.

"Looks like we both need to go," said Madison.

I nodded. "Indeed."

With seven dogs to drop off and less than an hour to go before my shift at The Family Table, I was running plenty behind.

"Thanks for walking with me," I said.

"I love our walks, even when you're late, and we can't go to the boardwalk like you said we would." Madison laughed. "See you before the benefit?"

"See you then," I said, forcing a smile I didn't feel. The last thing I wanted in my life was to go anywhere that Ryan Jones would be.

TWO

Ryan

"I'м sick of being a Hollywood heartthrob," I said, cringing at how ridiculous the words sounded now that I'd made the mistake of letting them escape my mouth.

"You're sick of being rich and famous?" My manager, Maggie, started furiously opening desk drawers.

"What are you doing?"

"Looking for a tiny violin." She slammed the drawers shut. "You don't get to be sick of your career. Who do you think you are? Leo?"

But I was sick of being a Hollywood heartthrob.

The relentless flash of paparazzi cameras.

The forced smiles with autograph seekers when they interrupted family dinners.

Every unflattering angle of my face plastered on tabloids, Photoshopped to give me a double chin, extra acne, and a brain-dead stare. Every mistake I made was blown up. I was tired of walking on eggshells.

I only had a month in between wrapping my last film, *Cold Fury*, and starting my next one, *Barcelona Mosaic*. The two movies had little in common, other than that they both took place in Europe. When I booked the part, I could not have been more excited to fly back to Spain.

But now?

The thought filled me with anxiety, thanks to the paparazzi and an unfortunate video of me yelling at the director of my last film. When you were a public figure, it was always your worst moments that went viral.

Admittedly, the video had caught me at my worst, but it wasn't like André hadn't been begging for someone to start yelling at him for the first five weeks of that excruciating shoot.

After what he did, that jerk deserved every vitriolic word that he got.

Problem was, André barely got anything, while I ended up with a lot more than a slap on my wrist. I still have no idea who on the set had the audacity to shoot that video, let alone release it, but I had everyone and their sister suddenly breathing down my back just hours after it was leaked.

Maggie stood at the other side of the desk and let out a long sigh. She had a stature not an inch over five foot one, but she was a diminutive dynamo, with her presence like a Hollywood marquee. A cascade of midnight black hair framed a face adorned with large round glasses, through which her eyes sparkled like the diamonds she loved to buy.

Not that Maggie didn't work hard for her money. She might have been the hardest working person I had ever met, and her office was a testimony to that reality. The room was an oasis of elegance and success. Polished mahogany danced with the city lights filtering through floor-to-ceiling windows, each beam illuminating signed headshots and glinting off her golden awards. The room crowed with her countless successes, framed by walls adorned with blockbuster posters. Plush leather chairs nestled next to a glass coffee table where she had sealed deals over shared smiles and the clinking of glasses. A few family photos rested on a table full of fresh flowers, but most of the photographs in Maggie's office were of people who had graced the covers of countless magazines.

"You need to understand the situation you're in," she said.

"I do."

"Do you? Sit."

Maggie was a bully, but I loved it when she was playing attack dog on my behalf, and I was pretty sure that she had somehow strong-armed the studio into not canceling *Barcelona Mosaic* on the assurances that she could rehabilitate my image before the movie needed promotion.

So I was being a good boy and listening to every word she said.

"We're not going to get anywhere with this situation until you can finally start accepting responsibility for what happened," Maggie said. "You lost all of your emotional fitness, Ryan. And the world got to see it. You love it when they see your volatile emotions scripted for their entertainment. Now you have to deal with people being entertained by your unscripted emotions."

Harsh words, but Maggie was right.

"What can I do for you?" I asked.

"I just wanted to confirm that you're still planning to go through with your weekend plans."

"I appreciate you keeping the words 'ill-conceived' out of your question this time."

"Are you still going to this thing or not?"

"Nothing has changed on my end. Also, this sounds an awful lot like a question that could have been asked in a phone call. Or a text. Maybe an email."

She shook her head. "I don't understand why you would want to go back to that place."

"Ocean Springs is where I grew up."

"I went to a small town once to get gas. It felt like it took a year. Never again." She shuddered.

"Where did you grow up? I want to say insulting things about the place that made you."

"I grew up in San Diego. Gorgeous beaches, fabulous weather, and only a few Angelenos. San Diego is my home, Los Angeles is my slum, and anything smaller than that is too boring to mention. Now, tell me again why you're doing this?"

"It's complicated."

Maggie sighed. "You actors are like designer handbags: expensive, high-maintenance, and everyone wants one until the next season's option comes along. But whatever, I guess."

"Is that it?" I asked.

"When it comes to you keeping the mystery all to yourself? Sure, I can scratch that right off my to-care about list. But I would also like to talk about our strategy for the weekend."

"Do we really need a strategy for this weekend?"

"I know that you're only toying with my emotions by pretending that we don't need a strategy for everything, especially now, after your little blow up last—"

"It has been well established what happened last month. Repeatedly and literally every single time we talk. So again: I am sorry for what happened, and I will continue to do whatever it is that you need me to do so that everyone stops being unfairly mad at me. Can we stop bringing it up now?"

"As soon as you stop using the word 'unfairly.' Even around me. You need to accept responsibility for what happened with André, or the boys and girls with the big bucks won't want to hire you. Got it?"

"I'm fine if the boys and girls with the small bucks want to—"

"Got it?"

"Got it," I agreed with my words, but not my spirit. "So what's the plan?"

"I want to play up the small-town angle. Boy becomes big screen actor — goes home to save the small theater where he learned to act. So—"

I stopped Maggie with a shake of my head.

"What?" she asked. "What's not to love about that?"

"It's way too obvious. Everyone will know that I'm doing this to scrub my image." And then to really drive it home, "It's pandering."

"Publicity, pandering, who's to say what the difference is. No one will judge you for it."

"Some people will judge me," I argued.

"More will judge you for not playing the game."

I hated that she had a point. "I really hate this."

"And I hate that you nuked your own career, but here we stand. I'm working for you here, because I know what you want out of your career, even if that's like twenty percent of what it could be."

"You're talking money, right?" I asked.

"Of course I'm talking money." Maggie returned to her plan. "I suggest that we don't do a press release. We can leak it to the paparazzi that you've gone home with your tail tucked between your legs. Then it will be a big reveal when everyone sees that you've actually gone home to do this incredibly selfless thing."

"Why does everything always have to be a lie in this business?"

"I don't even know how to answer that question." Maggie laughed with a shake of her head. "Darling, you're an actor; you make a living pretending to be someone else. Lies are your ply and trade; it's just about spinning the right ones. When we sell the right illusions, people love us for it."

"It's not the same."

"You keep telling yourself that, Ryan. But act annoyed when the press finds out about—"

"That won't be acting."

"Great. Then we agree."

"That is an awfully liberal use of that word."

"Come on, Ryan. This is PR gold, and you know it."

"I'm agreeing to do it, Maggie, but that doesn't mean I have to like it."

"It's going to be great."

"Better than you realize," I said.

"What's that supposed to mean?"

"I got Lucas Stone to participate. He's coming to emcee the night."

"Seriously?"

"Seriously. But all he knows is that it's a cops and robbers themed party. And that he'll be performing in a one-act play."

"The press is going to eat this up." Maggie was delighted.

Even her joy was exhausting.

I sighed as my phone buzzed.

I pulled it out of my pocket and looked at the screen. Lydia, sending me an update: *We've sold a lot of tickets, but we're still far away from our target. So I set up a 'celebrity auction' after dinner. With you of course. To the highest bidder. I hope you don't mind!*

"What's that look on your face?" Maggie asked.

I sighed again. "It looks like I am going to be auctioned off after dinner."

Maggie made a face. "Oh, that sounds very 1977. Has fashion made it to the '80s yet in Ocean Springs?"

"You're such an elitist."

"Maybe, but even an elitist can recognize when something's stuck in the past."

I felt so suddenly far away from the heights where I had been living just one-half of a movie shoot ago. "This isn't something I want to do. It's something I have to do."

Maggie said, "You tell me no all the time, so what makes this something you have to do?"

"It's hard to explain."

"A lot of things seem hard to explain for you this morning."

"It's all the same thing."

"You have nothing to worry about. I'll be there with you."

"How does that help me?"

"I'll simply buy you at the auction for however much you go for, and then you can reimburse me after the fact."

"That's actually a great idea."

"I'm full of them. And when you listen to me, they work."

"Are you flying out with Lucas then?"

"No." Maggie shook her head. "Whatever time Lucas is flying out, I'm sure that I'll be going later. I have a day full of meetings that I can't get out of, but don't worry, only one of them has anything to do with damage control for you."

"I wasn't worried."

"I promise that I'll be there in time."

"Great. Thank you. Am I dismissed?"

Maggie laughed. "You're dismissed."

I nodded as I stood, texting Lydia on my way into the hallway: *Sounds great. Super excited. Can't wait to see you tomorrow!*

I exhaled on the other side of Maggie's office door.

Now that I was out of there, I could finally look forward to getting out of Hollywood and going back to Ocean Springs for a deep breath of fresh air.

Home for a spell.

THREE

Olivia

THE AFTERNOON CREEPED ALONG, and as it did, the sinking feeling in my stomach got worse. Ryan Jones had been a fantasy of mine — which was easy to figure out when you saw his movie posters tacked to the walls of my childhood bedroom. He was the hometown boy who made good, and though he'd dated a lot — and I mean A LOT — he always came off like a good guy. Maybe a little shy, even.

Until that video had come out.

A month ago, if someone told me Ryan Jones was coming back to town, I would've been the first in line to meet him.

But now, just the idea of being in the same room with him made me sick. I didn't need any more reminders that even the man of your dreams could turn out to be a nightmare.

I was just about to text my friends and tell them I was feeling too sick to go to the benefit when I heard the doorbell ring.

Moments later, Mom called out, "Olivia, I'm sure it's for you."

I ran down the stairs and looked through the peephole, not exactly surprised to see Madison with Brooklyn and Ashleigh standing on either side of her.

I opened the door. "Since when do you guys use the doorbell?"

"Since I barged in on your mom baking naked," Madison muttered, grimacing.

I winced. "Sorry. She thinks her skin looks healthier when she air-dries."

"I just wish I hadn't caught when she was using the blow-dryer," Madison said.

"She had her leg up on the counter," Brooklyn added.

"Thanks for that," Madison said, clearly desperate to shake the image from her head. "We have something more important to talk about. Like my most recent shopping trip. Check it out!"

She held a large bag in each hand, but my x-ray vision wasn't working, so I couldn't see inside them.

"Let me guess. Your big bag is full of much smaller bags." I opened the door all the way to let my friends inside.

"Living room or your bedroom?" Madison asked.

"Definitely my bedroom. Unless you want my mom to come in and start offering you jeans from when I was a little girl."

"How little?" Brooklyn wanted to know.

"Too little," I told her as I started toward the stairs.

A minute later, the four of us were crowded on my bed as Madison emptied her two bags of what were apparently costumes onto my comforter.

"Cops and robbers," Madison explained.

Not that I needed her explanation. The costumes were perfectly obvious at less than a glance. The police officer was dressed to uphold the law with a flirtatious twist, a tailored, figure-hugging police uniform with handcuffs and a badge, both of them plastic.

"Wow, it's the only police uniform that could break the law," I said.

"I'm ready to patrol the party!" Brooklyn grabbed the officer costume and held it up to her body. "I hope it comes with a license to thrill, because I'm writing citations all night."

The girls laughed, and I begrudgingly laughed along with them, even though I wished I could say to hell with cops and robbers, and Ryan Jones.

Then Madison took out the robber costume.

Ashleigh said, "With a sleek, form-fitting black outfit complemented by a mysterious eye mask and a swag bag prop, the wearer of this costume is set to steal all the party's attention."

We started laughing again.

But then I shook my head and said, "No."

"What do you mean, no?" Madison asked.

"I could say it in a bunch of different languages, but it usually sounds the same. No."

"You're not allowed to say no," Brooklyn informed me, because she could sometimes be too much.

"And I let you leave work early the other day," Ashleigh said. She'd let me off my waitressing shift an hour before close because the place was dead. "You owe me."

"I thought you were being nice."

"I was being nice. With conditions." Ashleigh smiled hopefully.

"Is it being nice if there are conditions?"

"Would you prefer for me to be mean without conditions?" Ashleigh's smile widened, and she gently grabbed my wrists. "I also made sure not to schedule either of us tonight so that we could go to the fundraiser. Half the town is going to be there."

"Slobbering over Mr. Hollywood."

"Like you don't want to slobber all over Mr. Hollywood," Madison said, nodding towards the nearest bedroom wall, which was, of course, covered in posters of Ryan Jones. I'd have to take those down, soon. And maybe burn them.

Brooklyn sighed. "We all know you'll eventually agree to go out with us and have a good time. So why not get to the good part right now and skip all the moaning?"

"Usually the good part and the moaning are related," Madison said.

Brooklyn rolled her eyes. "I'll get started on your hair and makeup."

I shook my head. "I'm being stubborn about this. And you've all said that you love my stubbornness."

My friends blinked, exchanged glances, then burst into laughter.

"We like when you're determined," Madison said.

"Same thing."

"Determined is climbing a mountain in sneakers. But stubborn is doing it in high heels," Brooklyn said.

"Fine," I finally relented.

But my friends were right, because just a few minutes into Brooklyn doing my hair and makeup, I started to feel better, more like going out, sharing memories on my bed. Until the remembrances turned to Ryan, at which point I wanted to leap out my bedroom window.

"I don't remember him at all," Ashleigh said.

"That's probably because Olivia was hogging all the memories." Madison laughed.

"That doesn't even make sense," I said.

"How's that?" Brooklyn asked, finished with my hair.

"Olivia was in love with Ryan Jones," Madison finked on me. "Like she wanted to have all of his babies and get matching tattoos of each other's faces and travel the world in a van covered with photos of their favorite moments with each other—"

"Literally none of that is true." I turned to Brooklyn. "My hair looks great. Thank you."

"Totally in love with him," Madison said as if I hadn't interrupted at all.

"I was not in love with him. I danced with him in the fourth grade at the sock hop because no one else would."

Brooklyn shrugged. "I'm actually surprised he became an actor."

"Me too," said Brooklyn and Ashleigh in unison.

"Why?" I asked. "He was always so expressive."

Not that I cared or wanted to admit that I thought of Ryan Jones as expressive.

"He, like, never talked," Madison explained.

"Like, ever," Brooklyn added.

"These don't look as slutty as I thought they would," Ashleigh said, looking at all four of us dressed as cops and robbers — she and Brooklyn were both bad guys, while me and Madison were playing girls in blue.

"Do you want to look slutty?" Brooklyn asked.

"I don't know." Ashleigh shrugged. "Maybe tonight."

We all laughed, and by the time Madison was driving us all to the theater, I was actually looking forward to the evening. It would be fun. I was out with my girls, back home in Ocean Springs where I belonged, and the odds that I would actually run into Ryan were slim to none.

Even if I did, of course Ryan Jones wouldn't remember me.

Why would he? I read all the rumors and was more versed in his many supposed trysts than I should be. I wished I was more ignorant on the subject, instead of a reluctant scholar on his dalliances.

"How many A-list actresses do you think Ryan has slept with?" Brooklyn asked.

"All of them," Madison and Ashleigh answered in unison.

Then they both started laughing together.

I didn't want to play their reindeer games.

But Madison wasn't about to let me out of it. "How about you, Olivia? What do you think?"

"I definitely don't think about who Ryan is sleeping with. Like, not ever."

"Liar!" my friends all shouted as Madison pulled up to the theater.

It seemed like the entire town was there. Not surprising, given Ocean Springs' hometown hero was in attendance. Still, the sight made it all feel like a scene I did not want to be a part of.

"This looks like fun," Brooklyn said.

"Like a party that's been waiting for us," added Madison.

"See? Aren't you glad I let you off work early?" Ashleigh asked.

"It looks like a zoo," I replied.

"Check it out." Brooklyn pointed as Madison rounded the corner and the front of the theater came into view, thronged by paparazzi that hadn't been visible on the other side in front of all the crowds.

"Wow," I said. "That's a lot of cameras."

"I bet this is the most reporters that have ever been in Ocean Springs at one time before," Ashleigh said.

"Nope," Brooklyn shook her head. "There was a time when that squirrel was seen in the park wearing a tiny top hat and bow tie."

"His name was Sir Nuttersworth," I reminded them. "Now can we get this over with?"

Ashleigh said, "Olivia is the grumpiest slutty robber I have ever met."

"And how many slutty rubbers have you met?" I asked.

We all got out of the car, laughing, and started toward the theater.

It was just like I would have imagined for the paparazzi to be in real life, with all the cameras flashing, and even the wide-open space felt suddenly claustrophobic. They swarmed outside the little theater like a hive of restless bees, all jostling for position, lenses glinting and cameras flashing.

"I can't imagine being stalked by cameras all the time like that," Olivia said. "It must be a constant nightmare."

"Are you kidding?" Ashleigh scoffed. "I would love that."

"No, you wouldn't." Madison shook her head. "I mean, you might love it for a hot minute, but then it would get boring."

"I bet Ryan probably called the paparazzi himself," I said.

"Cynical much?" Brooklyn laughed.

Then everyone else laughed along with her.

I managed a smile, but even that felt like a lie.

FOUR

Olivia
_____

MY FRIENDS and I shuffled into the theater, and I instantly felt claustrophobic. Despite the theater being large and opulent back in its day — although the years had worn the place down, hence Lydia's never-ending work to maintain and improve theater — it didn't matter how big the theater was or how high the ceilings might be. This many people in any size space would make me feel claustrophobic.

I sat in between Madison and Brooklyn, with Ashleigh seated on Madison's left. The buzzing crowd was louder than anything I ever remembered hearing in an enclosed space, including the pep rallies at Ocean Springs High. No one was shouting or jumping around or anything, but there was an unending storm of commotion from all the locals who had come to support the theater.

Or, if everyone was being honest, get a glimpse at Ryan Jones.

I looked at the program and read the logline of the unimaginatively titled _Cops and Robbers_ while I waited:

A small-town cop finds himself in a high-stakes game of cat and mouse when a notorious bank robber targets a jurisdiction. When the robber leaves a series of riddles and clues at each crime scene, it becomes clear that he's challenging the cop specifically. This exclusive one-act play unfolds in real time as the cop deciphers the clues, uncovering a connection between the robber and his own past, leading to a tense standoff where both their true motivations are revealed.

A hush fell over the crowd as Lydia took the stage.

Once the quiet had finally died, noise erupted again, with only a second-long pause in between cacophonous chatter and uproarious applause as the theater's beloved caretaker prepared to speak.

"Welcome," Lydia said, "and thank you everyone for coming. This is going to be a very special night. As I'm sure you all know, we have a special guest. Ryan Jones is not just the star of films such as *Tears in the Rain*, *Shadows of the Past*, and *Beneath Unbroken Skies*. He was also played a delightful poultry in his performance as Chicken Little, once upon an I'm not telling you how long it was ago."

The crowd laughed.

Then Lydia continued. "What most of you don't know is that Ryan isn't just a special guest tonight. He is our actor of honor and will be playing the robber."

She stopped for a round of applause, then continued. "We have Ryan's good friend, Lucas Stone, here with us tonight. He will be playing the cop before fulfilling the emcee duties afterward as we start our auction with a special surprise at the end, which I am sure will surprise none of you."

More laughter. More applause.

Lucas Stone was a towering presence with his chiseled physique (he probably spent two-thirds of his life in the gym). His wavy blond hair framed a rugged face adorned with a charismatic smile.

Lydia warmly waved to the crowd, then exited stage right as the red velvet curtain rose behind her.

I watched the play, surprised to find myself invested fast. Sure, there were a few seconds of begrudging shifting around in my seat before recognizing my own determination to feel soured on the performance.

And of course, that was something Madison had pointed out a few times.

So I paid attention to the play, and by a half hour into it, I had to reluctantly acknowledge that I was enjoying the show. It shouldn't have been a surprise. Ryan Jones was still an entertaining actor. I appreciated talent, and even in something as silly as this one-act play, his gifts were evident.

But my enjoyment over the man wasn't about him being a good actor. Not anymore. I could never see him the same way again after watching that two-minute video of him screaming at the director like he was king of the world.

It had disgusted me because it was disgusting. Whatever people were saying on social media about him when the story broke sounded about right to me.

Seeing and hearing him yell at the director like that made me realize that Ryan Jones was not the same person I knew back in elementary and middle school. I had always seen him as shy before, but maybe he was just stuck up.

We didn't talk much after the dance, and then he moved away in seventh grade to go and live with his grandparents, so I never heard from him again.

Although, of course, like the rest of this country (and I'm sure a lot of the world by now), I had still seen Ryan Jones plenty.

"Olivia!" Madison nudged me.

I looked over and realized she was staring at me,

waiting to stand like everyone else around us, already on their feet and applauding.

Somehow, the play was over, and I had gotten seriously lost in thought. Bad enough, missing the punchline of the performance. Even worse was that I knew Madison was going to give me crap about it later.

I leaped to my feet a beat after she did and loudly clapped along with everyone else.

"Drinks?" Brooklyn asked, already wiggling her way down the row of seats so she could hit the aisle and head toward the bar post-haste.

We wandered over to where an array of cops and robbers-themed appetizers and drinks awaited us. A Burglar's Bounty platter with miniature loot bags full of spiced nuts and gold-foiled chocolates; Handcuff Hors d'Oeuvres, shaped like police badges and filled with smoked salmon or creamy cheese; and Cell Block Canapés (savory tarts shaped like little prison cells, with edible bars made from crispy breadsticks, encasing a prisoner of gourmet meat and cheese).

The drinks were no less inventive. The Getaway Car was a tantalizing mix of gin, lime juice, and a dash of black pepper, while the Detective's Delight was a concoction of bourbon, bitters, and a touch of orange zest, served with a fake mustache on the rim for an extra touch of intrigue.

I went through two loot bags while downing my Getaway Car and was on my way to experience the Detective's Delight when Lydia reclaimed the stage.

It was finally time for the auction.

She quickly explained how everything would work, even though the explanation was in no way necessary. Not only had most of the people in attendance been to fundraisers like this before, especially at this theater, but even if they hadn't, auctions were a trope seen on TV enough for everyone to understand them at a glance.

The applause for Lucas Stone as he walked out onto the stage wasn't quite as thunderous as the clapping had been at the end of *Cops and Robbers*, but after the crowd had downed all those Getaways and Delights, a few of the individual whoops and hollers sounded almost comically loud.

Lucas usually played an action hero on the big screen, but today he was playing the auctioneer from our little stage. Surprisingly, it seemed like a role he was born for.

It was impressive how fluidly he had that auctioneer's patter down. I wondered if he had practiced for tonight. Did something like that come easily for natural born actors? Because surely this little night in Ocean Springs was not a role that had been worth preparing for.

Lucas rat-a-tat-tatted his auctioneering through a chorus of lively bids and loud laughter. Baker's Bliss offered a year's worth of free birthday cakes, which were indeed delicious, but at only one cake per month, the prize seemed to go for a few hundred dollars more than I would have expected, while the Harbor View Day Spa weekend package went for low enough that I wondered why I hadn't bid on it.

My month of dog walking went for an admirable sum, sandwiched in between an offer from Ocean Springs Auto Care for six months' worth of car washes and a one-year membership to Main Street Fitness that was probably impossible to get out of.

Once the community offerings had all been auctioned off, Lucas redirected the theater's attention to Lydia, who was about to announce a special surprise that not a single person in the venue was bound to find surprising.

Ryan was ushered out onto stage by Lydia as Lucas brought the gavel down and asked the crowd to calm itself while the theater director made another couple of announcements.

"It has been my honor to have our Ryan back home in the town that raised him," she said with enough pride to make her face glow.

Then she delivered the totals for how much money they had already made for the theater tonight, with an additional message reminding the attendees about how much they still needed to bring in before they could consider the job was finished.

The clapping started, and Lucas smiled as he raised his gavel again, but Ryan seemed surprisingly nervous by the proceedings, leaning over and whispering to Lucas.

But Lucas simply shrugged, then banged the gavel, and started his opening spiel as Ryan stepped to the side and cast his gaze across the audience again, peering into the crowd as if searching for someone specific.

He looked worried enough that Lucas apparently had to hesitate. His opening spiel was now over, but the auction had yet to start.

Whispers rippled through the crowd:

"What's going on up there?"

"Why does Ryan look like that?

"Maybe he's about to donate something big…"

"Maybe it has something to do with that video of him yelling at André Dosh."

But then Ryan smiled to let the audience know he was ready.

And Lucas grinned as his gavel came down for more of his spectacle, clearly in his element, and still displaying a talent for auctioneering that to my mind beat his acting by quite a lot.

"Our next item, ladies and gentlemen, is a rare opportunity. An exclusive dinner with the man of the evening,

Ryan Jones himself! Who wouldn't want to dine with the star of *Shadows of the Past* and *Beneath Unbroken Skies*? Shall we start the bidding at $100? Do I hear $100?"

A hand shot up from a woman in a bright red dress.

Lucas looked at the name on her paddle and said, "Brenda must be a dear friend of the theater and a fan of vintage Hollywood if she's kicking us off tonight with $100!"

Another hand went up, a gentleman in a finely tailored suit. "Tom has a taste for the finer things with $150!"

The bidding escalated, with the quick and melodious patter from Lucas ringing out through the theater.

"And Sarah is a true patron of the arts raising us to $200!"

Throw in Willow and Kathi and Francis and Emily, and the bidding was up to $500 before I realized that Madison had a paddle, and that my best friend was bidding.

"$575!" Madison called out.

"What are you doing?" I asked.

The crowd was electric as a woman named Henrietta started duking it out with Madison, running the bids up to $800.

Henrietta looked like she wanted to snarl at Madison when the bidding reached $900. She made one last stab at $950, but Madison's next bid at a thousand dollars was clearly too rich for Henrietta's blood.

"SOLD! To Madison, for $1000! A truly spirited bidding, and all for an excellent cause! Let's give a big hand to Madison and to all our generous bidders!"

The whole thing was so surprising, from the winner to the winnings to the event itself. If I had guessed ahead of time, I would have expected for Ryan to go for ten times that much, probably to some old rich biddy who just wanted him to paint her toenails for like $10,000 or whatever.

But even more surprising, perhaps even downright shocking, was that Madison had bid enough to win, let alone bidding at all. She didn't care about Ryan Jone as an actor, and she wasn't the kind of person who needed to showboat. So what was this all about?

Madison was up to something, and I was going to figure out what.

"I'm surprised the dinner went so low," I said.

"I'm not." Madison laughed, obviously not trying to keep the truth a mystery. "I told everyone that they could have free parking for a month downtown if they let me win the auction."

"Isn't that cheating?" I asked.

"How is that cheating?"

"Because your husband is the local bylaw officer, and you probably shouldn't be promising city favors in exchange for personal services."

"I don't know what you're talking about," Madison said, shaking her head as she smiled. "Whatever you're talking about, it never happened."

"That's not how the law works," I said.

"This isn't New York. It's Ocean Springs. We like to help each other out here. Remember?" Madison laughed again.

But I didn't even really care, because she was right. Ocean Springs wasn't New York, and this was an auction, not a bank robbery. Despite the theme of the night.

I was just curious about why she had done what she did.

"Why did you want to bid on a date with Ryan Jones? You don't even like him as an actor and—"

Madison cut me off as she handed me the bidding

paddle. "We all pooled our money to get you a dinner with your favorite actor."

"What?" I said in disbelief, lost as to what I should do with my face.

Brooklyn and Ashleigh appeared on either side of Madison, with all three of my friends now staring at me.

"Did you tell her?" Brooke asked.

"What did she say?" Ashleigh chirped.

"What is going on here?" I asked, suddenly feeling sick.

"We figured that if dinner with Ryan Jones couldn't cheer you up, then probably nothing could," Madison explained.

But I was beyond horrified.

I had no idea what to do.

Or what to say.

Or what to feel.

Then there was a round of applause and everyone was looking at me, not just my friends, but maybe half of the theater.

This was like that classic nightmare about showing up at school in nothing but my underwear, except worse because Ryan was back on the stage and staring out at the crowd.

This time his gaze wasn't wandering; it was fixed right on me.

And then Lydia was running over. She grabbed me by the wrist, then dragged me down the aisle and up onto the stage.

I felt a full-body shiver of nerves.

What had my friends gotten me into?

FIVE

Ryan

I STARED out at the crowd, squinting while working to remember why the woman standing in the aisle seemed so familiar.

She looked a little like this moody girl who acted like I had cooties during a fourth-grade dance. I was so painfully shy, the look on her face had felt like a punch to my stomach. We'd danced at the sock hop together, neither of us saying a word for the entire dance.

My phone rang. I looked down at the screen and saw it was Maggie. Not that it mattered. Even if my manager was right outside, the damage had already been done. I was still obligated to a dinner that was filling my marrow with anxiety.

"Where are you?" I asked instead of saying hello.

"I'm so sorry, Ryan, but my plane got grounded for fog."

"Fog in LA? It's not like you're flying from San Francisco."

"You know I have no control whatsoever over the weather, right?"

"You seem to move half of Hollywood sometimes," I said.

She laughed. "I'm sorry, kiddo."

I could hear that truth in her voice.

"I know you are."

"It looks like I'm going to miss the auction for sure."

"You've already missed it."

"I'm sure you'll be fine. It's just a dinner, no big deal. It will probably be some rich lady who just wants to watch movies with you and have you autograph all of her furniture. Don't just smile your way through it. Try and have a good time."

"I'll do my best."

"Ryan!" Lucas shouted my name.

I turned around and saw my buddy smiling wide at me.

I followed his gaze to see Lydia bringing the prize winner up on stage.

And I couldn't stop staring at her.

Because it was the woman I had been looking at earlier.

And I was right — she was the girl from the sock hop. I still remembered her name: Olivia. You never forget the first person you dance with.

She still had the same wavy auburn hair. Same light brown eyes. Same full lips, although now they were painted a shade of deep rose.

But she wasn't the same stick-thin, awkward girl who Lydia had pushed at me back then. She'd gotten curves times ten, and she wore that clingy robber costume with a natural confidence that suggested she wasn't acting, she was just being herself. Nothing like the aloof poise that my ex, April, affected whenever she was out in public.

She'd be jealous of Olivia's lips — April who snuck off to the "spa" to maintain her bee-stung look with filler injections and who'd never risk forehead wrinkles by frowning at me like that.

Like I'd bid on a date with *her*, and she was disappointed that I'd won. "And our winner for the dinner with Ryan Jones is Olivia Bloom!" Lydia announced.

A chill rippled through my body. From my crown all the way down to every single one of my ten toes. Her name was under my skin. She'd grown up to be more beautiful than I thought possible. The only flaw — if you could even call it that — was the tight, pained smile she wore for the crowd. I knew it well — it was the same smile I used when I was walking the red carpet and dealing with the paparazzi.

Why did she look so unhappy accepting her prize? Her face was pinched, just like it had been when Lydia suggested that we dance together in fourth grade.

"Thank you all for coming," Lydia said as she looked out at the crowd. "Please, we're only a few thousand dollars short of our goal. If you can afford it, consider donating. Even if you can't afford it, you should consider donating anyway." She laughed. "I'm only half kidding about that last part."

Lydia let the moment settle, then smiled wider than she had all night. It was a Cheshire Cat grin if I'd ever seen one.

She was up to something.

"This evening cannot end until I unveil our final surprise." Lydia was almost giggling as she grinned through the elongated moment. Then, like she was a magician's deranged assistant, she produced a pair of handcuffs from behind her back. "In honor of our cops and robbers theme, Ryan and Olivia will be handcuffed for the duration of their dinner."

The audience laughed.

Olivia's already forced smile became more pained.

This had to be a joke.

"Wrists, please," Lydia said, dangling the cuffs in front of her.

A murmur of excitement rippled through the theater.

I did not know about that part of dinner with the winner in advance, and I would not have agreed to do it if Lydia had told me. It was just pulling too many of my triggers.

Something like this needed to be prepared for.

Maggie was supposed to keep things like this from happening.

Lydia could see the look on my face. "You'll have fun with it, I promise."

But I was gritting my teeth, chewing on a smile I could barely hold on my face. I had known going in that tonight would feel like work, but this was the kind of hard acting that put me down for days afterward. I never imagined going in that a fundraiser in my hometown would feel like actual labor.

Or that it would involve being handcuffed to someone who clearly didn't want to get any closer to me than she had to.

"I'm having fun already," I said through gritted teeth as I offered Lydia my wrist.

Olivia did the same, her forced smile matching mine.

At least we had that in common.

But why would someone pay a thousand dollars to have dinner with someone they didn't want to?

"Looks like we've got a problem," Lydia said, more to the audience then to us. "They both want the same hand free. Decisions, decisions."

The audience laughed.

"Can I hold them?" Olivia asked, holding out her hand for the cuffs.

"Sure." Lydia shrugged and gave them to her.

"These are real handcuffs." Olivia seemed to be weighing them in her hand.

"They sure are," Lydia said. "I got them from my grandson. He said I could borrow them for this special event."

Real handcuffs. Not stage handcuffs, like I'd hoped — the kind that had a built-in mechanism for unlocking them. Actual handcuffs that we wouldn't be able to sneak out of.

"I need my right hand," I said.

"And I need mine!" Olivia said quickly.

"I'm an actor; I gesture with my hands. I use them to talk. My hands are like my second voice."

"So you need your right hand to have another voice? I'm a professional dog walker. My right hand is literally how I make a living."

"Are you planning to walk dogs during dinner?"

"Are you planning to gesture wildly while I'm attached to you?"

The entire theater was watching us.

I made a show of rolling my eyes and chuckling as I offered Lydia my right hand.

She cuffed me, the handcuff surprisingly cool. And arguably tighter than it needed to be. It wasn't cutting off circulation, but it wasn't comfortable, either. She cuffed Olivia next, then after parading us around the stage, ushered us out stage left and through the back door into the parking lot.

"We can take these off now, right?" Olivia asked.

"Sorry, dear." Lydia shook her head and held up the key, gleaming metal with a weird little groove in it. "Not until the end of your meal."

"It's not like anyone will know," I said.

"I'll know, and that's all that matters," Lydia replied, her tone ending that particular part of the conversation. "I'll meet you both at the hotel with the key, but not until after your dinner. The *Ocean Observer* will be taking some photos of you guys, so grin and smile through all of them."

"Like this?" I flashed my Hollywood smile, the one I used to make Maggie happy more than my directors.

"Exactly!" Lydia clapped and turned to Olivia. "How does it feel to be the top bidder for tonight's fundraiser?"

"Awesome," Olivia replied in a monotone.

"And here's your vehicle," Lydia said as a black Audi pulled up next to us, then waited to whisk us back to the Fisherman's Finest, where our meal awaited us in the restaurant.

Adjacent to the main lobby, Cannery Grill paid additional homage to the building's illustrious history with reclaimed wood and metal accents. Floor-to-ceiling windows that once looked out on bustling docks now framed a breathtaking ocean vista.

I had enjoyed every meal I had ever had in the place. But tonight would surely be an exception. Even if the restaurant was still serving Truffle Lobster Mac and Cheese, Beer-Battered Fish Tacos with Pickled Red Cabbage Slaw, and Shrimp Pot Pie with Puff Pastry and Seasonal Vegetables, I would still be cuffed to someone who looked like she'd rather be in prison than suffer through a meal with me.

Getting in the car was awkward.

Olivia climbed in first, although it took her a couple of tries as she attempted to maneuver in that short skirt that stopped halfway down her bare thighs. I averted my eyes, not wanting to be caught ogling, but my gaze slid down the curve of her knees and to the straight sweep of her shins.

She scooted across to the other side of the seat without warning, dragging me into the limo. I failed to duck in time, dinging my head against the doorframe just before my butt hit the seat.

"Ow!" I clutched my head with my free hand, yanking my legs inside a half-second before the driver shut the door.

"Sorry," Olivia said, frowning again now that she was safe behind tinted windows. "I don't have a lot of experience being handcuffed."

I deliberately did not linger on the image that flashed through my head.

"I'm fine." That was a lie. "I'll be fine."

There we sat in the backseat, our silver bracelet linking us together. I was trying not to hold it against Maggie for packing her day so full that there was no way she could make the fundraiser. I understood Maggie was probably going to bat for some other actor, same as she was always swinging that bat for me.

"Thanks for buying me," I said. Then, trying to lighten the mood, "Do you think I'll fit in with your other furniture?"

"Don't know. I'm going to store you in the attic."

Olivia made a little gesture and sound, something like a half-scoff, as if withholding the full extent of her judgmental expression so I could witness a restrained version of her disapproval before adding, "It wasn't my idea."

"What do you mean, it wasn't your idea?" I asked.

"This dinner was a gift from my well-meaning but ill-informed friends. So if you want to cut the evening short, I'm good with it."

Only permanent deletion of that humiliating video from the internet sounded better at that moment. Because if she didn't want to be here, then why should I want to be here?

Because I promised Lydia, I immediately remembered.

Lydia meant the world to me.

"No. A deal is a deal." I shrugged. "And besides. Taking you out for dinner is the least I can do to repay you for the dance at the sock hop."

Olivia blinked, and for a microsecond, her pinched expression softened. "That was a long time ago."

"You never forget your first," I said. "But if you want to call it off, we can."

Olivia hesitated, the pained expression returning to her face.

"You were a gift from my friends, and I would hate for any of them to think I was ungrateful. So I guess that I am also excited to have dinner with you."

Again in a monotone.

"Great." My smile felt excruciating. "Me too."

But we didn't trade another word on our way to dinner after that.

SIX

Olivia

_____

WE ARRIVED at the Fisherman's Finest in complete silence.

The hotel was gorgeous. It had been refurbished in the past five years and was now the place to stay if you were spending any time in Ocean Springs. Everything about it screamed wealth, from the vintage furniture to the polished lobby to the way everyone addressed you as either "sir" or "madam."

I wondered what room Ryan took. Probably the Presidential Suite or whatever it was called in this place. Something like His Maritime Majesty suite. Not that it mattered — I would never see the inside of Ryan's room anyway.

But I would be eating at the Cannery Cafe, which served waterfront inspired comfort food at prices that cost too many walked dogs for me to spend on an appetizer. The host, barely able to hold a smirk in when he spotted our handcuffs, took us out to a semi-private balcony that overlooked the water.

It was an awfully romantic spot for two people who didn't know each other at all made even more awkward by our jockeying for position at the table, with each of us trying to figure out the best way to sit.

"Can you just—" I started.

"Just what?" Ryan tried to slide into one of the chairs, but when he went to pull his chair in, he accidentally yanked on the handcuff, nearly pulling me onto his lap.

"Careful."

"I'm trying—"

"If you just—"

"If you can just move like a skosh to the right, then I'll be able to sit down."

"A skosh?" I repeated.

"What? Is something wrong with that word?"

"I don't know." I shrugged. "It's a little outdated? I'm half expecting to see a slap bracelet or a Tamagotchi."

"Wrong era," Ryan said, looking at the table and chair set up. "I'm working on a period piece. My lexicon is all over the place."

"You and your lexicon are very fancy." With my free hand, I grabbed the centerpiece — a silver crab cradling a bottle of wine in its claws — and set it on a different table. It was one less thing for us to worry about knocking over with our handcuffs. "Maybe we should just stand for dinner?"

We both looked down at the table. The simple act of sitting suddenly felt like a game of Twister. Ryan tried to take the seat on the left, but that meant my cuffed left hand was uncomfortably stretched across my body.

"Why don't you sit on the other side?" His eyes darted to the chair he thought would work best for me.

I tried to move, but the tether between us made for an awkward dance. "If I sit there, our arms are going to be stretched out in the middle like a clothesline."

"When was the last time you used a clothesline?"

"What does that have to do with anything?" I asked.

"Just seems like clotheslines were in use right around the same time as the word skosh."

Ryan tried to slide the nearest chair closer to me, knocking into the table and causing the water glasses to wobble dangerously.

"Maybe you should sit first."

"Fine." I gingerly lowered myself into the chair, and we both contorted our bodies until we found a semi-comfortable position.

And to think — Madison had actually paid for me to have this experience.

Ryan sighed and sucked in his lips. "Bad news."

"More?"

"I have to go to the bathroom."

I didn't owe Madison. She owed me.

I tried not to frown or pout at him. "You have to be kidding me."

"I'm not kidding at all, but funny."

"You're going to have to hold it."

"I can't hold it." Ryan shook his head. "That's not how my bladder works."

"Then I suggest you don't drink any water. Or wine."

"I usually have to go a lot when I'm nervous."

"Then don't be nervous." I paused, considering what he'd just said. "Why would you be nervous?"

"Am I not allowed to be nervous?"

"I'm the one who's supposed to be nervous. Having dinner with Mr. Hollywood Big Shot." I watched Ryan carefully, and for a breath, the movie star facade slipped away. The movie star looks — the ones that made my stomach do all kinds of uncomfortably delightful things — were still there. But he looked less polished and more human, less like he walked out of a magazine and more like he walked down main street.

But I wasn't going to get attached — I'd seen his polite facade slip away before, and behind it was a torrent of rage reserved for his director.

"It's just a lot," Ryan said. He gestured towards the handcuffs. "All of it."

"We can call Lydia. We don't have to get dinner."

"I want to have dinner." Ryan didn't look at all like he wanted to have dinner, but then he tried on a smile that he surely didn't mean, because a famous movie star like him sure didn't need to be slumming it with a hick from the hometown he'd ditched in seventh grade. "Look. We've started out on the wrong foot. Let's start over. On the other foot."

"My other foot is my best foot," I said, hoping my lame joke would diffuse the tension I was feeling.

To my surprise, Ryan laughed. Not a deep belly laugh, but a quick, light, sincere one.

I glanced at the menu, unsure what to make of this new development. "Have you been here before?"

"Every time I'm in Ocean Springs."

"When was the last time you were here?"

"Six months ago."

"Six… why didn't I hear about it?" Ryan Jones returning to his hometown seemed like something I definitely should've heard of. Maybe he came during that week where I wasn't sort of tracking his flights.

"I keep a low profile when I can, and the people here keep my secrets."

"Oh," I said. "Then, what do you recommend?"

"Honestly, everything is excellent here."

"What do you like to order? You must have a favorite."

"The first several times I ate here, I always asked the

server what their favorite thing on the menu was, or what they ask the cook to make in the kitchen if it's not on the menu."

"That sounds dangerous."

"It doesn't always work out," he admitted with a laugh. "But sometimes I end up with one of the best meals I've ever had."

"Has that ever happened here?"

"No." He shook his head and picked up the menu, glancing down as he gave me audible reviews of the appetizers he had tried before, citing his favorites as the lobster mac and cheese bites, seared scallops, crab-stuffed mushrooms, and clam chowder shooters.

"I did not care for the baked brie with sea salt crostini," he added at the end.

"So which appetizer would you like tonight?" I asked.

"Whatever you want. Order one of everything. I mean that."

"I could never be that wasteful." He opened his mouth, but I kept going because I didn't need to hear about how buying one of everything on the menu for him was like me paying extra for coconut milk in my coffee. "Which of these appetizers would you order if you were all alone? The lobster mac and cheese bites?"

"None of them." Ryan laughed. "I would order crab, just pure clean crab."

"I love crab!" I exclaimed, surprised by how delighted I sounded by the suggestion. Everything about eating crab, from the cracking the shell to savoring the flavor had been a favorite culinary experience of mine ever since I was a little girl and my mom used to take me to buy them fresh from the dock.

"Well then, crab it is." Ryan smiled, and it was the first

time the expression had looked genuine on his face since all night. "And let's order a lot of it."

Small talk was usually hard enough for me, and I was sure that this next bit was about to get excruciating, but our server came walking jauntily over to the table and interrupted us before the small talk could get started.

Paul (according to his name tag) was late 30s or maybe even early 40s, but with cherubic cheeks and a boyish grin that wanted to lie about his age, and twinkling eyes that suggested he was in on a joke he was just about to share with the table. His slightly tousled hair looked effortlessly cool, and I could already feel myself wanting to tip him.

Not that tipping was my responsibility. For a thousand dollars, Mr. Fancy Pants Movie Star could cover the cost.

"Welcome back, Mr. Jones," said Paul before turning to me. "And welcome to the Cannery Cafe. Have you dined with us before?"

I shook my head. "I have not."

"Well, you're going to love it." Back to Ryan. "Can I start you off with some mac and lobster bites?"

"We'll start with the Dungeness crab, and let's make it a generous portion, Paul. We're here to indulge tonight."

"How generous?"

"Ten pounds," Ryan said.

"Ten pounds," I repeated.

Paul repeated it too, but the two words sounded a lot different coming out of his mouth.

"Ten pounds." He nodded. "I'll get that started for you." And then he was gone.

"That's a lot of crab," I said.

"Life is short; eat the crab."

"Is that a catchphrase from one of your movies?"

"My movies don't have catchphrases."

"'Every hero needs a horizon,'" I quoted.

"That wasn't supposed to be a catchphrase. The memes were unfairly out of control on that one." Ryan looked embarrassed.

I agreed with him back when it happened, the memes were out of control, but that line had been beautiful in the context of the movie.

But then I heard him yelling at director André Dosh, and after that, I figured Ryan Jones deserved every meme he got.

Our gaze fell to our handcuffed wrists in tandem and then, as if in rehearsal for a play, we shared a mutual sigh.

But then I suddenly remembered something and got an idea.

"Wait!"

"I wasn't going anywhere." A dry smile lit his lips.

"Do you see this costume?" I pointed to my robber outfit.

Ryan nodded and gave me an appreciative smile. "Indeed I do."

A thrilling trill that I didn't even want to admit was there in the first place rippled all the way through me. I slapped the handcuff accessories fixed to the belt at my waist.

"This costume came with handcuffs, so of course it also came with a key. I'll unshackle us, then you can go to the bathroom. I'll reattach us when you come back, and Lydia will never know that they were ever even off."

"Isn't that cheating?"

"It's cheating for you to go to the bathroom?"

"We're supposed to be bound through dinner. We're not supposed to have a key to the handcuffs."

"But we do, and you need to pee," I argued. "You're obviously doing this as a favor to Lydia. And my friends roped me into this dinner, no offense. So you should go to the bathroom and then come back to the table, and we'll enjoy the obnoxious amount of crab you just ordered together. Sound good?"

Ryan looked both relieved and reluctant as he nodded. "Sounds good."

I reached into my purse and pulled out the small hand-cuff key that had come as part of my costume. But confidence that it would do the trick was clearly misplaced, because when I inserted that key into the lock and twisted it, something was obviously not right.

No matter how much I turned or wiggled it, the key refused to cooperate.

"Thank you for trying."

"I thought it would work. For some reason."

"Optimism. You're just that eager to get rid of me."

I didn't say anything, because what was there to say?

There was a dull quiet between us.

Ryan broke it with the words I'd been dreading. "I still have to go to the bathroom."

"You know that can't happen."

"Well, it's going to happen. If it happens right here in my lap and someone takes a picture — you're in that picture tomorrow morning. That picture will exist for the rest of eternity, you next to me with pee all over the front of my pants. If you're really okay with that happening, then I guess we can make that choice together. But I would greatly prefer, and I'm sure that Maggie, my manager, is totally with me on this, and same for Lydia: it would be best if we could find a way for us to somehow migrate to the restroom right now so I can relieve myself."

After giving him a long stare, I felt like I had no other choice. "Fine."

Then we got up from the table and went into the men's restroom.

I had to plug my ears and sing "Twinkle, Twinkle, Little Star" while he peed. Or, as I sang it in my head, "Tinkle, Tinkle, Little Star."

It was the least romantic moment of my life.

He finished and washed his hands, though it took him a few seconds of looking around aimlessly before he was willing to make eye contact, then said, "I can do the same for you if you want to go into the ladies' restroom."

"No thank you, absolutely not. My bladder will pop like a balloon before I let that happen."

"You'd rather die?"

"One hundred percent."

"So that's a no. I hope you don't get thirsty while eating all of that crab."

"I could go the rest of my life without drinking."

"More wine for me, I guess."

We got back to the table, and I was surprised to see how much crab we had actually ordered, even though I was at the table when Ryan had ordered it. The table was practically groaning under the weight of all that glistening Dungeness crab, their spindly legs splayed out like a convocation of majestic, armored spiders from the deep, creating ten pounds of opulent spectacle.

"I'm not sure we thought this through?"

"Is this about how much there is again?" Ryan asked.

"No. It's about how we ordered crab and we're hand-cuffed together."

"Oh." He got it. "That's right."

I wondered how this was going to work. We each needed both of our hands to effectively eat crab.

"I can do it," I offered. "I'm an expert crab cracker. Been doing it all my life. Let me at it."

And he did. Cuffed together like we were, Ryan and I faced our culinary challenge with unexpected grace. With me in the lead, crab cracking was a shared dance as I deftly prepared our plates.

Our cuffs softly clinked with our movement, the backs of our hands brushing against each other every time one of us shifted. Ryan's occasional fumbles and laughter eased into the rhythm, and his bewilderment at my expertise was both obvious on his face and enjoyable to see.

The constraint of our handcuffs had somehow gone from being a nuisance into feeling like an intimate connection between us, making me almost uncomfortable with the sense of this unspoken dialogue, with this trust through teamwork suddenly established between us.

But the good vibes didn't last. By the time we were a quarter way through all that crab, I realized that Ryan still wanted to order entrees, and there was no way we could come close to finishing our shellfish appetizer off. What I had seen as extravagant twenty minutes before, I suddenly saw as so incredibly wasteful.

It made me sick to my stomach that Ryan didn't care at all. That he was indulgent to the point of obnoxiousness, leaving all that crab aside while ordering surf and turf without a care for both of us.

And yes, the surf and turf was delicious. The succulent lobster tail glistened with butter, its tender flesh practically melting with each bite, contrasting beautifully with the perfectly seared, medium rare steak that boasted a rich, smoky flavor with every juicy forkful, just like Paul had promised, paired with a velvety béarnaise sauce and garnished with freshly chopped chives.

Ryan kept trying to play the role of good host through to the end of our meal, seemingly sorry for his earlier indifference toward me and doing everything he could to make it right.

"Dessert," he asked as our plates were cleared. "We have to have dessert."

I wasn't about to say no to dessert at the Cannery Cafe, so we ordered some ice cream, even though that seemed like the least exciting option on the dessert menu to me.

But he loved ice cream, and his favorite flavor was vanilla.

"Do you like it?" Ryan asked, and the expression on his face suggested that he really wanted me to say yes.

"It's okay," I smiled but had no reason to. "Nothing great."

"What don't you like about it?" He sounded more surprised than injured.

"It's just a little too bland for me."

"It's vanilla."

"Right," I agreed, "but vanilla doesn't have to be bland. The taste is pleasant but uninspiring, like a song you've heard a million times before."

"But this restaurant has great food."

"You're absolutely right, and it's gorgeous. But they played it safe with their ice cream." Then I couldn't help but add, "And I kind of figured they would."

"You have a lot of opinions about ice creams."

"I have a lot of opinions about a lot of things, if you care to ask me."

"Well, I loved every bite of dinner, and I appreciated dessert, even if it was the oatmeal of ice creams." Ryan laughed.

And I laughed with him. "The ice cream was a culinary wallflower, what do you want me to say?"

"Now I want to see what you consider delicious ice cream."

I opened my mouth, not even sure of how I would answer him, but half-sure that I was about to surprise myself when his phone started jangling with "The Entertainer" as a ringtone and his expression grew instantly alert.

"That's Lydia. Do you mind if I take this?"

"She is the one with the keys," I said.

Ryan nodded and answered the call.

"Hey Lydia, we're ready to—" He paused, and something terrible crossed his face. Then he swallowed hard. "WHAT?"

SEVEN

Ryan

I HUNG up with Lydia to find Olivia still staring at me, same as she had been throughout the entire call.

"What?" she said. "Tell me what happened? Why does your face look like that? I feel like something really bad is happening right now."

"Relax," I told her. "You look like you're about to hyperventilate."

"Do I have a reason to hyperventilate?"

"Maybe." I tried to smile as I said the word, hoping to reassure her that everything was going to be okay — even though I had to give her some fairly terrible news. "Lydia lost the key to our handcuffs."

"Oh." She looked relieved, her entire body seeming to sigh as a fresh light returned to her eyes. "They're in her coat pocket."

"I'm not so sure." I shook my head again. "Lydia seemed pretty adamant that she couldn't find them. She said that she's been looking for a while, and I imagine her coat was one of the first places she would have checked."

"I'm telling you, I saw her drop it into her coat pocket,

and it was a deep pocket, so the key is probably just way down there at the bottom and in a corner or something. Call her back and tell her to check."

I was surprised by the sudden relief I felt. Olivia insisted that the key was in Lydia's pocket like that was a fact and not just her being hopeful.

I dialed Lydia, believing that we were minutes away from her finding the key and all three of us sighing with gusts of relief as we met Lydia in the lobby to unlock our shackles and get this evening over with once and for all.

Not that I had any ill feelings toward Olivia at all. The meal had its highlights, and though she still didn't seem like she wanted to be there, she'd been an enjoyable conversation companion.

And really — who was I to complain about being handcuffed to a beautiful woman all night?

"What's happening now?" Olivia asked, probably because of my worried expression.

"She's not answering her phone," I replied, dialing again after my first attempt rang four times before going to voicemail.

My second try rang four times before I heard the opening words to Lydia's outgoing message again. "Hello! The stage is my current calling, but your call is equally important to me, so please—"

My third attempt proved even worse, with the call going straight to voicemail for the first time.

I dropped the phone in my pocket and raised my hand to get Paul's attention.

"Just give me a second," I said to Olivia to quell her clearly swelling worry as Paul rushed over.

"Yes, Mr. Jones?"

"Please send the check to my hotel room and add 30 percent gratuity. And can you please box up all of this crab for anyone working the dining area or kitchen who wants any of it?"

"Yes, sir." Paul nodded. "Thank you as always."

"We're also going to need our car."

"Yes, Mr. Jones." Another nod from our server, and then he was gone.

Minutes later we were sitting in the car again, and things were back to being weird. The strangeness felt different this time. Now we had dinner in our rearview mirror but a different problem in front of us.

Being bound together had been horrendously awkward and barely tolerable during dinner. The conclusion of our meal was supposed to be the point where we reached the light at the end of the tunnel. Only in our case, the light at the end of the tunnel was an oncoming train. Now, with a key missing and the odds of the promise of escape still being in Lydia's pocket felt more like hope and less like certainty by the minute.

Our car pulled up to the theater, and we got out of the car, with Olivia defiantly leading the way by getting out on the driver's side, even though that put us on the street and walking around the car instead of just stepping out onto the curb.

Unlike before, the place looked mostly abandoned. The crowds had all dispersed, and without Ryan Jones in close proximity the paparazzi had no reason whatsoever to stick around. They were vultures circling a carcass, and once their source of interest was gone, so were they, every time.

But Lydia was still inside, looking upset with herself as she scurried down the aisle. There were a few remaining members of the cleanup crew. Three of them it looked like, all standing around with an air of waiting.

"I can't find the key anywhere," Lydia declared, her

voice cracking at the end and she finally broke, collapsing onto her knees as she started to sob. A bit dramatic, but that was Lydia.

"It'll be okay." I wrapped my arm around her and pulled my first favorite teacher into a hug. "We'll find the key." Then I took a deep breath as I adopted the role of a confident general. "There were plenty of 'cops' at this event tonight. I'm sure someone has a key that will fit. Either way, we'll get them off."

Not exactly solid logic, but I needed to believe so that everyone else could believe, which was necessary before we could work together to find the key.

"Do you think so?" Lydia looked up at me, her eyes suddenly hopeful.

And Olivia was looking over at both of us. She, too, was daring to hope.

So I had no other choice but to act the part and say something that I wanted to feel so much more than I was letting on.

"I'm sure we'll find the key."

But we didn't. Not even after we opened the vacuum bag and emptied everything out to discover only an earring and a baffling set of dentures, in addition to all the dust balls and strands of long-lost hair.

There was also no sign of the key after we searched through all the trash cans in the theater, and then the garbage dumpsters in the back alley because the cans inside had all been emptied.

We looked under the seats, checked Lydia's coat for the fourteenth time, and tried Olivia's costume key for the third, fiercely hunting for the key until we had finally worn the remaining theater staff's attention so threadbare that the theater manager — a tall and imperious woman with a stern expression — finally marched over and ordered us to leave.

"We all love you, Miss Lydia, and you know that we do or we wouldn't have been here since early this morning until now. But we haven't been able to find the key even after looking everywhere, and we have no reason to believe at this point that it's going to turn up. You more than anyone know how long a day it's been, and I'd like to ask your permission to go home now."

Lydia nodded, but she still looked frantic.

"Ten more minutes, okay?" The manager waited for her to nod again, then walked toward her two waiting compatriots.

"Maybe we could go to my friend Madison's," Olivia suggested. "Her husband, Mick, has tools we can use to cut the handcuffs off."

"That sounds like a great idea then," I said. "Please call him."

The phone was already in Olivia's hand, with her thumb moving wildly across the screen as she texted. Her phone buzzed the instant she sent the text. "Madison's on her way."

"We'll get out of your way now!" Lydia called out to the manager.

The theater manager whispered something to the other two staff members: a young usher with a bewildered expression and an ill-fitting uniform, and a seasoned veteran whom I remembered from when I was a kid, though his face now wore the wrinkles of countless intermissions and encores.

"We'll wait until your ride gets here," said the theater manager.

Ten minutes later, Madison pulled up to the curb, and

the theater staff audibly exhaled with relief as they scattered in a trio of directions toward their individual cars.

Madison got out of her Camry, then circled around to the trunk and got a pair of bolt cutters out.

"We can't do it out in the street," I said. "Anyone could be watching."

Madison looked around, first seriously, then a second time more dramatically. "Who are you afraid is watching?"

"The paparazzi are everywhere."

Olivia, Madison, and even Lydia all traded glances of disbelief.

"Look, I know it might sound paranoid, but you don't understand. Being seen in handcuffs at a charity event is one thing, it's playful, it's part of the act. But a photograph of me having them forcibly cut off in the street? That's a whole different story. It'd be spun into something it's not."

It wasn't just about the paparazzi. It was about controlling the narrative, especially in a world where whispers could outshine a spotlight.

"Where would you like to do it then?" Madison asked.

"Back in my hotel room. That's where we'll have the most privacy."

"Yes. We'll go to the hotel that the paparazzi knows you're staying at. That will provide us with oodles of privacy," Olivia said sarcastically. She tried to cross her arms to prove her point, but all she succeeded in doing was yanking the handcuffs still on our wrists.

"You give me a hard time for using skosh, but you're throwing out oodles?"

"Oodles is a perfectly normal word."

"For a grandma."

Olivia looked offended. "Do I look like a grandma to you?"

Madison clasped her hands together like an excited fan. "Look at you two. Bantering."

"We're not bantering!" Oliva and I said simultaneously.

I wanted to be anywhere in the world but where I was. "Look. I'll text my people at Fisherman's Finest. They'll drop a tip to the paps that I'm somewhere else. Scare them off. We can sneak in the back."

This time, there were no sarcastic replies, so we hopped back in the car. We drove in a caravan of two back to the Fisherman's Finest, with Madison in the lead, us in the backseat, and Linda following behind in her Mini Cooper.

The plan came to a screeching halt just a block away from the hotel when I caught sight of the unmistakable glint of telephoto camera lenses. The paparazzi slinked around like ghosts in broad daylight, their intentions as transparent as their actions were covert. With the knowledge that I would eventually make my way to the hotel, they lingered by the entrance.

"Guess your people weren't able to scare them off," Olivia said.

An encounter with them was the last thing I needed right now.

While the playful handcuff stunt at the benefit, orchestrated by Lydia, was all in good fun and publicized for charity, this was different. Seeing me handcuffed to Olivia in a casual, off-event setting would fuel salacious headlines.

"Duck down," Madison said. We did, unbuckling and sliding down to the floor in unison. She gunned it past the paparazzi and headed into the underground parking garage.

"Thank you. The two of us being seen handcuffed right now will go viral. A picture, a video, whatever. I know for a fact that I don't want that in my life, and I'm pretty sure that you don't want it in yours either." We got out of the car. "Believe me when I say that I'm doing this for both of us. We need to find a way to get upstairs without—"

A particularly aggressive paparazzo named Rusty, whom I had wanted to punch more than once in the past, suddenly jumped out from the shadows of a concrete column and started snapping photos.

"Got a spicy evening planned?" he jeered, eyeing our linked wrists. "I can see the headlines now: Tied up in passion? Hollywood's New Naughty Secret. Can't you just feel the clicks?"

"Get out of here," I growled.

"Or you'll — hey what are you—"

Lydia, who had parked a few spots away from us, had snuck up behind Rusty and deftly removed his camera from his hands. She popped out the SD card, let it fall to the concrete, then stepped on it with her heel. There was a satisfying crack.

Followed by a shriek from Rusty. "I'll sue you for that!"

"Thanks for letting me see your camera," Lydia said. She handed the camera back, but just before Rusty could take it from her, she fumbled it, letting it fall to the concrete.

There was another even more satisfying crack.

Rusty croaked. He collected his broken camera, swore, then scuttled back into the shadows.

Lydia leaned against the window, smiling, her eyes watery. "It was the least I could do for getting you into this mess."

"Rusty's going to tell everyone we're here," I said, already dreading the throng of paps that would be waiting at the garage exit. "We need to do this somewhere else."

"My house," Madison said.

"And get out of here without being seen."

"You can get in the trunk," Madison suggested.

"I'm not getting in the trunk," Olivia said. "I may be handcuffed but I'm not a hostage. And besides — there are no seat belts."

I raised my eyebrows.

Olivia rolled her eyes. "As if I should need a reason to not climb into a trunk."

"I'm not getting in the trunk," Olivia said again. Her eyes drifted over my body as if she was sizing me up. "There's not enough space for both of us."

"We need to get out of here. And we can't have people seeing us handcuffed. So unless you have any better ideas…"

"I'm not getting in the trunk."

EIGHT

Olivia
___

How HAD they convinced me to climb into the trunk?

We were trapped inside, two puzzle pieces forced together — Ryan had gotten in first, then Lydia helped me crawl in so I could curl into a half-fetal position. I barely fit into the space he didn't take up, forced to lie with my backside flush against him, so close that the thin, stretchy fabric of my costume did nothing to shield me from the warmth of his body.

Spooning with the man I once lusted after in the trunk of Lydia's car while he tried to find an inoffensive place to put his hand was almost as awkward as walking in on Taylor and that b—

Ryan's hand grazed my bottom.

"Sorry," he whispered as he yanked his hand back, yanking my hand back with it as he banged his elbow on something. "Owwww! Fork me!"

I scooted forward as far as I could, which was barely anything. Then I pulled my hand forward, guiding his arm so that it draped loosely around my waist.

"This is not an invitation," I said. "I just don't want to

be responsible for you showing up on set with elbow bruises."

"It's okay, Makeup will take care of the elbow bruises when they cover up my tramp stamp."

I couldn't help but smile, and thankfully, he couldn't see it. Madison was going to love this story when I told it to her tomorrow. I was having the worst "date" of my life, but she was definitely getting full entertainment value for her $1,000.

All this to avoid the paparazzi.

"How do you live your life like this?" I asked.

"This is the first time I've been trapped in a trunk," he said. His breath was hot against the back of my neck, which made every part of my body that could do a flip, do one.

"No, I meant how can you live your entire life spending every second worrying about what everyone thinks of you?"

"This trunk thing? It's not for me. It's for you."

"Right," I murmured, giving Ryan a nod he couldn't see, but in the confines of the trunk, he could likely sense my movement. "And I believe it exactly as much as I did the last time."

"I'm serious. If the paparazzi see us still handcuffed after dinner, they won't leave you alone, and you'll be subjected to a lot of uncomfortable gossip."

I scoffed. "Maybe for five minutes — which I guess is as long as most of your relationships. Maybe a minute longer."

"Only if you believe everything you read."

I ignored that. "You're the one who will be subjected to the gossip. You're the one who is obsessed what magazines say about him. Nobody cares what anyone has to say about a dumb little girl from Ocean Springs."

"You're not dumb." Ryan shifted behind me, trying to find a place to put his cuffed hand that wasn't completely awkward. I could feel the metal links in the small of my back. "Can we just not discuss my lack of love life right now? It's hot and claustrophobic enough in here. If you want to yell at me about something, fine. Can you wait until we get to your friend's house?"

"I guess," I said, wondering what he meant by his lack of love life. According to the tabloids, he cleaned up in that department. I knew that some of the relationships were probably just for publicity. But all of them?

Unlikely.

We kept jostling against each other with every bump and turn of Madison's Camry, the softly humming engine somehow sounding like a roar in the background. It was a shock to the system, how loud my own heart seemed to be pounding, echoing what I hoped was panic and definitely not something that had anything to do with the subtle touch of Ryan's warm breath on my neck.

I was hoping the goosebumps on my arms weren't related to that, either.

I reached out in the darkness, not for him, but more to adjust myself.

Our fingers found each other.

We stayed touching fingertip to fingertip for several seconds, surely much longer than either one of us meant to, or would have expected we even could have endured considering the many layers of tension that had settled between us in such a short time.

But it felt like a lifeline for me, and maybe it felt the same way for Ryan.

There were no more words until Madison stopped the car, and I assumed we had arrived at her house.

Then there was the sound of a garage door opening,

the feel of her Camry easing into the enclosed space, and the heavy whir of the garage door rolling back down.

"Guess we're here," Ryan said.

"Or she's kidnapped you and taken you to an undisclosed location."

"Don't you mean 'kidnapped us'?"

"Definitely not," I said. "I'm in on this scam."

Ryan snorted a laugh.

Two moments later, Madison opened the trunk, and harsh fluorescent light spilled down on top of us. I looked over at the sound of the kitchen door opening, then Madison's husband, Mick, appeared standing on the threshold.

Mick walked over to the trunk. Lydia, who must have arrived just before us, watched from the sidelines.

Madison handed him the bolt cutters. "I'm glad to see you. I was only pretending like I would be able to pull this off."

She laughed, and he laughed with her, but no one was even half-smiling several minutes later after every attempt to cut the handcuffs with his bolt cutters had been foiled.

Were these handcuffs enchanted or something?

I'd known Mick for most of my life, but I had never seen his eyes so determined. Chewing on his bottom lip with a grotesque certainty as his biceps struggled, he clamped down harder and harder and harder on the cuffs, certain that freedom was still just a snip away.

And yet, no matter how long the poor guy tried, or how much his muscles kept straining, the cutters could never slice through the metal.

"I've no idea why this metal is so strong." He scratched his head as he stepped back in defeat. "We could use the angle grinder."

"Um, no," I said. "We are definitely not using something called an angel grinder."

"Angle grinder," Ryan corrected me. Then he shrugged self-consciously. "I have a workshop attached to my house. Carpentry, mostly."

"Of course you do," I said. "Angle, angel — either way, we're not using something with the word 'grinder' in it."

"I think we should try. It's perfectly safe," Ryan said. Then he looked to Mick. "You have extra safety glasses?"

"If it was safe, we wouldn't need safety glasses," I replied.

"It's mostly safe."

"Mostly?"

"Like there's a seventy-five percent chance we'll both keep our hand."

"SEVENTY-FIVE PERCENT?"

Ryan laughed.

I swatted him. "Now is not the time for jokes."

"We'll try the angle grinder," Ryan informed Mick, who had already prepared it.

He fired it up. The noise was deafening, and the sparks terrifying. Even from across the garage, I couldn't imagine the fear I would feel with that thing so close to my hand.

"It should cut through the metal like butter," Mick promised.

But that same logic had failed with the bolt cutters.

"This is the best way to get rid of me," Ryan said. "Look. We'll cut the link closer to my wrist. So if anyone loses a hand, it'll be me."

"What about your 'second voice'?"

"I'll only play characters with one hand." Ryan grinned, and though the thought of being anywhere near the angel — correction, angle — grinder was terrifying, his smile was reassuring.

"I promise I know what I'm doing," Mick said.

"He's really good," Madison assured me.

"Fine," I finally agreed, even though I didn't like how nervous Lydia looked standing off to the side. "But if you cut my hand off, you'll be signing all my Christmas cards from now on."

I was only kidding. I didn't even send out Christmas cards.

But if he cut my hand off, I would start sending millions every year out of spite.

My laughter was full of nerves as Mick started the angle grinder.

But that still didn't work. And I really wanted (maybe even needed) to cry. If I hadn't been handcuffed to Ryan Jones, I would have been sobbing already for sure. I literally wanted to throw up. And realizing that I wanted to run into the restroom as fast as I could and hurl into the toilet, I also suddenly realized how badly I needed to pee.

"I guess we're going back to my hotel," Ryan said as Mick put the angle grinder away. "I bet the concierge can quietly help us figure something out."

"I have to pee," I told him.

But Ryan dismissed me. "You can pee at the hotel."

"I need to pee right now," I told him.

"Why didn't you go at the restaurant?"

"Because I didn't have to."

"I thought you'd rather die."

"I changed my mind," I said. "I'm always changing my mind."

"No, you're not."

"You've figured that out in the last four hours of knowing me?" Why was he being difficult?

"I've known you since the fourth grade."

"We didn't know each other in the fourth grade, dude."

"Sure we did."

"We knew each other's names."

"That's knowing each other in fourth grade," Ryan argued, while Madison, Mick, and Lydia all watched us.

"Do you remember when we were having dinner at the Cannery and you got all dramatic about how badly you had to use the restroom, insisting that you had to go now, now, now while stomping your foot?"

"I never stomped my foot."

"That's not how I remember it," I said, glaring. "I'm going to use the restroom. The small one in Madison's laundry room with the toilet right next to the door. You will stand outside that door while I stretch my arm as far as it can go so that you're not in the room with me while I take care of my needs. Agreed?"

"Fine. What song should I sing? 'Jailbreak'? 'Smooth Criminal'? I know, 'Take the Money and Run'!"

Together, we walked to the laundry room, and I slipped inside while he waited on the other side of the door and began to belt out: "That's the sound of the men working on the chain gang..."

Very funny. He'd ditched his shyness, but Mr. Hollywood had managed to hang onto his dorky sense of humor.

I tried to hang onto how annoyed I was with him.

Madison had an eye for decoration, and even the rarely used restroom felt thoroughly loved, decorated with vintage coastal accents, softly lit and filled with a gentle fragrance of lavender. An oddly charming space to harbor the peculiar awkwardness in this moment.

"I didn't hear a sink. You're not going to wash your hands?" Ryan said once I was back in the laundry room.

"No, I'm good." Then I wiped my hand on his face like we were still in fourth grade.

Ryan blanched but didn't otherwise appear to know

what he should do with that. It almost looked like he wanted to laugh.

I grinned. "That sink doesn't work. There's a bottle of hand sanitizer on the shelf."

We made our way back to the garage.

Mick came over.

"I have an idea," he said.

"And what might that be?" I didn't trust the look on his face at all.

"I have an oxy-fuel torch."

Ryan and I exchanged a nervous glance. While he'd been all for the angel grinder — angle, whatever — he did not look like he loved the idea of anything involving a torch.

"It's a high temperature torch," Mick said, puffing out his chest slightly. "It combines pure oxygen with a fuel source."

"That sounds dangerous," I said.

"Only in the hands of an amateur. The flame is capable of melting or cutting through nearly anything. We'll have to be careful, but it'll do the trick for sure."

"No way." I shook my head while making fists at my sides. "I said yes to that angle grinder or whatever and that was terrifying. This is a hard no, and you can't make me do it. I don't care how rich and famous he is, I'm not letting a 'high temperature torch that combines pure oxygen with a fuel source' anywhere near my flesh just because you're afraid of being seen handcuffed to me."

Mick looked to Ryan.

Ryan pointed at me. "I'm with her."

Mick's shoulders sagged with disappointment. He glanced tenderly at the oxy-whatever-torch. "Someday, my friend."

Lydia interrupted the moment by poking her head

through the doorway. I hadn't realized she'd left. "More bad news," she said.

"What is it?" I asked.

"I just got off the phone with my grandson, Elliot."

"The one who works for the Pentagon?" Ryan asked.

"And loaned you these handcuffs?" I added.

"A big giant bingo to both of you." Lydia nodded. "It turns out the handcuffs are prototypes made of a new kind of titanium alloy. They're not classified or anything. Apparently, these puppies are in full and heavy production. Elliot thought that I'd get a kick out of using something he helped bring into this world for my fundraiser. He was right, and I jumped at the chance, but now, unfortunately, I have to admit that I really screwed up by not thinking this through."

"Why exactly didn't you think it through?" Ryan asked, his voice terse, seeming more than mildly upset, but trying to hold himself in check.

"Well, there's only one key," Lydia explained. "And I'm embarrassed to admit that I don't have a contingency plan."

"So what does that mean?" Ryan kept pressing.

"That Elliot needs to make another key."

"How long will that take?" I asked.

"Making the key won't take more than a few minutes. The problem is that Elliot doesn't have the materials to make the key because he's currently out of the country."

"And when will he be back?" Ryan asked, his jaw hardening.

Lydia looked like she didn't want to say.

"Go ahead…" I put an encouraging hand on her arm. "You can tell us."

"Elliot won't be back for five more days," Lydia admitted.

Five days of peeing with the bathroom door open while Ryan serenaded me from right outside.

What about showering?

Were we supposed to sleep in the same bed?

I had barely made it through five hours chained to Mr. Hollywood. Five days would be impossible.

"Nope. Uh-uh. That is not going to work for me." Ryan shook his head, more adamant than I had seen him all night. "I'm sure we can put our heads together and find another solution. Might I suggest the concierge at the Fisherman's Finest again?"

"That's a terrible idea." Lydia made a face.

"Why?" Ryan asked.

"Because Angus can't help himself. He really does give it the old college try when it comes to providing his guests with discretion, but if they don't actually live here in Ocean Springs, then that man is an absolute gossip."

"But I was born in Ocean Springs," Ryan protested. "And he's kept my appearance a secret before."

"Which time? When you were here six months ago, or the time before that when you ate so much crab your belt buckle exploded?"

Ryan flushed. "That's not what happened. And how did you—"

"I talk to Angus. He brings it up."

"Oh." Ryan looked hurt. Genuinely hurt. Had he really thought Angus was keeping his appearances a secret? I hadn't known he was making secret appearances in Ocean Springs, but I never talked to Angus. I'd heard rumors but I thought they were just that — rumors.

"And there's nothing your grandson can do?" Ryan pressed. "There's no one he can communicate with here in the States who could make the key on his behalf?"

"I'm sorry," Lydia shook her head. "There's nothing he

can do until he's back home in Washington. We'll just have to wait."

Five days of that song.

I turned to Mick. "Use the torch."

Ryan's face went white.

Mick, torch already in hand, looked like a kid who'd just learned he was allowed to eat an entire chocolate cake to himself.

"I was joking," I said before Mick could light up his torch.

Ryan breathed a sigh of relief.

I resisted the urge to laugh. While this wasn't my ideal living arrangement, maybe I could at least have some fun with it.

"So what are we going to do?" Ryan asked.

Lydia frowned. "I don't know. But I do know we're all in this together."

"I think that Olivia and I are a little more in this together than anyone else right now," Ryan said jiggling our handcuffs.

"I think we should be discussing solutions right now," Lydia said.

"That's exactly what I've been trying to say." Ryan threw his hands up in the air, now clearly irritated by the situation. The handcuff pulled my one hand up with his, making me look equally exasperated.

"No," Lydia shook her head. "I mean, as much as you two understandably hate the position you're in right now, you will be handcuffed together for the next five days, and there is nothing any of us can do to change that. So I suggest we come up with a system for navigating the next five days."

"What kind of system?" I asked.

"For example, you both have to agree on anything that

you want to do."

Ryan and I traded a glance.

"Okay…" we both said.

"And maybe you each get three passes," Madison suggested.

Lydia nodded in approval.

"And how would that work?" Ryan asked.

Madison was suddenly in full lawyer mode. "You will each get to veto the thing that your partner wants to do in the event that you use one of your passes, but once you use that pass up, then you must go along with whatever your partner wants."

"Oh, I love that," Lydia said.

"Three passes doesn't seem like nearly enough," Ryan protested.

"Agreed," I said.

"But that's what makes the passes special," Lydia argued.

"I'm with Lydia." Madison nodded. "I think it should be three passes too."

"Okay, great," Ryan clapped. "Sounds like that's settled. Now, who wants to take us back to the hotel?" He turned to Lydia with a smile.

"What about Angus?" she asked.

"I'll—"

I cut Ryan off before he could provide his ill-advised plan on dealing with Angus. It was bad enough that I would have to sleep in the same bed with him. There would be gossip — and while Ryan could run back to Hollywood and ignore it, I would have to live with it for the rest of my life.

That's why I said what I said next. Not because I didn't trust myself to be alone in a hotel room with the man I'd fantasized about for years.

"I'm not going back there. I don't care how gorgeous the hotel is, I'm not spending the night in your room. I've slept in my own bed every night since I moved back here from Los Angeles. Peacefully. I'm not about to lay my head on another pillow tonight."

"Poetic," Ryan mocked me.

"I'm going home," I insisted.

"That's going to be awfully hard. With me attached to you like this." He raised our wrists to prove he was stronger than me.

"I'm going home," I repeated.

"We're going to the hotel," Ryan pressed.

But then I couldn't take it anymore.

So I said the one thing I could.

NINE

Olivia
_____

"Pass," I said.

Ryan chuckled like he thought I was joking. "We're not going to your house."

"Actually, we are. I just said 'pass' so that means you have to do exactly what I say."

Ryan cocked his head, raised his eyebrows, and took a quick glance at my still-too-revealing outfit. "So if I say pass, does that mean you have to do exactly what I say when we get to your bedroom?"

I glared as hard as I could, mostly to stop the heat that was creeping to my cheeks.

"I feel like you two need a room," Madison said, breaking the tension.

"We've already got one," Ryan said. "Apparently, we're spending the night in her bedroom."

"You make it sound like something it's not," I said.

"Just stating facts."

"Well… stop." I was still a bit flustered from the mere insinuation that a movie star would want to do anything with me in my bedroom. Never mind Ryan Jones. Six months ago, if someone had told me Ryan Jones would be spending the night with me — and wearing handcuffs — I probably would've passed out.

I cleared my throat and tried to shake some truly inappropriate images from my mind. "So. Are we going to my house?"

"Sure, if you really want to use your first pass right now. You'll only have two left."

"I can math," I said. "My house is three blocks away from here. I am exhausted, and as you won't stop constantly saying, the paparazzi are all over Fisherman's Finest. So if you want to stay incognito, the best place for us to be right now is my house and not your hotel."

Lydia said, "You know I love agreeing with you, kiddo, but Olivia is right. You should stay at her house tonight, and maybe we can figure out a better situation tomorrow."

"Fine." It looked like he didn't like being called "kiddo" at all. "But we're going to your house in the trunk."

There was a loud cry from upstairs.

Apparently, Kai had woken up.

Madison stared at Mick. "Your turn. The bottle is already warmed up. I'll be up in a minute."

Mick left to take care of his son.

"There will be no trunks," Madison said. "Kai at night is a two-parent job, so the Camry's off limits, and Lydia only has a Mini Cooper. You'll have to think of something else."

"It's only three blocks to my place. It's a nice walk. I make it once a day with a pack of seven dogs in front of me. I'm sure I can handle one hound." I jiggled the handcuffs and eyed Ryan. "You'll be a good boy, won't you?"

"Unless I see a squirrel — then I'm dragging your butt into the trees."

The absurdity of the image — Ryan taking off into the trees, his tongue lolling out of his mouth as he chased a squirrel — made me burst out laughing. Ryan's eyes met mine and he smiled.

"I'll walk with you guys," Lydia offered.

Madison loaned us a sweater, which we draped between my left hand and his right to disguise our situation as best we could while walking down the street. Lydia looked all around, either on Ryan's behalf to make him feel like she were being vigilant, or because she actually believed his nonsense about paparazzi hiding in the bushes.

Although, after leaving the house (and no, I would never admit this to Ryan Jones for any amount of money), I did feel an unsettling sense of someone watching from the shadows.

It had been Madison's idea to disguise Ryan in a balaclava as we left the house. Same as with Lydia looking all around as we walked, I wasn't really sure if the intent was to help Ryan disguise his identity like she said, or if Madison was messing with the movie star so that the two of us could laugh about it later. Either way, I was grateful for her being here to help me out tonight, even though Madison is the one who got me into this mess in the first place, along with Brooklyn and Ashleigh.

We were halfway between my place and Madison's when the glare of headlights caught us off-guard.

A police cruiser eased up to the curb, spotlighting our motley trio. Ryan's ski mask, initially amusing, now seemed like a dreadful choice.

And my so-called robber officer costume, which had felt like a daring thing to wear earlier this evening, now left me feeling exposed, with the chilly night air brushing against my bare midriff. But then my body tingled all over with the memory of Ryan looking at me so appreciatively during dinner.

"Strange time for a walk," the officer said from his cruiser.

"We were just at the fundraiser tonight. At the theater," I explained. "There was a cops and robbers theme. So that's why we're dressed this way."

"That's right." The officer nodded. "Ryan Jones is back in town. That explains all the commotion over at the waterfront."

"I'm sure it's a zoo," I nodded back.

Lydia stepped up. "I'm Lydia, and I'm the theater director. Olivia and her friend Mason here were just helping me out by cleaning up after the fundraiser. Our friend Madison drove us all over to her place on Ramona, and we were just walking home to Olivia's house."

I said, "My address is 2097 Hollyhock Lane, if you need to know it."

"Thank you for the information, ma'am, but it's not necessary." The officer smiled and gave us all a friendly wave. "You folks have a nice night."

Having a nice night seemed impossible at this point.

We made our way the last block and a half to my house, where my mom was waiting at the door to let us in, as if she could tell the future and knew that we were on our way. And knowing my mom, such a thing was not totally impossible.

"Hi, Mom." I greeted her with a wave, suddenly wondering if insisting that we come back to my place was such a good idea after all.

Ryan pulled the balaclava from his head and studied my mother, clearly wondering what to make of the free-thinking woman standing before him. Pure silver hair loosely pulled back, with a few wisps framing a face that always looked sun kissed, regardless of the lighting, her eyes still reflecting a soul that had danced barefoot through festivals and protest marches alike.

My mom was also loud, obnoxious, and embarrassing as all get out. But I still loved her more than anything.

"I'm Helen." Mom offered her hand to the actor standing on her front porch. "And you're the very famous Ryan Jones. Last time we met, it looked like you needed to pee your pants."

"It's good to meet you, Helen," Ryan replied in a kind voice as they shook hands. "I still need to pee all the time."

Then we entered the house, and I felt bad for not warning Ryan about the dogs at any point during our three-block walk over, once I saw what was clearly his barely stifled fear.

It was suddenly deafening, with a cacophony of barks and tail wagging from the assembly of motley rescue dogs that roamed freely around our house. The ancient and wise-eyed golden retriever; two energetic terriers; a gentle-eyed three-legged pit bull (staying back but eyeing Ryan from the corner); and an overly enthusiastic Dalmatian who wasn't present to paw at the movie star, but was probably asleep in the bathtub upstairs.

And then there was the cat, perched on his cat tower near the entrance, lazily glaring at us for disturbing one of his twenty hours of daily sleep.

"This is a lot of dogs," Ryan said, his voice uneven.

"You don't like dogs?" Mom sounded shocked. "Who doesn't like dogs? They're rescues. I can't help myself."

Ryan cowered back from the small army of canines sniffing and jumping and nuzzling him, their eyes wide and tongues lolling.

I almost felt empathetic as my heart rate spiked in sympathy and my palms started to sweat on his behalf, as he struggled to maintain his composure. All of those eyes on him from furry faces full of canine teeth and the unpredictable energy of dogs he didn't know.

But my mom just looked at Ryan with a smile and said, "Don't they just warm your heart?"

"They sure get my heart going," he replied with a clearly forced smile.

"I should explain." Lydia redirected us to the situation at hand with an awkward smile. "This is all my fault."

She pulled Madison's sweater up from our joined wrists like a curtain rising on a dramatic scene and said, "It was my idea to cuff them for dinner, but my massive folly that I lost the key."

"Oh," Mom said, eyeing the handcuffs. "Your father and I had a pair like that."

"Not the time, Mom."

While I shuddered from embarrassment, Lydia looked like she might start to cry again. Ryan reached out and set his hand on her shoulder, then smiled and winked. That seemed to reassure her.

"I don't see any problem here," Mom said. "I'm thrilled that Olivia brought a boy home. It's long overdue. You know how many months she's been moping around this house talking about Taylor, her stupid ex-boyfriend?"

"Mom!"

"Mom, nothing." She shook her head. "Mope, mope, mope, mope. That's all you've been doing for months now—"

"That's not all I've been doing!"

"—stupid Taylor this and stupid Taylor that and your former maid of honor sucks and you hope she somehow ends up inheriting a parrot that never stops singing 'Baby'—"

"Please stop."

"—Shark.' I'm sorry, honey, but make a new dream. Get another idea. Start a new life with someone else, someone better than Taylor. Maybe a movie star. You never know when you might meet one of those. Funny that you never did in LA, and now here the two of you are."

My mother started to cackle like she was actually funny.

"The two of us are only here because of a mistake," I clarified.

"I made a mistake once, then nine months later, you arrived," Mom said. She pretended to cover her mouth. "Whoops, said the quiet part out loud, didn't I? You are very welcome to stay here as long as you like, Mr. Jones."

"Ryan," he corrected, smiling like a movie star — but clearly unsure how to respond to my mom. She was a lot. For everyone.

"Ryan, you are welcome to stay in my home, so long as you don't mind that Olivia still has her teddy bear, Cappuccino, on her bed and insists on wearing mismatched socks because she believes it brings her good luck."

"Mom!"

But of course my mother kept going, and it got even worse.

"Even after you get the key back, you might want to keep the handcuffs."

"Mom, no."

"Well I'd be happy to take them."

"MOM."

"My daughter has always been uptight when it comes to talking about that stuff," she said to Ryan and Lydia, while I wanted to die eight times in a row from embarrassment. "I always thought the more honest I was with her, the freer she would feel. There are few things more damaging to the women of this world, to my mind, than shame around sex. But no matter how open I am, I can't ever get Olivia to appreciate it."

The conversation fell into a lull with her revelation. She stopped talking, and both Ryan and Lydia were clearly confused as to the most appropriate thing to maybe say next.

I just stared back at my mother, trying not to stew at her.

Damn right, she made it even harder.

"Do you need any condoms?" she practically chirped, making herself sound like she was actually trying to be helpful instead of dragging me down into a black hole of embarrassment.

"We'll behave," Ryan said.

"Well, I'll leave you alone then. Just ring the bell if you need me." Mom started to walk away, but then turned back at the bottom of the stairs and looked at Ryan. "I literally mean that. There are bells and wind chimes all over the house. Just ring one if you need me."

And then she was gone.

"Your mom is wonderful," Lydia said, once she was out of earshot.

"When I was in seventh grade, she volunteered to teach sex ed. Like actually," I said. "Who does that?"

"I like her." Ryan nodded. "Your mom is awesome."

He sounded like he meant it, too.

Which made him the first boy to come to my house and not be completely embarrassed, humiliated, or terrified of my mom.

That was something, I supposed.

Still standing at the doorway, Lydia reached out and touched both of our hands. "I'll be back to check on you two tomorrow. In the meantime, use your passes, and remember, communication is key. If words fail, use one of those bells to break the ice."

Lydia winked as she opened the door and disappeared on the other side of it.

Ryan looked around, fully taking in my house — or at least what he could see of it from the entry. Then his eyes met mine. "So. Should we take a look at this bedroom you were so desperate to stay in?"

"It's right upstairs," I said.

But when my foot touched the first stair, I remembered something truly horrible.

I was taking Ryan Jones to my bedroom.

My bedroom, which still looked like it did when I was in college.

My bedroom, which was covered with posters prominently featuring Ryan Jones.

Some of them where he was shirtless.

Like I was some kind of stalker who'd built a four-wall shrine to him.

I stopped. "Maybe we should go to the hotel instead."

Ryan frowned, confused. Then the confusion disappeared and his smile widened into something I could only describe as diabolical. He cocked his head to the side. "So just how embarrassing is your childhood bedroom, Olivia?"

TEN

Olivia
_____

I PAUSED in front of my bedroom door. "I need you to promise not to judge me."

Ryan was still wearing his diabolical grin. "What are you hiding in there?"

"Nothing that I should be ashamed of."

"So let me in."

"I can't."

"Why not?"

"Because I'm ashamed of it."

Ryan burst out laughing. "You know the anticipation is only making it worse, right?"

"Yeah, but…"

There was no but.

Ryan Jones was going to see my bedroom, the walls plastered with posters of him smiling. And a strategically positioned poster of him shirtless, on my ceiling, directly above my bed.

That had been my mom's idea.

She said it was to help me with my "explorations."

I sighed, closed my eyes, and pushed open the bedroom

door. I felt Ryan slip by, then heard a murmur of disappointment.

I opened my eyes.

My room was the same as it had always been — like diving headfirst into a time capsule, untouched pastel walls obscured by a collage of posters, trinkets, and memories from when I was seventeen and younger.

But, where posters of Ryan Jones had been, there were now blank spaces.

Several of them.

My phone buzzed in my pocket with a text from Mom: *I took down the posters when Madison told me what happened. I thought it might be embarrassing. And that you wouldn't need them now that you had the real thing. I'll wear ear plugs. Love, Mom.*

She always signed her texts. I felt a mixture of gratitude and embarrassment.

My phone buzzed with another text from her, but I ignored it.

"I thought you'd have… I don't know… something?" Ryan said, not bothering to hide the disappointment in his voice. "Why were you so worried?"

"Because this stuff is ancient," I said, allowing myself to be pulled along by his handcuff. "It's all from when I was seventeen. It's embarrassing."

"It's a part of where you came from. Easier to accept it than be embarrassed by it." Ryan tentatively poked around my room, limited somewhat by our handcuff. He eyed the door in the corner. "Oh, an en suite bathroom. Does it have a shower?"

Before I could correct him and tell him that was my closet — and that most seventeen-year-olds didn't have en suite bathrooms — he had yanked open the door.

And out came tumbling all of the Ryan Jones posters my

mom had removed from my walls. The posters went all the way back to his breakout role in *Heaven's Flight*. The poster featured Ryan with round adolescent cheeks looking upward, his piercing blue eyes full of wonder and determination.

To that poster's right was one from *Metropolis Dreams*, where a slightly older Ryan in his early 20s was perched high on a skyscraper beam with a sprawling cityscape below him, his chestnut brown hair tousled by the wind.

Ryan wore a leather jacket and looked ready to conquer the world in *King's Rebellion*. That movie had been my favorite look for Ryan, with his long flowing locks and smoldering eyes, wielding a sword to go with his medieval armor, standing defiantly on a hill with an army amassed behind him, fiery skies in the background hinting at epic battles to come.

Ryan's mouth made an "oh" shape that barely concealed the grin I could already feel was beginning to form.

"Those aren't mine," I said quickly and way-too-casually, like a high school student who's been busted with something they shouldn't have. My cheeks now on literal fire, I pulled out my phone and did my absolute best to avoid eye contact. I read the text from my mom.

P.S. I put all the posters in your closet. Oh, the cut-out is in there, too. Love, Mom.

Fear wrapped me in its shivering embrace as I looked to see—

Ryan, kneeling, sorting through the posters. "I'm sure these aren't yours. You're just keeping them for a friend, right?"

Then, before I could do anything, my life-sized cut-out of Ryan Jones — shirtless, smiling, and with a fake wedding band I'd scribbled on his ring finger — teetered out of my closet and bonked the real Ryan Jones on the head.

Ryan blinked, seeing double.

Then he howled with laughter.

Like, howled.

This could have only happened to me.

Ryan, who would've been rolling on the floor if not for my handcuff holding him up, was practically breathless as he said, "Do you want me to sign any of these?"

I gritted my teeth so hard I'd need dental work the next morning. "If you'll excuse me, I need to crawl under my bed and die."

"And I," Ryan started, pulling out his phone and taking a selfie of himself with his life-size cut out, "need to talk to Lucas."

While I steeped in humiliation, Ryan spoke with his friend.

"Yo … Yeah, I was hoping you could bring me a change of clothes … Right? … Sure … I'm at Olivia's house… the winner. No. I am not 'getting lucky.' It's not like that… Believe me, dude. There is nothing fortunate about this situation. Maggie owes me big time. Can you come? Thanks."

"Can he help?" I asked, pretending my cheeks weren't still burning.

"I dropped him a pin. He's going to swing by."

"I want to try removing the handcuffs again," I said. "Do you have any ideas?"

"Other than do everything we possibly can to try and get them off before your friend gets here? No."

"Just tell me where you think we should start."

I led him into the bathroom and motioned to a countertop lined with an assortment of bottles: soaps and lotions and oils.

I grabbed a bottle of lavender-scented oil. "If we lubricate ourselves up enough, it should slide right off."

"They're on pretty tight."

"Do you have a better idea?" I snapped. I didn't mean to snap, but I'd just been humiliated by a cardboard version of Ryan, so I wasn't about to take any lip from the live-in-the-flesh version.

He stuck out his wrist. "Lube me up."

I poured a generous portion of oil on his wrist and rubbed it in with my thumbs, trying to force the oil between his skin and the metal of the handcuff. I tried not to think about how warm — and surprisingly soft — his skin was. Nor did I want to think about how close I was to him, and what it would be like to rub this perfectly scented oil all over his body.

Or vice versa.

"Okay. Pull," I said, my cheeks now hot for a completely different reason.

Ryan pulled, but try as he might, the cuff wouldn't slide past his wrist.

"Ugh. Maybe it'll work on me. My wrists are smaller." I passed the slippery bottle to Ryan and stuck out my cuffed wrist. "Pour the oil on and do me fast."

Ryan raised his eyebrows so high they touched the ceiling.

"You know what I meant," I snapped.

"Of course." Ryan squirted the lavender-scented oil onto my wrist. Then, with his hands, he began trying to work the oil under my cuff, the same as I had done for him. His grip was strong and his thumbs firm as they rubbed along my forearm and pushed the warm oil up to my wrist. I felt myself relax under the massage and almost groaned.

Thankfully, I stopped myself.

Now that would've been embarrassing.

We spent the next several minutes in a blur of bending, tugging, and pulling, using every ounce of our mutual strength to no avail.

Despite our joint efforts and much to our growing dismay, the stubborn cuffs refused to budge. I finally surrendered a moment before Ryan's phone buzzed with a text.

He looked at the screen and said, "Lucas is at the door, but he doesn't want to ring your doorbell."

"Good. The less he sees of my mother, the better. If she finds out Lucas Stone was here, she'll never shut up about the time her daughter had two movie stars over in one night."

We went downstairs, and I opened the door to find myself face to face with the second movie star that night. So life in Ocean Springs was definitely getting weird.

Lucas greeted me with a cheeky grin. "So you're the superfan."

"I am not!"

He pointed at Ryan. "Are you the real Ryan or the cut-out?"

"I'm the cut-out," Ryan quipped. "The real Ryan is locked upstairs in her closet."

"I hate both of you right now," I muttered.

Lucas reached out and touched the cuffs, then quickly pulled back his hand in disgust. "Why are you wet?"

"It's oil," Ryan said. "We were trying to get them off."

Lucas burst out laughing.

"It's not funny," Ryan said.

"It's kind of funny," Lucas argued. "Maybe even really funny. You should definitely stay away from the paparazzi."

"Don't worry, Ryan has already articulated his allergies to the press."

"Not the press," Lucas corrected, "the paparazzi. The paparazzi are not journalists, they're like gnats that never leave you alone at a barbecue."

"Or vultures with cameras instead of beaks," Ryan said.

Still chuckling, Lucas said, "So, I'm assuming this is a lost key sort of situation."

Ryan nodded. "Lydia has no idea where she left it."

"And her grandson apparently made the handcuffs," I added. "He can't make another key until he's back in the country, five days from now."

Lucas laughed again.

"I'm glad you find this entertaining," Ryan deadpanned.

"Entertaining? This is the best thing that's ever happened in life. Absolutely hilarious."

"It is the opposite of hilarious," Ryan said.

"It'll be hilarious someday once the handcuffs are off of you guys, and this is a story you both get to tell."

"I won't be telling the story," I said.

Ryan turned and looked at me with raised eyebrows. "I'm sure that you're going to tell this story every chance that you get."

"I'll just leave that to your 'trusted people' at the hotel."

Ryan's playful grin quickly faded. Had he seriously been that hurt by finding out that Angus had been gossiping about him at every opportunity? He couldn't be that surprised — he was a movie star, after all.

"I brought your clothes. And bought some more from the gift shop. They're inside, too." Lucas set a rolling suitcase inside the door, then looked at me. "Don't kill my buddy. I know he's a lot, but he's a good dude. And he has a big career waiting for him back in Hollywood once he cleans up his messes."

"You should stay in town for a few days," Ryan said quickly.

"Can't. I'm off to scout a location."

"Location scouting? Why?"

I looked between the two friends, clearly not picking up on something.

Lucas smiled. "I'm going with Roman. He's helping me to scout a location for a script I just optioned."

"You optioned a script?"

Lucas winked. "Sure did."

"Dude, that's awesome!" Without thinking about the handcuffs, Ryan pulled Lucas — and me — into a group hug. It was weird to be part of a group hug when I wasn't part of the group. "You're moving up in the world."

"I'm going to produce. Be in charge of my own career. Find new roles."

"That's really awesome," Ryan said, finally releasing the hug. "What script? Anything I know?"

"It's a surprise."

"When are you planning to take it out of the box?"

"Maybe when Roman and I get back from our trip," Lucas said.

"So Roman gets to know before me."

"Roman already knows, so yeah," Lucas replied without apology.

"Where are you scouting?"

"Washington state."

"Washington state will still be there a few days from now. We could hang out until then." Ryan looked sadly hopeful.

Lucas raised his eyebrows again. "It's not fair to Roman."

"I'll pay his daily rate," Ryan offered. "Double, triple, quadruple, whatever he normally charges as a location scout. Just stick around until we can figure this out."

"Everyone has a price," I mocked him.

Lucas shook his head. "Sorry, man. I really wish I could help you, and if you had put this mishap on the calendar alongside the fundraiser, you know I would have been there for you." He laughed. "But right now we're on a tight schedule, and I need to be 'producer Lucas' instead of good time actor Lucas right now. Are you picking up what I'm putting down now?"

Then Lucas was gone, and Ryan was taking a bag full of clothes that Lucas had bought from the Fisherman's Finest gift shop up the stairs and into my bedroom. He set his suitcase at the bottom of the bed like he was staying in a hotel.

"So. Before bed, there's one more thing I want to do."

"What's that?" I asked.

"We need to wash off all this oil." Ryan's eyes met mine. "We need to take a shower."

ELEVEN

Olivia

"WE DON'T NEED TO SHOWER," I said way too quickly, now standing in the bathroom with him. I opened a cupboard, pulled out a navy-blue hand towel, and handed it to Ryan. "We can get the oil off with this."

Ryan looked at the towel doubtfully. "I don't think this is going to cut it."

"You haven't even tried."

He sighed, took the towel, and tried wiping the oil from his cuffed wrist. "Even if we get most of it off, there's still going to be some left. And it's going to get uncomfortable when we try to go to bed."

I'd been trying to avoid thinking about going to bed with him. How were we going to navigate that hurdle? I liked to toss and turn — not something easily achievable when you were handcuffed to someone else. And what if he snored?

Or worse — what if I snored?

Ryan rubbed the towel over the handcuff, but at best he was just smearing the oil around. "If we could just shower—"

"It'll absorb into your skin if you wait long enough."

"Why won't you let me shower?"

The question was more complicated than he thought it was. My brain, the part of me that knew the somewhat charming image he'd presented to me most of the night was a facade, and that the real Ryan was the one who screamed at directors, didn't want to end up in a compromising position. I didn't want to open myself up to someone who was secretly a jerk. Not again.

My eyes and my body, however, were very open to the idea of getting into a compromising position with Ryan. Did it matter if he was a jerk if he was only around for a few days?

Ryan handed me the oil-soaked towel. Despite his best efforts to scrub himself dry, his wrist still glistened. "Do you—"

"Fine, you can shower," my mouth snapped. My body celebrated. My eyes were already roving across his body, just wondering exactly what we'd find when we stripped him out of his costume.

Satisfied, Ryan started to take off his shirt, and he'd just pulled the hem up to where I could see his movie star quality abs when he stopped.

"What's wrong?" I squeaked. Like my voice actually squeaked as though I were one of Cinderella's mice.

"I won't be able to take this shirt off while I'm wearing handcuffs."

He was right. Unless he physically pulled me through his sleeve, there was no way his shirt was coming off.

His eyes begged me for a solution.

I grabbed a pair of scissors that I used to trim my hair from the bathroom drawer. "We'll have to cut it off."

"We can't. This is a costume I borrowed from the studio archives, so—"

It was too late, my scissors had already snipped into the fabric and were quickly doing their work. I heard what he said but had to keep going.

"What are you doing?"

"You know what I'm doing, and it's too late to stop me."

With each cut of the fabric, another piece of Ryan's costume fell away, and more of his absurdly toned body was revealed. He had muscles in places I didn't even know you could have muscles. Soon half of his shirt was in ribbons on the floor, and after he pulled the other half off, I was standing in my bathroom with a completely shirtless Ryan Jones.

My stomach was doing flips.

My heart was setting off fireworks.

And my eyes were trying to high-five each other, which probably made me cross-eyed.

And dizzy.

This egotistical hometown hero was so gloriously gorgeous that I needed to lean against the bathroom counter to keep my balance.

"There," I said, my words far more breathless than I would've liked. I handed him another towel. "Now you can shower. Just don't get me wet."

"I don't make promises I can't keep." He climbed into the shower and drew the curtains closed. I took a seat on the toilet next to the shower, my hand dangling through the curtain but pressed against the wall. I didn't want to accidentally touch anything.

Or maybe I did.

Which was more of a problem.

Ryan slid his neatly folded pants through the far side of the curtain, letting them fall to the floor in a heap. There was a rush of cold water.

Ryan yelped.

"It takes a while to warm up," I said, grinning. I could have warned him that the tap water in mom's house was ice cold, and would take minutes before it got hot, but where was the fun in that?

"It's … refreshing," Ryan said through chattering teeth. "Just get it over with."

He turned, pulling my arm further into the shower, and a spray of icy cold droplets splashed the inside of my wrist. As I shivered, the scent of coconut and vanilla hit me a moment before a blob of body wash splatted against the palm of my hand. I instinctively pulled back, and my knuckles dragged over skin before soapy fingers tightened around my wrist.

"Hold still," he said. "If you get handsy with me, I'm not autographing your cut-out."

I was so grateful he couldn't see how red my face was. "I wasn't expecting you to dribble soap all over my hand."

"It's a *shower*. Soap and water are implied."

"This is not how showers usually work for me, believe it or not."

But I couldn't help wondering how often fans did get handsy with him. Imagine having a stranger come up to you and grope you, and having to smile and be polite because someone was probably live streaming the whole encounter to social media.

Ugh. That might be even worse than being stalked by paparazzi. At least with them, everyone understood that you were being harassed. A meltdown at a fan could be even more damaging than—

I made the mistake of glancing up, derailing that train of thought, and my ability to have thoughts at all.

His sculpted body was a silhouette on the other side of the curtain, soaping and lathering around our bound wrists and trying fruitlessly yet again to slip the cuffs off them.

Even though I technically couldn't see anything but the outline of his body, my brain wanted to fill the details in anyway, imagining every inch. The false privacy of the shower curtain made this moment feel even more invasive than it would've if I'd accidentally peeped at him naked.

Just a few more seconds. Then I would give him as much actual privacy as I could.

He finally turned the water off and pulled the towel off the curtain rod. He wrapped it around his waist and pulled back the curtain.

To find me staring.

And I couldn't stop.

I hated the reality, but I could not deny it: yes, I still very much found him so very attractive. Every sinew and muscle on his torso were defined, from the ridges of his abs to the broad sweep of his shoulders. Wet hair clung to his forehead, somehow amplifying the intensity of his eyes and the ruggedness of his jawline.

Yes, the gorgeous actor was standing mostly naked in front of me, but now that I could see everything, I couldn't stop picturing the shaky footage showcase his popping veins and angry face as he berated André Dosh.

Half of me wanted to rake my gaze — and my finger-nails — over his body until he could no longer stand it and pulled me into a passionate embrace, smooching me with his leading man kisses. The other half wanted to race back to Madison's and demand Mick use his oxy-torch to melt through the handcuffs and get Ryan out of my life forever. Or at least before I did something really stupid.

Unfortunately, no matter what I tried now or in the future, Ryan Jones would never leave my memory.

And had this man ever eaten anything fried?

How many hours a day, week, and month did he spend in the gym?

He must have a personal trainer. Or trainers. And nutritionists.

Who else did you need on your team to look that good?

"What are you thinking about?" Ryan asked.

Because of course I was still staring.

"Nothing. Why would I be thinking about anything? It's late. I'm tired. You're the one who's thinking about something."

He looked at me for a long time, seeming to consider several responses before he finally settled on, "I'm thinking about going to sleep. I'm exhausted too. Can we get ready for bed now?"

"You can't go to bed yet," I told him.

"And why not?" Again, he looked surprised.

"Because I'm soaked, thanks to you. And now I need a shower too."

Ryan sighed like I was thoroughly exhausting him. "Can you please take your shower so I can go to bed?"

"So *we* can get to bed. Unfortunately."

"This has been the longest day of my life."

"I'm sure a big star like you has had much longer nights." Together, with him only wearing a towel, we went to my bedroom and pulled a pair of pajama pants out of his suitcase. He put them on, and then it was my turn to shower.

"You'll need to cut off my top," I said.

Ryan didn't reply on our way into the bathroom. He grabbed the scissors from the counter and went to work, cutting one straight line through the side of my costume. I felt the fabric pull away from my skin, loose, and wondered what Ryan was thinking as he saw a lot more of me than my already-revealing costume had showed.

"Can you close your eyes or something?" I said.

"You want me to close my eyes while wielding scissors?"

"Can you?"

"I might cut you."

"I'll risk it."

"Okay," he said hesitantly. He closed his eyes and continued cutting ever-so-slowly up the side of my shirt, using his fingers to figure out where exactly he was, until finally the side of my shirt fell away.

Freedom.

At least temporarily.

"You're done."

Ryan sat there, his eyes closed, scissors still in his hand. I removed the scissors and set them on the counter, then found myself a towel. The last towel. Laundry would be a must, ASAP.

I climbed into the shower, the hangers screeching against the curtain rod. Then I closed the curtain. "You can open your eyes again."

"Sure," Ryan said quietly.

I showered as best I could with one hand and tried to ignore the tingling that echoed through my body. I was showering with my former celebrity crush right next to me. There was his hand, right there, stuck against my shower wall. If he moved even a little bit—

I shook the thought away.

I was definitely not supposed to be thinking about anything like that.

Not now.

Not ever.

"If you were…" Ryan started. Then, "Never mind."

"Never mind what?"

"It's nothing."

"Just tell me."

"Why did you ask me to close my eyes?"

"I don't know? Because?" I scrubbed at the oil on my wrist.

Ryan waited patiently, drawing me out.

"Because I was self-conscious, okay? You get out of the shower, and it looks like you've never eaten something fried in your entire life. Then there's me. Even under the most flattering light, you can still see evidence of the donut I ate three weeks ago. It's hard to be mortal next to a god."

"Oh," Ryan said.

I attacked the oil on my arm with renewed vigor.

Then Ryan spoke again. "I don't know if it helps, but you don't have anything to be self-conscious about. You're very beautiful."

TWELVE

Ryan
_____

WE WERE FINALLY BOTH SHOWERED, dressed, and ready for bed, but I had to do something that Olivia either did not or could not understand.

"What do you mean you have to meditate?" she asked.

"I'm saying it in English and using the only word I know how to use. So I will say it again: I have to meditate."

"I don't have any difficulty understanding what meditation is. I just can't understand why you need to do it right now, as exhausted as you keep saying that you are. Am I supposed to just stand here and watch while you meditate?"

"You liked staring at me when I got out of the shower, how is this any different?"

"I wasn't staring."

"That's what it looked like to me."

"Maybe you were staring," Olivia said.

"Maybe I was," I shot back.

Olivia instantly went quiet.

Had I said something wrong?

Before I could ask her, she said, "Okay. _We_ meditate."

"We?"

"Yes, we."

"Okay. We." I shoved aside her movie posters and the cardboard cut-out to make a clear space for myself on the floor. Olivia followed suit, sitting across from me.

I took a deep breath, then closed my eyes.

Meditation was a positive for everyone, even though most people turned their back on the practice, even when knowing better. And yet I had never met anybody who wasn't better off after finally trying it. Everyone was always too busy in Hollywood, and most people acted like they couldn't afford a simple 10 minutes to simply clear their mind each day. Invariably, it was the people who insisted that they couldn't afford the time to meditate who needed the meditation practice most.

The day's events had left me mentally frazzled, and the only way I would be able to find any semblance of peace was through the stillness of my mind as I sat cross-legged on the floor.

I could feel Olivia watching me as I tuned into my breath, searching for that familiar rhythm that would transport me to a place of calm.

But even after a while, I still wasn't getting there.

Every inhale brought the scent of soap and oil escapades from earlier, and every slight shift of my wrist served as a reminder of our predicament.

It was a struggle, trying to find serenity amid the chaos of our situation, but I persisted, hoping to touch even a fleeting moment of stillness before sleep.

When I opened my eyes, I was not terribly surprised but certainly happy to see that Olivia's eyes were still closed, her breaths perfectly controlled. She probably did yoga.

Her eyes fluttered open.

Mesmerized, I saw that her eyes weren't just brown, they had golden flecks that shimmered faintly as she focused on me. She wasn't wearing specialty contacts — I've spent plenty of time staring dreamily at actresses on set who used them to enhance their own looks, but Olivia was beautiful without them. Without botox and lip fillers and lash extenders. Olivia was real, and that made her infinitely more gorgeous.

"Better?" she asked.

"Better."

We stood and looked at the bed. It was a double, big enough for one person, but barely big enough for two, unless you wanted to spend most of the night pressed up against each other. Not that I would've minded.

She would've, though.

"I'll sleep on the floor," I said.

"Can't. Won't work with handcuffs — your wrist'll be stuck in the air all night."

"So you want to share a bed?"

"Don't say it like that."

"How do you want me to say it?"

"We're not sharing a bed, we're just sleeping together."

"You think that sounds better?"

"No," Olivia muttered. "We're … sleeping companions. Co-sleepers. And I have rules for my co-sleepers."

"Of course you do."

"You need to sleep outside of the covers and I'll sleep inside."

I shrugged. "That sounds perfectly fine with me. My only rule is no talking after the first rule is stated, on account of it being past my bedtime."

Olivia didn't reply as we got onto the bed, with me staying on the outside and her getting under the covers.

The next quarter hour was a misery of tossing and

turning. I never thought Olivia was being intentionally obnoxious, but she sure did seem to itch a lot.

"Can you please use your other hand to do that? Every time you scratch, you're yanking my hand over to your body."

"Why don't we switch?" she suggested.

"What do you mean?"

"You can be under the covers and I'll be outside."

"Why?"

"Because I'm too hot."

"So you expect me to be too hot?"

"You do want to sleep?" Olivia asked. "Don't you?"

"Desperately."

So I agreed and got under the covers.

And it was like lying in a furnace. How could one person generate that much body heat?

"This is miserable," I said, after ten minutes that felt like twenty or more. "Can't we just both sleep on top of the covers? That's not intimate … if that's what you're afraid of."

"I'm not afraid of anything! Except for maybe spiders and bees. And running out of wi-fi in the middle of a binge."

Olivia grabbed a stuffed teddy bear, presumably Mr. Whatever his name was, and set it dead center in the middle of the bed.

"This is the invisible line down the bed," she said. "Neither one of us can go past this imaginary line. Got it?"

"Don't make a move or the teddy bear will bite me, got it."

Lying on our backs, we closed our eyes and tried to get some much-needed sleep.

But just a few moments later, I began to hear a strange scratching sound.

I assumed it would go away, just another bump in the night, but the scratching persisted.

It became intermittent, and that was somehow worse. Every time I was settling into some semblance of calm it would come back, incessant and grating on my already frayed nerves.

"Your cat is scratching at the door," I finally said.

"Just ignore him." Her tone made it sound like I was being unreasonable.

"How can you sleep with that?"

"I'm actually a lot more bothered by the Hollywood actor handcuffed to me in bed."

"Will he stop if we let him in?"

"There's definitely a better chance of him stopping if we let him in than if we don't," Olivia replied.

So then we got out of bed, opened the door, let the cat into her room, and closed him in with us.

Just a few minutes later, the cat, of course, wanted back outside.

And then it wanted in again.

"We would've been better off at the hotel," I said.

"Too bad — I used my pass."

"I invoke my pass against your pass. We're going to the hotel."

"Nope." The tone in her voice was a nail in the coffin of this conversation. "That's not how it works."

"Fine, we'll just sleep with the door open then, and your dumb cat can go in and out of the room at his feline leisure."

"You'll regret that," she warned me.

"Why?"

"Just a hunch." Olivia made it sound like a dare, and I took it. But sure enough, less than 10 minutes later, I did regret it, as I was now sharing the bed with three dogs and cat.

Still, exhaustion was eating me alive, so I closed my eyes, put myself back into a meditative state, and repeated a mantra in my mind that now was the time when I would find sleep.

But minutes later I felt an odd yet delicate sensation tickling my scalp. It went away and came back, a couple of times.

"It feels like something's crawling on my head," I said.

"That's probably just Felix. Must have got out of his cage."

"Another dog?"

"No," Olivia said. "Tarantula."

I bolted out of the bed and swatted at my scalp.

Thanks to the handcuffs, Olivia came with me.

And the dogs started barking.

The cat, however, looked less than impressed, lounging at the head of the bed, his long tail drifting over the side. It was a second, separate cat.

How many animals did this farm have?

Olivia should have been upset. But she was laughing. Hard.

"That was just Bells swishing his tail from the nightstand."

Olivia started laughing harder, pointing at a second cat sprawled out on the nightstand. I didn't want to give her the satisfaction of seeing me upset, so I slipped back into bed without another word.

But I couldn't stop my heart from pounding.

And even after we were both back in bed, I still couldn't sleep. After that straight shot of cortisol to my system, I was suddenly too wired.

There was a long moment of stillness, and then she said, "I'm sorry for laughing."

"It's okay," I said. I probably deserved it, after laughing so hard at her closet full of me.

"I get it. But I promise that I wasn't at you."

"Are you kidding? Of course, you were laughing at me. But it's fine. I've always wanted to be better at comedy."

Olivia laughed. "I thought you were funny in *Dude, Seriously*."

"Thank you." The smile spread all the way across my face. Not that she could see it in the dark. Comedy was hard, and *Dude, Seriously* was one of my favorite roles. Deeply underappreciated when it came to the critics. "It was always harder for me to be funny on-screen than it was to be sad."

"I think the critics got that one wrong," Olivia said.

Her words made me feel even lighter.

"Me too," I replied in barely a whisper.

"Do you have a favorite movie that you've been in?" Her voice was suddenly so gentle.

"I love them all for different reasons."

"I'm not a reporter. And this isn't a magazine interview. I'm sure you have a favorite."

"*Modern Memories*," I said.

"Really?" She sounded surprised. "That's my favorite too."

"What did you love about it?"

"Everything." And Olivia sounded like she meant it. "I loved the exploration of love and memories. How intertwined and fragile they can be. The concept of choosing to leave someone when you know it's time, and all the pain and joy that comes with those memories was so beautifully portrayed … and you were so great in it."

She yawned at the end of her sentence, then asked another question.

"What did you love about making *Modern Memories*?"

"The raw vulnerability of having to navigate through those emotions and all of Adam's memories. Beyond the character, I really loved working with a team who was just as passionate about telling that story as I…"

But then I stopped talking.

Because just a few sentences into my answer, I had bored Olivia right into snoring.

THIRTEEN

Olivia

A BEAM of morning sunlight spilled across my face and pulled me from sleep. For a blissful moment, I felt only the softness of my pillow.

I tried to reassemble the odds and ends of my strange dream: the revealing cops and robbers costumes, the disastrous dinner date with a Hollywood movie star, the infernal handcuffs that had kept us bound together.

I wanted to laugh at the nightmare as I exhaled into the morning, my eyes still closed as the sun kissed my skin.

I thought more about the dream, and the version of Ryan Jones in it. He had been exactly as I expected — entitled and arrogant, accustomed to getting his way. Yet despite his difficult demeanor, I'd gotten glimpses of his humanity.

A flash of humor, a moment of sincerity, a pang of vulnerability.

Was there more to him than the temperamental movie star I saw yelling in that viral video? Could the cocky leading man also be a real person deep down, complex and flawed like anyone else? Or was he just a cardboard cut-out?

The dream made me wonder if I had judged him too quickly.

I went to scratch my itching nose and realized (like a punch to the stomach) that my wrist was still wearing a titanium bracelet.

I must have been delusional not to feel that upon waking up.

I rolled over to the edge of the bed and peered down on the floor.

Ryan's tall frame was contorted, knees tucked to his chest, one arm pillowing his head while the other was suspended in an awkward angle above him, our hand-cuffed wrists dangling in the air. His face was pressed hard against the carpet as if trying to sink into it and disappear.

I almost felt bad seeing him looking so miserable — the big shot movie star scrunched up on the floor looking like a stepped-on spider.

"What are you doing down there?"

"It beat sleeping in the bed," Ryan replied.

"Why?" Whether or not he meant it that way, he had said it like an insult.

"Because you kept trying to snuggle me all night."

"I absolutely did not."

"Okay," he said.

"Don't okay me! I don't snuggle."

It was true. I had never been into snuggling. That was one of the things that me and Taylor always agreed on, even at the end.

"Well, you kept trying to snuggle up with me last night," Ryan insisted as he stretched out on the floor, his body uncurling from a broken comma into a fully erect exclamation point before he stood.

I suddenly became very aware of his shirtless torso again.

I felt a flush spread through me that I wished wasn't there. This was the same arrogant movie star who had frustrated me to no end last night. Yet seeing him now, muscles flexing as he stretched, it was hard not to notice how attractive he was.

I scolded myself even as my eyes traced along his chiseled abs and broad shoulders. Get it together, Olivia. This guy is a jerk.

But the memories of seeing those movies for the first time came rushing back — watching a fresh-faced Ryan Jones on the big screen, watching him emote through his late adolescence.

I had crushed on him hard for years, until that awful video.

I had to defend my honor. "Well, I'm sorry that you find me so repulsive that the bare threat of my touch would send you out of bed and onto the floor, where you slept like a dog."

"Slept like a dog?" Ryan laughed, glancing at the two canines still asleep at the foot of my bed. "The dogs in your house sleep better than the people do."

"The dogs deserve to sleep better than the people do."

"Are you referring to me, or yourself?" Ryan asked, his voice genuine.

His comment was way too introspective for me to deal with before I'd had breakfast. "Do you really want to start today with an argument?"

Ryan put his hands up in surrender. "Not at all. I would love to start my day by going to the bathroom. I have been waiting patiently for you to wake up."

"You don't look so patient."

"I've been down on the floor bunched into a ball so I

didn't go all over your floor. I don't know how much more patient you could expect a man to be."

"Especially a man like you?"

"And what kind of man am I?"

"One who is rich and famous and probably only uses a bidet."

"I've used a bidet exactly thrice," Ryan defended himself.

"Thrice?" I repeated with a laugh. "Are you practicing Shakespeare?"

"Can we just go now?"

We shuffled into the bathroom together, and after a few minutes of back-and-forth deliberation, came up with a system for taking care of business that neither one of us strongly objected to. It involved tossing a towel over the other person while they blocked their ears and loudly sang "Twinkle, Twinkle, Little Star."

Post-bathroom antics, dressing was our next hurdle. The logistics were even trickier than I expected. Being able to cut off my sports bra was a saving grace, but then I had to figure out what to put on its place. So I rummaged through my collection of tube top swimsuits. Meant for sun-soaked afternoons when I was looking to avoid tan lines, they were now saviors in this awkward debacle, in tropical prints, flamboyant patterns, and soft pastels.

I settled on a design of sandy beaches with bright green palm trees. It wasn't my most flattering piece, nor my worst, but indecision plagued me.

Was I trying to impress him?

Or did I want Ryan to remain indifferent to my appearance?

His situation was a lot more challenging.

The thought of a shirtless Ryan accompanying me

throughout the day was a tantalizing torment, but I needed to get him dressed in something else.

"What are you doing?" he asked in shock as I grabbed a plain white tee from the bag that Lucas had brought over and started cutting it into a garment that Ryan could easily wear.

"How else are you going to get it on?"

"I'm supposed to walk around all day with a huge hole in my right side?"

I hadn't thought about that. "We could tape it shut."

"Tape it shut? That's Gucci!"

"It's a white T-shirt."

"I'm sure Lucas spent a small fortune on that."

"A small fortune?" I repeated, and then I started to laugh because I just couldn't help it. "Yes, I'm sure this stupid T-shirt cost something dumb like a hundred bucks or whatever, but are you really calling that a small fortune? Didn't I read that Lucas Stone got paid like a billion dollars for his role in *Debt of Shadows*?"

"Twenty-two million. And that's not the point."

"What is the point, Ryan?"

"It's wasteful."

"Like ordering 100 pounds of crab?"

"It was 10 pounds. And yes, that's different. All of that food went to somebody, so—"

"Oh, enough." Why were we bickering like we'd been together for twelve years when it had only been twelve hours?

"I want to go back to the hotel." Ryan said after a performative breath. "That feels like a smart home base for us. We can wait in my room while we figure out what to do next. I need to call Maggie. She's the best problem solver I've ever met, and I'm sure that after 10 minutes on Zoom with her, we'll have a plan and both of us will feel better."

"Zoom works great at my house. We don't need the hotel for that."

"We need to go back—"

"I can't go to your hotel today."

"And why not?"

"Because I have to work. I have a job to do. Rent to pay."

"I'm sorry that you'll have to miss a day of work, but I would be happy to talk to your boss, cover your shift, or do whatever I need to—"

"I don't buy my way out of problems," I said. Even if I had felt a genuine connection with Ryan last night, lying in bed and talking about movies, it was gone now. We came from different worlds. In his world, he could throw money at any problem that came up and emerge without a stain. In my world, I had to work for everything I had.

"Look, I hear you, and I'm sorry about all of this, okay? I promise that I have both of our best interests at heart. Let me go back to the hotel. Get dressed in something better than this. I can't walk around shirtless for the next five days." He looked at the ruined Gucci tee, then back to me. "Maggie can help us solve this problem, then you can go into work without having to drag me along behind or beside you. Okay?"

I took a deep breath. "Okay."

I only relented because Ryan sounded legitimately worried. And his worry made me worried. Or maybe I was just empathetic. Whatever.

I guess I just felt like I should maybe try and listen or help, and I wasn't about to use a second pass just to avoid going to his hotel.

I dragged us over to the tiny desk where I'd stared dreamily at a poster of Ryan's face instead of doing my homework and ransacked the drawer until I found a roll of Scotch tape, which I tossed to him.

"Let me just call Ashleigh and let her know that I'll be a little late," I said as he started looking for the end of the tape.

After I called Ashleigh, Ryan grabbed his rolling suitcase.

"Are you ready to go now?" he asked.

"What about breakfast?"

Ryan waved a dismissive hand. "I don't really believe in breakfast."

"You don't believe in breakfast? It's pancakes, not Santa Claus. Didn't your nutritionist tell you that it's the most important meal of the day?"

"I intermittent fast, so I don't eat between 8 p.m. and noon."

"Intermittent what now?"

As we made our way to the kitchen, Ryan explained the idea behind intermittent fasting and how it helped optimize his energy and focus as an actor. I found myself actually listening with interest instead of jumping to make fun of him.

"Why?" I asked, more curious than I wanted to be.

"Because our brains use a lot of energy, and I want as much of my energy available to me as I can get," he sort of explained.

But I looked at him, obviously wanting to understand.

So he kept going. "It takes a lot of energy for your body to digest food, and whether you're eating an almond or a bag of them, your digestive system is either on or off. As an actor, I want instant access to a full spectrum of my emotions. You can make fun of me all you want, but that's exhausting work, and I need my brain and body at peak efficiency at all times. I'm paid a lot of money, and I want the people signing my checks to get at least, if not more than, what they pay for."

"Do people still sign checks?" I asked, instead of telling him that sounded interesting, which is what I really thought.

"Yes. I specifically request that they give me the giant novelty checks with each movie deal."

I laughed, then cut my own laughter short so he wouldn't think he was too funny. I fetched a frying pan out of the drawer beneath the oven. "You sure you don't want anything? You're going to change your mind when you start smelling it."

"That's highly unlikely," he said.

I was stuck using only one hand to crisp the bacon and whisk the eggs, all while Ryan awkwardly tried to keep pace and give me enough space. I swore I heard his stomach grumble, but when I confronted him about it, he moved swiftly into denial.

Ryan glared at my plate of food.

"Did my bacon offend you?" I asked.

"My nutritionist would kill me," he said, staring at the brown crisps. He discreetly wiped the corner of his mouth. "There's a lot of saturated fat in that."

Was he drooling?

"Then I'm sorry my little breakfast isn't up to your nutritionist's standards," I said, popping a piece of bacon into my mouth. "Mmm, saturated fat. Delicious."

His stomach grumbled so loudly that the chair rumbled and the cutlery on the kitchen table jingled together.

"I'm not hungry," he repeated.

"Obviously," I said, digging back into my breakfast.

As soon as I finished my last bite of egg, Ryan was on his feet, clearing the table and rinsing my plate in the sink before putting it in the dishwasher — even though he practically had to drag me through the kitchen to do so.

"How are we getting to the hotel?" he asked.

"We're walking."

"What if somebody sees us?"

"Of course someone is going to see us. You're a famous actor."

"Then I don't want to walk. I don't want anyone gossiping about where I spent the night."

"There you go." I rolled my eyes. "Protecting your reputation again."

"I'm actually worried about protecting other people." From his gaze, it was clear that he meant me.

But I didn't need protecting, so I just rolled my eyes. "This again?"

"If word gets out that you're connected to me, literally in this case, that story will follow you around for the rest of your life."

"Haunting," I said sarcastically.

"I mean it. Every future boyfriend will wonder about our time together. Being associated with me comes with baggage."

"I'm off boys, so no worries there."

"You're off boys?"

"I quit boys."

"How can you quit boys?" Ryan asked.

"I quit boys, I quit relationships, I quit kisses. I just don't do those things anymore."

"You just don't do those things anymore? How?"

"It's like intermittent fasting. But for relationships."

"Jeez. Who hurt you?"

"Taylor," I said matter-of-factly. Ryan had meant it to be a rhetorical question, but before I caught onto that, I had already answered.

Ryan stopped walking, meaning I had to stop walking too. He looked me in the eyes with a pleading expression. It would have been easy to mistrust because the man was an actor, but I could feel his energy and it felt as honest as his posture. "If you want to quit relationships, that's up to you. But if you ever get out of retirement, you're forever going to be known as the girl who was handcuffed to Ryan Jones. If any of your future boyfriends have even the slightest insecurity..."

Before I could answer, my mom appeared.

"I'll drive you," she offered.

Ryan nodded in appreciation. "Sounds great."

"Just give me a couple of minutes and I'll meet you two at the car."

We went outside and waited, standing in utter silence together.

FOURTEEN

Ryan

"I'M REALLY glad that I called Ashleigh and told her I would be coming in late," Olivia said. "This stakeout makes me feel like I'm living in a real-life spy thriller."

"I'm not sure that your sarcasm is helping, dear," Helen said.

I felt grateful for Olivia's mother. Without her, the last half hour would have been even more stressful.

Paparazzi were still hunting in a pack out front of the Fisherman's Finest, despite Maggie having reported the problem as solved multiple times by now. I texted her as Helen was backing out of the driveway, asking if there was something she could do to get rid of them before we got there. Maggie texted back that she was on it, but the wolves were still on the lookout for prey when Helen pulled up a block away from the hotel.

And now, Olivia squirmed impatiently on the seat beside me. "You said that your manager was the best problem solver you knew."

"She is," I replied, already knowing what Olivia was going to say next.

"Well, I hope it's not a spoiler for you, but this problem has definitely not been solved."

"Olivia, dear," Helen said, and Olivia flushed with embarrassment, looking away.

"Sorry," she muttered.

I couldn't blame her frustration — I'd been dodging paparazzi for years, but when I'd first become famous, having to organize even the simplest errands around avoiding them made me feel like a prisoner.

But I'd chosen fame knowing that I would be giving up a lot of privacy. Olivia had been thrown into this without a choice.

"There must be something we can do besides sitting here in the car like this."

This time, Helen was finally on her side. "While I would love to play super-secret stakeout all morning, I do have plans today. Morning meditations at Yoga Vida, and then a sensual dance class later this afternoon. And my daughter's dinner doesn't make itself, so I need to get groceries in between my activities."

"I get dinner out sometimes," Olivia weakly defended herself.

"Would you mind texting your manager again?" Helen finished.

"Sure." I got out my phone to message Maggie again, but it buzzed in my hand with a text from Lucas.

You two still cuffed? he wanted to know.

I took a picture of our bound wrists.

"What are you doing?" Olivia asked.

"Lucas wants to know if we're still handcuffed together, and I wanted to show him in real time that our nightmare lives on."

Lucas texted a laughing emoji back.

I knew he didn't mean anything by it, but still, it rankled me.

Maybe I should join Helen for her morning meditations.

I should be feeling gratitude that someone could find the situation funny and therefore mine enjoyment from my predicament.

Instead, I was annoyed at the heckler sharing the backseat with me.

I suddenly realized that I no longer trusted Maggie to get me out of a bad situation, and for the first time ever. But even if Olivia and I were stuck in this dilemma together, her mom shouldn't be obligated to stick around.

"You can drive around back." I pointed toward an alley behind the hotel, where a kitchen door opened onto the street. "I've used that exit as an entrance a few times before. It goes into the kitchen."

"Why didn't we try that when we got here?" Olivia asked.

"Because I thought Maggie had it under control. And using that door is just trading one problem for another."

"I'm sure the chef in the back is just waiting to talk about the time the rich and famous Ryan Jones—"

"You always mention rich."

"What?"

"Whenever you're teasing me, you always mention how rich I am. Like it bothers you."

"Olivia suffers from some limiting beliefs about money," Helen said.

Olivia didn't answer, but her mom gave me a glancing smile in the rearview mirror.

"Thank you," I told her as we got out of the car.

"Of course, I hope the two of you get married, and I see you again at Christmas," she said, winking.

"Unbelievable," Olivia muttered.

"She only does that because she loves you," I told her as we started walking toward the kitchen door.

"Thank you very much for explaining how my relationship with my mother works for me. I super appreciate it and definitely would not have been able to figure that out without your help."

"At least she wants to see you at Christmas."

"Are you saying you don't come home to your family for Christmas?"

"We haven't spent Christmas together for years. My parents retired to Florida, my sister's always traveling, and my little brother became a foreign exchange student in Norway and never came back."

"Oh." Olivia's expression softened. "Do you miss them?"

I did, but it felt like whining to complain about how we were never in the same place together when I could afford to visit them individually between movies.

"Sure, but we text all the time."

"That's not the same as family Christmas."

It wasn't. "It's better than nothing."

I rapped my knuckles hard on the door a few times before it opened to a wide-eyed cook in a bright white uniform.

"Mr. Jones," he said.

"We'll just be walking through," I explained with a smile.

Then the two of us entered the kitchen.

I weighed the atmosphere and subtly scanned our surroundings before deciding to take her hand. What initially felt like a strategic move turned undeniably comforting as our fingers intertwined.

"Why did you do that?" Olivia leaned in and whispered as we walked through the kitchen, with chefs in stark white darting among the gleaming countertops amid a vibrantly colorful palette of fresh produce.

"Because now we look like a couple. It's less for people to gossip about."

"How is that less for people to gossip about?" Olivia asked.

"Believe me. It's less of a story than being accidentally handcuffed together."

"Please tell me that you have some idea how little sense you're making right now."

I stayed silent, swiftly guiding us to a hallway exit and then to the elevators, unable to discern whether the rush I felt through my body was born from the spark between our braided fingers or from the exhilaration I always experienced when stepping into a new role and feeling it mold to me like a second skin.

"Sorry." I let her hand go, feeling suddenly guilty for taking it.

"No, it's okay." Olivia reached out and reclaimed it.

As we reached the hallway, I couldn't help but notice the warmth and grace of her hand; holding it felt like finding a missing piece of a puzzle that I didn't know was lost, or that I had been looking for it.

Then we were standing in front of the elevator, and I was looking wildly around, certain that at any second, someone was going to see us.

"Someone is going to see us," Olivia said, as if reading my mind.

I shoved my hand into the bag Lucas had given me last night, grabbed another white T-shirt, and dropped it over the handcuffs.

"That's the perfect disguise." Olivia laughed. "It doesn't look suspicious at all."

"It's worse, isn't it?" I laughed with her.

"It's definitely not better, but I'm not sure that it's worse. I say we leave it."

The doors dinged open.

The elevator was empty, but just as we entered, three people started toward the elevator, each coming from a different direction.

The closest one made it and held the door for the other two.

As the elevator doors closed, recognition flickered in the eyes of the closest individual, a clearly star-struck young woman.

I had been in this situation countless times before.

But inside the elevator, with Olivia cuffed to my wrist and a stupid T-shirt draped like a towel on a hook in between us, I had never felt so deeply uncomfortable.

"You're … you're Ryan Jones!" The woman began to fumble in her purse.

I nodded, attempting to angle my right hand away. "I am."

She handed me a pen and a piece of paper.

"Will you sign this for me please?"

"Of course." Though doing it with my non-dominant hand made the handwriting look more like hieroglyphics than my signature.

The elevator door dinged open.

"Can we?" asked the passenger who had held the door, a short man with a five o'clock shadow and a tuft of hair in the vague shape of a well-used eraser holding out his phone for a picture.

"Of course," I said again.

Olivia tried to sidestep out of frame, after the man made it obvious that he wanted his picture with me alone.

The third passenger, an older woman, was clearly impatient to get the show on the road.

Eraser Hair waved as the doors closed.

Two more floors, then the doors dinged open again, and both the older woman and the star-struck admirer got off.

A minute later, we were in my room.

"Do you feel better now?" Olivia asked once the hotel room door had closed behind us.

"I will in a minute. Scratch that. Yes, but I'll feel even better in a minute after I take my vitamins and do some yoga."

"How do you expect to do yoga like this?" Olivia raised our wrists, just in case I had turned stupid and didn't know what she meant.

"I was hoping we could do it together."

I expected another fight, because so far that was how Olivia apparently rolled, but instead she agreed, and her reluctance felt almost like an act.

Morning sunlight filtered softly through the curtains to cast the room in a gentle golden glow. We had no yoga mats, but Olivia knew her postures, and we were able to do them side by side. Sort of.

We started with a seated spinal twist, cross-legged on the floor, back to back as each of us turned to look over the other's shoulder. I was doing a great job of pretending I was leaning against a wall instead of Olivia, until she put her free hand on my knee to brace herself as she twisted farther. She pulled it back immediately, mumbling a quiet *Sorry*, and moved it to the floor.

But now all I thought about was the faint sweet scent of coconut and vanilla combined with something flowery that might have been coming from her hair. I twisted another half inch, getting closer to her ponytail. Definitely her shampoo. And beneath it, Olivia herself, which somehow put the other scents to shame.

I had wanted to do yoga to center myself, but doing it while cuffed to Olivia was having the opposite effect.

"Let's try boat pose," I suggested. Surely the pain of holding a non-stop abdominal crunch for several minutes would distract me from how amazing she smelled.

And how those few straggling hairs that didn't make it into her ponytail trailed down to the curve where her neck became her shoulder.

And how those cute dimples framed her lips on the rare occasions when she actually smiled.

But that boat pose wasn't any better — balancing in a V-sit as we faced each other and held hands, the soles of our feet pressing together, left me looking deep into those gorgeous eyes again. Instead of clearing my mind, doing yoga with Olivia was filling it with thoughts she definitely wouldn't want me to act on.

Thoughts about asking her to put last night's costume back on so we could put on our own personal play about cops and robbers. Except that I definitely wanted the handcuffs off, so I'd have both hands free to—

"Hey, we haven't done warrior pose."

I dropped my feet and rocked forward, letting go of her free hand a little too fast. She lost her balance coming out of the V, flailing as she fell sideways, dragging me down on top of her legs with my face pressed into her stomach.

Which did nothing to calm or center me.

"Get off!" she said, giving my shoulder a shove, sounding more outraged than angry.

I pushed myself back up to kneeling. "You're the one who pulled me down."

"Because you didn't warn me before you let go."

"Maybe this was a mistake." And maybe I should cut it short, before I added a new kind of embarrassment to this whole experience.

But she got to her feet and offered me a hand up. "Let's try warrior."

This one was the easiest so far, and required the least amount of physical contact, although we were still forced to lean into each other for support as we stood there, side by side, with our hands overhead.

We wobbled and our stifled laughter broke the meditative serenity.

But less physical contact just made me more aware of the places where our bodies did touch. And wish they were touching more.

"Okay, I think that's enough," I said.

Did she actually look disappointed? Or was that wishful thinking on my part?

"Now do you feel better?" she asked.

"Twenty minutes worth of Twister-like stretching later, I do."

"Shockingly, the same is true for me. When is Maggie going to Zoom in?"

I smiled.

"Why are you smiling at me like that?" Olivia asked.

"That's the first time you've used her name. You usually say 'your manager' like a curse word."

"I do not."

"You kind of do," I said, lightly laughing to let her know it was okay.

"So when is she calling?"

I glanced at my watch. "Eight more minutes from now."

"That's very exciting."

I couldn't tell if Olivia was mocking me or not.

She solved the mystery. "I actually mean that. I've seen Hollywood managers in movies before, of course, but it will be different to see how one really acts in real life."

We shared a lingering silence. I spent it with my thoughts drifting, first tracing the contours of our recent interactions, and then wondering what she was thinking right now.

Then it was five minutes later, and we were sitting side-by-side on the couch. It felt intimately familiar as we waited for Maggie to appear on Zoom.

Like we were waiting for results of a pregnancy test together.

Where did that thought come from?

"So," Maggie said the second her audio connected. "What's the emergency?"

"Why are there still paparazzi outside the hotel? You said you were going to get rid of them."

"No," Maggie corrected me in front of Olivia with a dismissive laugh. "You texted me and said that there were paparazzi outside and that I needed to get rid of them. I told you there was only so much I could do. You pressed, and I said that whatever was in my power to do had already been done."

She took a long breath before she continued.

"I would like to apologize for falling short of my duty and not clearing away the vultures from outside your hotel, but I think it's smarter to reserve my sorries for those times when I actually mean them, so my sincerity is never left in question."

Maggie didn't wait for my reply before glancing over at Olivia, the shift in her gaze obvious even through Zoom.

"Hi!" Olivia waved. "I'm Olivia. It's really good to meet you."

I raised our wrists to show Maggie the handcuffs. "My

dinner date from last night and I accidentally got hand-cuffed together."

"So get un-cuffed," Maggie replied.

"I'm working on it. But it's going to be at least five days until—"

"You don't have five days. You need to be in LA in 20 hours for your premiere."

"That won't be a problem. I'll just have to bring Olivia with me."

"You will not be bringing Olivia with you," Olivia cut in. "I'm not going back to LA. Not now. Not ever."

Except that she was. Because she had to.

Maggie didn't reply, looking at both of us and waiting to see what I might say next.

"Get Olivia a ticket for the plane and on the guest list for the premiere," I said to my manager.

"I'll get right on it," Maggie replied. And then to Olivia, "It was nice to meet you."

"Nice to meet you too." But now Olivia was gritting her teeth. And the second Maggie was gone from the Zoom, she turned to me and said, "Is that what you call solving the problem?"

FIFTEEN

Olivia

"I'M NOT GOING to Los Angeles," I told Ryan again when he ended the Zoom call.

"We have no other choice." He looked defeated.

"We have lots of other choices. And I choose to stay here until Lydia's son comes here to unlock us."

"I'm under contract. Failing to show up at the premiere will tank my career."

"I highly doubt that. You were caught screaming and yelling at the director of your movie, and your career survived."

"How can you say my career survived?" Ryan asked, looking injured. "You're only proving my point. The premiere is for *Cold Fury*, the movie where that video happened. I'm already on thin ice with the studio. If I do anything to mess this up, they will never work with me again."

"Can't you find another studio?" Surely Mr. Box Office Draw was someone that other studios would want to work with.

"You're being awfully dismissive of my career. And

that's not how it works. If I piss off one studio, the others will all hear about it."

"Sure, but that doesn't mean they stay away," I argued. "I can think of plenty famous actors who got to be jerks and still—"

"I'm not a jerk."

But now I felt like one. It's one thing to decide someone's a jerk when the only time you ever see them is on a screen, but another thing to say it to their face. Especially when you're going to be handcuffed to them for four more days. "I just meant that everyone makes mistakes, and mistakes eventually get forgiven."

A long beat of silence, then Ryan said, "I just hope that Maggie can get you on the invite list."

"Your manager is sounding a lot less powerful than I originally imagined her to be."

"She's back to being my manager?"

"If she gets us out of the handcuffs, then she can be Maggie again," I huffed. "So, are we supposed to just sit here and worry the morning away about whether or not you'll score me an invite to this premiere that I don't want to go to?"

"I don't have any control over—"

"I get that this is a big deal to you, but I can't just sit here and worry the morning away. I still need to work. I told Ashleigh that I would be coming in late, not that I would be a no-show."

"Where do you work?"

"I'm a waitress at The Family Table. Do you have a problem with that?"

"Why would I have a problem with that?" He shook his head and continued, not giving me the chance to answer. "I'm sorry, but you'll have to let Ashleigh know that you can't come in today."

"I can't leave her short," I argued.

"Do you really think that we are in a position to help her like this? We'll be in the way more than anything."

"I'm not calling and canceling on her. If anything, we have three hands. We can be more efficient."

"I'm not sure I agree with your logic."

"What's your real objection? Afraid to wait tables?"

"Do you know how many tables I waited before I made it as an actor?"

"Good. Then you're experienced." She sighed. "Look, I'm trying to save money to open my own coffee shop, so I'm not about to miss a shift, and I'm not letting Ashleigh down either. I need to keep my commitment. Plus, I need those tips. And if you even think of suggesting that you could write me a check so that I 'don't have to worry about it,' I will use these handcuffs to choke you."

"I don't think you're nearly as violent as you pretend to be, and I wasn't going to suggest any such thing, because I know exactly how you would have responded, but I don't understand how you think this can work."

"How what is supposed to work?" I asked.

"You already know how I feel about the public seeing us handcuffed together. If we're waiting tables, then everyone in the restaurant will see us. I grew up in Ocean Springs, so I know exactly how fast gossip travels around this town."

"We can't stay in this room all day." I felt like I was begging him, but the pleading refused to leave my tone. "Isn't there anything that you can think of for us to do?"

He looked thoughtful, like he was really, truly considering my question.

Then he finally nodded with a reluctant yet grim-looking smile.

He walked over to the phone, gently dragging me behind him.

He picked it up, and someone answered on the other end.

"Yes. Hello there, Carmela. Would you be so kind as to send the most beautiful scarf from any one of the shops downstairs up to my room?"

Another long pause, then he nodded and smiled. "Thank you, Carmela. I look forward to seeing your choice."

He hung up the phone and turned to me, still smiling. "A scarf is on the way."

"Is it like the invisibility cloak from Harry Potter? Because otherwise I'm not sure that that's really going to do the magic you seem to be imagining."

"You wanted an idea? That's the best one I have. Let's try it. Okay?"

And that time, his Hollywood smile actually melted me.

He called for a car, and it drove us to the restaurant, a silly scarf now covering the handcuffs despite there being zero chance that it would actually accomplish the impossible of hiding them forever like Ryan was obviously hoping they would.

The Family Table was nestled by the shimmering coastline and offered an array of homestyle dishes. It was all weathered wooden tables, nautical decor, and a warm, familial ambiance. Ashleigh's family had been running the restaurant for three generations.

Ashleigh was surprised to see me coming in, still in lockstep with the movie star she had chipped in for me to dine with last night. But she was welcoming and promised to keep our predicament a secret.

"If you can pull it off, then who am I to blow your cover?" She laughed.

I was even more surprised than Ashleigh that a day I was dreading only slightly less than my reluctant compatriot turned out to be not only be fun, but one of the best days ever at the restaurant, for both me as a server and Ashleigh as its owner.

Not only did Ryan seem to get more relaxed throughout the day, we quickly figured out a pattern to our work, with me clearing dishes and him wiping the tables down, or him delivering the food while I poured the coffee.

He hadn't been lying. He clearly had lots of experience doing actual work. I didn't want to admit it, but I was impressed by how he handled the chaos of the lunch rush, while treating each customer to that signature smile that melted hearts in every movie he'd ever been in.

Not my heart. But lots of other people's hearts.

Everything was going swimmingly until Stephanie entered the restaurant.

Ugh. Taylor's sister was my total nemesis, even before things went kaput between me and her brother. Stephanie was rude and supremely unpleasant. She was a big part of the reason why I felt like I had to move out of Ocean Springs, even though Los Angeles had been Taylor's idea, and never felt like my kind of place.

Stephanie knew which section I was working and claimed a table without waiting for the hostess to seat her. She had always reveled in her role as my tormentor-in-chief. From malicious rumors spread about me throughout high school, to publicly belittling my choices (including clothes, taste in music, or even the way I laughed), or mocking me to make her friends laugh, during my teenage years and then in my life with Taylor, Stephanie was the literal worst.

And from the moment she sat in my section, Stephanie made it her mission to make her meal hell for me.

"This fork is filthy," she complained loudly to no one in particular. I hurried to her table with a fresh set of silverware, which she made a show of examining like it was a hundred-dollar bill she suspected of being counterfeit.

I sighed and turned away, meaning to check on the single mom with two kids two booths down, but Stephanie snapped her fingers. I turned back around.

"What?"

"My water tastes stale."

"That's not—" Ryan started, but I cut him off and grabbed the offending glass.

"I'll get you a fresh one."

As I dragged him back toward the kitchen, Ryan asked, "What's her problem?"

"She goes away sooner if we just do what she asks."

"That wasn't my question."

I dumped her water out and tossed the glass in a bussing tray, then grabbed a water pitcher and gestured for Ryan to take a clean glass from the stack.

We approached Stephanie's table again. Ryan set the glass down and I poured.

Then I pasted on a smile and said, "If there's anything else—"

Stephanie smiled right at me and knocked the glass over, like a cat that wanted to see how many tchotchkes it could knock off the mantel before it got the spray bottle.

"Oops," she purred.

"I'll get a rag."

Gritting my teeth, I turned and headed back to station where we kept the cleaning supplies in a small credenza, but Ryan grabbed my hand and pulled me to a stop.

"You know there's no way she's going to leave a tip, right?"

"It's not about that," I said.

"Then what's it about?"

"It doesn't matter."

"I think it matters," he said, and the expression on his face took me off guard. It wasn't the pity I expected. It was like ... like he actually cared that Stephanie was being mean to me.

A loud whistle pierced the air, startling several customers and scaring an infant, who started crying.

I looked back at Stephanie, who held up her empty glass and waggled it.

Grabbing a rag and tucking it into my apron pocket, I hurried to fetch another glass of water, which I brought to her table.

"I strongly suggest that you leave the restaurant if you're going to bother the other customers," I said to Stephanie, setting the glass down on the table just out of her reach instead of dumping it onto her head.

"I'm not sure what you mean," Stephanie said in a voice that suggested I was crazy or paranoid, or somehow misreading a situation that was crystal clear.

"I don't understand why you're doing this." I stood straighter, embarrassed that I had to be having this confrontation at all, let alone with Ryan right next to me. "Taylor cheated on me. I don't see how I'm the enemy here."

"Ha!" Stephanie exclaimed, looking over at Ryan for the first time. "Is that what you want him to believe?"

"I don't care what he believes. That's what happened. Taylor started sticking it to my maid of honor, and then they stole my business together."

"You mean you cheated on him with Matthew—"

"Our packaging vendor?"

"—and left him saddled with a business he never even wanted to begin with, but his name was on the lease—"

"Because he kept me off of it!"

I realized I was yelling just as Ryan put a comforting hand on my shoulder.

Then he turned to Stephanie. "If you can't be pleasant, then you need to leave."

"You don't work here," Stephanie said, obviously offended and stating the obvious.

"Get. Out." Ryan stared her down alongside me, the pair of us holding our gazes.

Then Stephanie finally got up and huffed out of the restaurant.

"Thank you," I said, blinking back unexpected tears.

Taylor's betrayal had hurt, but at some level, I had known that he was not the man I'd been pretending he was.

My former BFF's betrayal had hurt worse, because I'd leaned on her friendship when Taylor and I had gone through rough patches, not realizing that she was one of the reasons for those rough patches.

But coming home to be continuously humiliated by my high school bully hurt worse than both those betrayals combined.

And Ryan was the first person who'd ever noticed how much I was hurting.

Ryan nodded. "I can't stand bullies."

Ashleigh appreciated Ryan coming in for the shift so much that she worked triple time to make sure that the paparazzi stayed out of the restaurant. If anyone looked unfamiliar to her, she assumed they weren't local, and today was a local's only day at The Family Table.

By the end of our shift, we were a well-oiled machine.

It was one of the best days ever for the restaurant, and the best day for me and my tips by far, for all the obvious reasons. I couldn't deny that half of my haul belonged to Ryan.

"Here, this is yours," I said, extending his share after I counted the total.

"You know I'm not going to take that."

"I insist. You earned it. Giving it to you will make me feel good."

"I should feel bad so that you can feel good?"

"How does it make you feel bad to take home your half of tips which you earned?"

"Because I don't need the money and you do."

"So, because you're rich—"

"You just told me earlier today that you were saving to open your own coffee shop, which is an admirable goal. So why would I want to deprive you of inching any closer to that target when you specifically said that all of your tips mattered?"

I didn't know what to say and was suddenly stricken so hard by Ryan's words that I was afraid I might start crying if I open my mouth.

Fortunately, his phone rang and saved me from any potential embarrassment.

He looked at the screen and said, "Maggie is calling me back. Is there somewhere private we can go to take the call?"

I nodded. "The cafe bathroom. It used to be a closet, so it's a little cramped with us both inside, but it's private for sure."

"Let's go." Ryan nodded, then followed my lead as he answered the call, now rolling into its third ring.

Maggie appeared on his phone as I closed the bathroom door.

"Hey Maggie," he said. "According to your face, you have bad news."

"André is refusing to attend the LA premiere if you're there."

"What?" Ryan looked stunned. "Can't the studio just make him go? They make me do whatever they want me to."

"They're siding with André. He gave them an ultimatum that if you walk the red carpet, he walks."

"Unbelievable," Ryan fumed.

"There's more. The studio is forbidding you from attending the official premiere at all."

"You have to be kidding me."

"Sorry, kiddo. Not this time. But on the bright side, you hate going to these things."

"You know that's not the point," Ryan replied.

And the movie star looked defeated.

SIXTEEN

Ryan
_____

I WAS upset but trying not to show it.

"You look like your entire family just died," Olivia said, then turned to Maggie and surprised me with the end of her thought. "And you don't look much better. Rehearsal is over. You both need to stop moping."

"I'm not sure you really appreciate the gravity of this situation," I told her.

But Olivia just shrugged. "Or maybe you don't appreciate the possible opportunity that this opens up for us."

"Opportunity?" Maggie and I repeated together.

"Right. A big one, if what I'm about to suggest is possible."

"Then suggest it," Maggie said as I braced myself.

"What if we held the premiere here in Ocean Springs? A second red carpet, without André."

We both stared at Olivia, and again replied in unison: "What?"

Then Maggie added, "On less than a day's notice?"

"We have a theater. And it's one of the nicest on the California coast!"

Now Maggie really seemed to be listening to a bunch of stuff I already knew as Olivia continued.

"The Ocean Springs Theater opened in 1938 and was the only theater for a hundred miles. That art deco facade and neon marquee will look great for all the red-carpet pictures, the grand lobby is gorgeous despite a few needed repairs, and the auditorium seats 1,500 people. So maybe you could hold the premiere here?"

Because it made sense to relocate an hour away by plane.

"Thank you for trying to help, Olivia. We really appreciate that." I used my kindest voice, both because I truly did appreciate that she was trying to help and I didn't want to look like a jerk in front of Maggie.

But Maggie had yet to reject the idea.

And that rejection didn't appear to be pending.

Instead, she looked thoughtful, as if she might seriously be considering Olivia's outlandish suggestion.

"What are you thinking?" I asked Maggie.

She grinned, and I knew what was coming. I could hear the words "PR Gold" before she said them.

"I think it's a brilliant idea!" Maggie exclaimed. "It's PR Gold."

I sighed as Olivia smiled.

"Are you sure?" I asked because I absolutely was not. "Doesn't that seem like it's asking the studio and the press and everybody else involved to jump through an awful lot of hoops just to accommodate me?"

"Sure, absolutely," Maggie agreed with a vigorous nod, "if that's what we were doing, but it's not."

"Then what are we doing?" I asked.

"Creating PR Gold," Olivia answered, still smiling.

I didn't love how pleased Maggie obviously was with Olivia.

"I can sell this twice," Maggie said. "It's simple, Ryan. This isn't about moving the premiere here to Ocean Springs so we can accommodate you. It's about doing what's best for the project, and what's best for the project in this instance is getting *Cold Fury* as much positive attention as we possibly can."

"How will the attention be any more positive by moving it here? Seems to me that all we would be doing is making me look like a prima donna for stomping my foot and bringing the movie back to my hometown."

"Exactly," Maggie nodded, "bringing the movie back to your hometown. You want to get away from this image that the viral video started of you? Great. What better way to do it than with a loud proclamation that proves you're no longer that person."

"I was never that person," I had to interject.

"You're just a small town boy who wants to do small town things at the end of the day."

"I'm not sure that's what moving the premiere here would say." I disagreed with Maggie's logic.

But Maggie kept going, while Olivia observed our back and forth.

"We can highlight your childhood home — or how about that acting teacher that you were telling me about yesterday morning in my office?"

"Was that just yesterday?" I asked.

"Was Lydia her name?"

"Yes," Olivia answered for me. "Lydia is awesome."

"Maybe we can even throw in a bit about you reconnecting with an old flame," Maggie suggested.

"Sorry to disappoint you, but I don't have any of those."

"Are you kidding?" Maggie laughed. "You have plenty of those. Do I need to remind you about—"

"You most certainly do not," I cut her off. "And to clarify, I don't have any of those in Ocean Springs."

"What about that girl you took to that sock hop in fourth grade?"

Maggie's question made me want to keel over and die.

Surely my face must have withered with embarrassment.

"What?" Maggie asked, not understanding what had just happened. "What did I say?"

Olivia turned slowly to me, a bemused smile spreading across her face. "You told her about me? Before the handcuffs?"

Maggie blinked. "She's the girl you bring up every time you talk about this place?"

"You bring me up *every time?*" Olivia asked.

"No, I do not bring you up every time."

"He does," Maggie insisted. "Mention Ocean Springs, and he tells the story of the sock hop."

Olivia couldn't have looked more delighted. Probably enjoying this as payback for me laughing at her closet full of posters with my face on them.

But this was ten times more embarrassing for me. Because Olivia's posters were obviously the remnants of a teenage girl's fantasies. Whereas I'd told the story of the sock hop last month, shortly before the incident that had ruined my career.

Maggie started laughing, cackling really. "Well then, isn't that just perfect?"

"How is it perfect?" I asked.

"It's perfect because it sounds like this whole thing was meant to be."

Olivia and I traded a glance, and finally it felt like we were on the same team.

"It was definitely not meant to be," I said.

"Definitely not," Olivia agreed.

"Can you do this?" Maggie asked Olivia, ignoring me.

"Do what, exactly?" she asked.

"Go along with all of this."

"Go along with what, exactly?" Olivia tried to clarify.

But Maggie was wiggly, and I had seen her worm her way out of answering direct questions countless times before.

"I'm asking if you can go along with your own suggestion," Maggie said.

"You mean to have the premiere here?"

I wasn't sure if Olivia was playing dumb or she simply wanted Maggie to say what she wanted out loud.

"This event will generate an incredible amount of publicity for Ocean Springs," Maggie continued, still without being explicit. "You would be doing your town a tremendous favor."

"Doing my town a tremendous favor if I did what?" Olivia pressed.

I was proud of Olivia for refusing to let Maggie slip out of it.

"The theater will be able to get the rest of its funding. Ryan, didn't you say that the fundraiser was still several thousand dollars short of what your teacher said it needs? Of course holding the premiere here will put you over the top and then some. In fact, I'm sure the studio would be happy to write an additional check for ten thousand. What do you need? It's half done already."

"You seem to be making a lot of promises for people who aren't here with us right now and able to agree," I said.

"You should hear all the promises I make about you." Maggie turned to Olivia. "So, can you do it?"

"Just tell me what you want me to do."

Then she finally did.

"I want you to pretend that you and Ryan Jones have known each other since elementary school, and that when he moved out to Hollywood, you realized that your relationship was never meant to be. But Ryan has never stopped pining for the girl back home and the way he made her feel all those years ago."

Olivia opened her mouth but paused before speaking.

My heart started pounding with a need to know what she might say next.

Maggie could sense that she was on the fence and needed one final nudge.

"Whether or not you realize it, Olivia, Ryan Jones is one of the best actors of his generation. And I've worked with a lot of big names, honey."

She leaned toward the camera. "I'll bet every award on my shelf that Ryan will be one of the all-time greats. But we are in a pivotal point in his career. Maybe *the* pivotal point. And you can help. Ryan can do most of the acting here, but if you're willing to help him, then I can promise your performance will lead to a big payoff for the town, and for you. So, are you willing to help us?"

Olivia still looked uncertain, but I thought it seemed like she wanted to.

"Yes," she finally said, "I'll help."

"Great." Maggie beamed. "Just hang tight. I'll talk to the studio tonight, then fly out to meet you guys in the morning."

"What time do you think you'll be in?" I asked.

"Early. I'll be on the first flight. As early as I can get there."

Then Maggie disappeared from my FaceTime, and I suddenly realized how enclosed it was in the confined space of that tiny restaurant bathroom with my body pressed so close to Olivia's.

I felt an urge to escape the tight quarters, in a flight from either the claustrophobia or from my confusing emotions toward Olivia.

We stepped outside the bathroom.

"I'm surprised you told people about the sock hop," Olivia said.

"Why?" That dance was as clear to me as any childhood memory. Peggy Lee vamping her way through "Fever." Olivia in a thrift store poodle skirt that swirled around her ankles as she held my hand. The sweet taste of fruit punch lingering at the back of my suddenly dry throat as my heart beat faster. "That was one of the best days of my entire school life."

"It was?" She seemed surprised, then touched a second later.

"School was terrible for me. I hated it, but that day was special."

"What made it special?"

"I knew that Lydia was watching out for me," I told her, remembering how alone I had felt before that day. "She made sure I wasn't left out or made fun of. For that one afternoon, I felt like I belonged."

"That's a really sweet story." Olivia's voice softer than I had ever heard it before. I tensed, wondering if she was setting me up for more mockery.

But her eyes were kind as she said, "You look a lot better than you did a few minutes ago. Are you sure you're okay with having the premiere here?"

"I'm warming up to the idea," I admitted, realizing it was true. "But I want to stay at the hotel. Would that be okay with you?"

It looked like Olivia wanted to argue, but my question had given her pause. After a moment, she nodded.

"Okay, sounds good. I'll text Madison and ask her to pack me a bag. I don't want to keep going back and forth to my house. I get why you want to be back at the hotel." She shrugged. "I've never had to go through fancy pants withdrawal before, but I imagine that it's rough."

"There is no such thing as fancy pants withdrawal." I smiled despite myself. "I'm just hoping that the climate control and white noise machine in my room will help drown out the sound of your snoring."

Olivia made an outraged noise and mock threatened to strangle me with the handcuffs. But she was laughing, and so was I.

Perhaps too loudly.

Ashleigh appeared, giving me a friendly but pointed look. "I love the little movie moment happening here in my restaurant, but can you please not block the thoroughfare."

Chagrined, I let Olivia usher us outside.

Her phone rang on the other side of the door: Madison calling her back.

"Yes…" Olivia started, keenly aware that I was standing right next to her and could hear every word.

I felt guilty for listening, but I was also curious with nowhere to go.

"Right … because there's been a change of plans … no, I wouldn't call it that … pack whatever you think … NO!"

Olivia twittered with an embarrassed little giggle.

Then she covered her mouth, cheeks flushing as she continued.

"Stop calling it that! Please just pack me a bag. Yes … no … probably. Thank you!"

She hung up, looking shy. An almost imperceptible shift in her demeanor into a softer, coyer version of herself.

Our eyes caught and skittered away like magnets repelling and attracting.

We tried to maneuver past one another, but our movements were suddenly constricted by the handcuffs.

Olivia got caught off guard. She lurched forward and collided with my chest. Instinctively, my arms circled her.

Time seemed to halt, our gazes locked, and an electrifying tension permeated the air between us.

But then we quickly pulled away from each other.

A brief and uneasy pause.

What Olivia was thinking.

SEVENTEEN

Olivia

I FELT a pang upon hearing Ryan's dismissal of what had made the sock hop special for me, but I wasn't exactly sure why.

What had I been expecting? That he would say dancing with you was the highlight of fourth grade for me?

That was ridiculous.

Because being handcuffed to a movie star was making me act ridiculous.

As much as the situation made me feel like a silly teenager fantasizing about her crush, the whole thing was beyond absurd. I was a 24-year-old woman, not the starry-eyed girl staring up at posters and pining for a boy from her past. I had lived a lot since fourth grade. Engaged, rejected, stolen from, lied to. Even bullied by my ex's sister.

I wasn't the small-town bumpkin Ryan probably thought I was.

But had he even said that, though? Or called me small town?

No. I was getting worked up over nothing.

"When is Madison getting here?" Ryan asked.

And I swear, being around that man sometimes felt like being on a Hollywood set, the way things always seemed to go exactly on cue.

There was a knock on the door. Three quick beats, just like Madison always did.

"She's here now," I said. "Come on."

And this time, when I dragged him along with me, I yanked on our cuffs with the kind of flair and drama that a true thespian like Ryan Jones could appreciate, or at least mock.

"What was that?" he asked.

"That was me acting."

"Acting like what?" He laughed.

Like a girl who wants this guy to like her? Or at least find her funny?

I really needed to get out of my head, because Ryan Jones wanted nothing to do with me, and I wanted nothing to do with him. Not in that way.

Or any way, really.

"Hey, Madison," I said as I opened the door.

She raised the bag full of clothes and other assorted goodies that she had brought over and started loudly laughing when she looked down at the cuffs.

"I'm glad that you find it so funny. You can take the next shift being chained to Casanova here."

Madison laughed harder as she entered. "I find the entire situation hilarious to be honest, while of course supporting you a hundred percent." She dangled the bag again. "I've also done you a solid."

"Thank you. I really do appreciate you coming here. Not just coming here, but for bringing me all of this."

Madison grinned as she pulled out a stylish blouse from

the bag, its side seam cleverly modified with a discreet line of velcro. "I thought tube tops weren't really your style, so I altered one of your blouses that I borrowed but never returned."

"Genius!" I exclaimed. "Thank you!"

"I also brought you an extra present you weren't expecting."

"And what is that?" I asked, not wanting to play Madison's games, and suspicious that this next gift might be a monkey paw kind of present, like my last little surprise from the girls.

"Guess," she said.

Ryan raised his hand. "I'll guess."

"Yay!" Madison exclaimed.

"Is it a set of keys for these handcuffs?"

"No," she smiled.

"A subscription box for monthly handcuff accessories? Now that we have them, you want us to enjoy them?" Ryan asked.

Clearly, he wasn't being serious.

But you wouldn't know it by Madison's reply. "You mean like a gift certificate for the subscription? Because I couldn't actually have the first box delivered yet."

"Of course." Ryan nodded, like that was exactly what he meant. "Is it a gift certificate for a subscription box full of assorted handcuff accessories."

"Nope." Madison shook her head, still laughing like this whole stupid thing was funny when it wasn't.

"Is it a poster of me to add to her collection?"

Madison laughed a little too hard at that one.

"Just tell us!" I snapped.

They both looked at me.

But I didn't know why I was acting that way any more than they did.

It surely couldn't be that I was feeling jealous — because why would I ever feel jealous of Madison?

My best friend was married with a baby.

But more importantly than the fact that Madison would never like Ryan, because she loved her husband and family more than anything in the world (and no rich and famous movie star was ever going to change that), I would never like Ryan like that. Sure, he was the kind of guy who'd stand up to my childhood bully and give me his share of our tips, but what about that video of him melting down on set?

It was getting harder and harder to reconcile the Ryan I knew from the news with the Ryan I'd literally been cuffed to.

But maybe that was how jerks kept getting forgiven. They did sweet, charming things for the people who thought they were jerks in between meltdowns.

I needed some serious recalibration.

"I brought you a pair of noise-canceling headphones," Madison announced, finally pulling her surprise present out of the bag.

"Oh my God, thank you!" I cried out, grabbing the headphones and immediately putting them over Ryan's head.

"Wait, no," he protested, but I wasn't about to give him a choice. Once they were firmly on his head, he relented with a sigh. "Fine."

And I finally got to have a heart-to-heart with Madison.

"So tell me everything, or at least what you can get out in the next couple of minutes before he takes those off. How is it going for real?" Madison asked.

"I'll feel a lot better when I finally get these handcuffs off."

"That doesn't answer my question. How is it going, you know, with him?" She smiled and glanced at Ryan, as though the subject of her query wasn't painfully obvious.

"I don't know, Madison. He's a typical Hollywood star."

"Thank you for painting such a vivid picture! I almost feel like I've been handcuffed to him myself. I know so many Hollywood stars, after all, and everything is so crystal clear to me now. Good thing I dropped everything to rush over here."

"What do you want me to say?" This was so uncomfortable.

"I want you to tell me about your dinner with a movie star, Olivia. What do you think? The girls and I were dying to give this to you. So, what's he like?"

What was Ryan like? I glanced at him. He was currently smiling obliviously, eyes closed, bobbing his head and pretending like he was at a rock concert. When we'd first met, I'd assumed so much about him. I'd assumed he'd be full of himself. But...

"He's ... unexpected," I said.

"What does that even mean?"

"I'm not sure anymore."

How did I know if the Ryan I was getting to know was the real Ryan, or if he was playing the nice version of himself so that I wouldn't run straight to the media to trash-talk him for cash?

And how would I ever know, if that was how his world works? How honest would I be with anyone, if I had to worry that they'd tell all my worst secrets just for the money?

Or worse, for the attention?

I wanted to believe he was the guy who'd stand up for

me because I deserved to be treated better, and who'd think that dancing with me at our fourth-grade sock hop was one of the best days of his life.

But what if he was saying all those things because he wanted me to tell them to the press in an interview — something that made him look good to help repair his tattered reputation?

"C'mon," Madison said, giving me a playful poke. "I'm not asking whether he wears boxers or briefs. Although, I'm not *not* asking, if you wanted to tell me." She lowered her voice, as if she was worried he was going to hear her next question, even through the noise-canceling head-phones. "Is he who you hoped he would be?"

I shook my head. "I really appreciate what you all did for me by buying me dinner. And I love you all so much, but this experience has been a lot."

"It's not like we had no idea that you were going to get handcuffed together, especially when it comes to the emergency part of that situation."

"Of course not." I smiled at Madison, really wanting her to know how much I loved her before I kept going with the answer she wanted, that surely sounded like a complaint even though it totally wasn't. "But Ryan was a lot before the handcuffs, or really, before the fundraiser even started."

"And why is that?" Madison looked confused. "I thought that Ryan Jones was your favorite actor ... and has been forever?"

I'd been bursting to tell her before, but now it felt like a betrayal.

But it was only a betrayal of Nice Ryan, who might be imaginary.

Meltdown Ryan totally deserved it.

"He used to be," I confessed, "but after that video of him yelling at his director went viral, I could never look at him, or even think of him in the same way. Even when I wanted to give Ryan Jones the benefit of the doubt and thought that maybe the video was unfair or somehow taken out of context, like maybe he'd had a really bad day or something, I still don't understand how a person could yell at someone like that just because they weren't getting their way. The way he put his needs in front of everyone else on that set…"

I shook my head and finished the thought. "It was unconscionable."

"I'm so sorry." Madison flinched away, looking embarrassed before she blinked again and turned her gaze back to me. "Why didn't you just tell me how you really felt about him?"

"I didn't think it was a big deal. We were all having fun and going to the fundraiser, and you guys brought over all the costumes, and we were laughing so much. I didn't want to bring anyone down."

I drew a breath before I continued. "Of course, I would have said something if I'd known that you were all going to spend your hard-earned money on buying me dinner. And again, I appreciate what you guys did so much. I promise to pay you all back for the auction, because I know you never would have—"

Madison cut me off. "That is *so* not the point here. I don't want the money back, and neither will Ashleigh or Brooklyn. We all love Lydia and the theater and would have donated our share anyway."

"You wouldn't have donated that much."

"Probably not," Madison admitted. "But none of us are sad that we did. I'm the one who feels bad about putting you in this predicament."

She glanced down at the handcuffs and then over at Ryan dubiously. "I don't even know how I'm going to tell Brooklyn and Ashleigh about this. They're both going to feel so terrible."

"You don't have to tell either one of them how I feel about Ryan." I shook my head. "This is my fault if it's anybody's fault."

"Can it be nobody's fault?" Madison asked.

"Fine. It's nobody's fault. But if it is somebody's fault, then it has to be mine, because I should have told you how I felt ahead of time. I could have, and didn't, so I'm sorry about that. But there will only be four more days of this at the most." I shrugged. "It's nothing compared to what I went through with Taylor."

"I know, sweetie." Madison opened her arms for a hug.

And I fell into her embrace. "Thanks for all the stuff. Especially the headphones."

"You know it's my pleasure. I can't wait to catch up later."

"Me too." I withdrew from the hug.

Then Madison left.

But as soon as I closed the door, I could see the apparent hurt carved onto Ryan's face.

"What's wrong?" But of course, I knew. And now I felt like the jerk.

Except maybe I wasn't the jerk. Maybe he did deserve what I'd said.

"I'm sorry to hear how you felt about me."

"I thought those were noise-canceling headphones."

"They're noise-canceling, not noise eliminating. And besides, you talk a lot louder than you think you do."

"Sorry I don't have an actor's perfect control over the volume of my voice. And why were you listening?" I snapped. Which made me even more of a jerk, but I couldn't rein the defensiveness in.

"I'm right here. What was I supposed to do, Olivia?"

"I don't know. Maybe cut in? Interrupt? Let us know that you could hear?"

"I could barely hear anything at first. Then I either got used to it or you started talking louder. I honestly don't know. But what was I supposed to say? You were already going on and on about what a jerk I am."

"I didn't say that you were a jerk," I insisted.

"Maybe not in those words. But come on, Olivia. We both know exactly what you think of me."

"If you didn't hear the whole thing, then I'm sure you missed a lot of context, Ryan."

"You mean like the context in my video?"

"What?" I didn't follow.

"That set video from *Cold Fury*. Remember, you said that no matter what the context of that video might be, I was still just looking out for myself."

"Sounds like you heard more than a little."

"Like I said, I only heard the conversation after you got loud."

"I'm sorry I hurt your feelings." And I meant that. "I would have said that all differently if I had known you were listening."

"I usually prefer the director's cut of a movie, and I want it even more raw and unedited in real life."

"You already knew how I felt. It shouldn't have been much of a surprise."

"Suspecting a plot twist isn't the same as the sting of seeing it play out."

"Can you please stop talking in movies?"

"Sure." Ryan nodded. "No problem. I'll just change who I am."

"I used to like you, a lot. How could I not? You're clearly an amazing artist. I always feel something when I watch you in a movie. And I used to love how much you could make me feel. But then I saw that video, and you made me feel something that I never want to feel again."

I shook my head.

"And what was that?" Ryan asked, his jaw firming.

"Disappointment, I guess? Hurt that you weren't who I thought. Anger that someone else I had seen as an exceptional human being was really just another jerk."

"So you do think I'm a jerk."

"I think you're a lot of things, Ryan. I do think you're a great actor, and I think that the spectrum of emotions you carry is phenomenal. But we are from two very different worlds."

"We're actually from the exact same world."

"You know what I mean."

"Unfortunately, I do." Then after a moment of silence, he said, "I would like to be alone right now."

"What? You need to meditate?" I didn't even mean to sound like a jerk that time.

"No," Ryan shook his head, looking defeated. "I just need to be away from you."

Ouch. That one hurt, even if I deserved it.

"I'm happy to give you the space, but how are we supposed to do that?"

Ryan led the way without answering.

A few minutes later, we were sitting on either side of the bedroom door, with him inside of the room and me outside on the floor.

Ten minutes of silence was excruciating.

Twenty felt like it might break me into pieces, the guilt like bags of sand pressing down on my shoulders.

"I'm really sorry," I said from my side of the door. "I never meant to hurt you."

"So you told me."

"Do you accept my apology?"

After a long pause: "I accept your apology."

"I want to make it up to you. Will you let me make it up to you?"

"I'm agreeable to you making it up to me." I imagined his smile. "What do you have in mind?"

"Do you feel like a walk?"

"I would love a walk."

"How about a long walk?"

"Even better," he said.

So we started down the same route I walked with all the dogs on my way to meet Madison. But this time I walked along the coastline to my favorite spot with Ryan Jones by my side instead.

We stopped at a small ice cream shack, where he insisted on buying us cones. Cold brew for me and chocolate for him. The descriptions were better than the dessert itself, but the shack still did ice cream better than what the Cannery Cafe had passed off as gourmet ice cream for sure.

Still, the cones could have been crunchier, and the ice cream most certainly could have been creamier. The balance between sweetness and bitterness in my cold brew was slightly off, with too much sugar drowning the rich depth of the coffee. Ryan's chocolate lacked the deep cocoa richness of an artisan scoop, but I still loved that he let me lick it.

We paused to enjoy our ice cream under the shade, then continued on until we finished our walk at my favorite spot.

Ryan broke into a smile when he got there. It might

have been the prettiest one I had caught on his face so far. The kind that would have hit me heart and soul if I was seeing it on the silver screen.

"I love this spot," he said.

"Why do you love it?"

"I used to watch a little girl fly a kite here when I was little."

"Really?" I asked, feeling my heart start to gallop.

"Yeah," he nodded. "I was always jealous because my mom would never get me a kite no matter how many times I asked."

I was stunned. For several long seconds, I couldn't make any words.

"What's wrong?" Ryan asked. "Are you okay?"

"I was that little girl. I always used to fly kites here in this spot."

In a motion both instinctual and sentimental, I led him to another modest shack across the road, brimming with nostalgic treasures.

Without a word, I selected a brightly colored plastic kite and bought it for him, with cash from our haul of tips.

When I offered it to him, the excitement that spread across his face reminded me of how he'd smiled at me after our first and only dance. It was just a kite, but he accepted it like it was his first Academy Award.

Thankfully, he did not give a little speech thanking God and his mother and several dozen other people before tearing into the flimsy plastic bag and dumping all the pieces out onto the grass.

Sitting cross-legged on the ground, we assembled the kite, and I didn't mind how often our fingers collided or the way the backs of our cuffed hands kept rubbing against each other. Once it was flight-worthy, he helped me to my feet. He grabbed my hand, then we ran together, trailing the kite behind us on its string and laughing when the breeze finally caught it and lifted up it.

Then back at the spot, our spot now, we stood side by side as his new kite kissed the sky, bridging our pasts with the present in a silent dance.

EIGHTEEN

Ryan

I woke up in bed the next morning to find Maggie staring down at us, inspecting our handcuffs.

My system flooded with adrenaline, and I shouted out in surprise. "What the hell?"

It was loud enough to jostle Olivia awake — slowly for the first few seconds, and then quite suddenly as she realized that we weren't alone. She leaped backwards so quickly she banged her head against the headboard.

"I wouldn't have startled you if you were up at a reasonable time," Maggie said.

"Define reasonable," I asked, sitting up in bed.

"You're bare-chested," Maggie observed.

"You're welcome," I said.

Maggie glanced at Olivia with a grin but kept any opinions to herself.

"Nice to meet you in person," Olivia said, offering Maggie her unrestrained hand.

"You too, dear." Maggie shook her hand, then addressed us both. "I'm sure you'll need a few minutes to get your morning business taken care of. And while I do admit to a strong curiosity around the particulars of how you both manage to get the various activities from brushing your teeth to the essential ones and twos accomplished, I'll respect your privacy if you want to keep the sordid details to yourself."

"You know, there's a line between manager and invasive species," I said, "and I think we just crossed it."

"Take the time you need, but not too much of it," Maggie replied without responding to me. "I got on an early flight, and I'm already exhausted with ninety-four things to do and no time to do them, so—"

"Is that a real number?" Olivia asked.

"No, dear. It's an under-estimation." Maggie shook her head. "Meet me in the other room as soon as you can."

"She's a lot," Olivia said, once Maggie was gone.

"I know. But we're in good hands now."

It was too early in the morning for me to start going on and on about the magic that I had seen my manager repeatedly make, but if there was anyone I trusted in this world to guide us through the beyond awkward nature of this situation, it was Maggie.

The only reason people even knew I could act in the first place was because for the last ten years, she had done everything in her power to get me performing in front of the world, fighting tooth and nail to get every script that she thought would develop my talent in front of me. Sometimes it was the story she thought I should be doing, and other times it was a director I should be working with.

That formula had been foolproof until this recent fiasco with André.

I suppose we were both wrong in our own way about that one.

"You ready for this?" I asked Olivia as we entered the bathroom.

"I guess?" she replied with a smile.

Everything about her seemed softer this morning, kinder, more willing, or at least less reluctant to be constantly standing next to me.

Maybe it was that long walk and the lingering time we spent eating ice cream and flying kites, which made our stroll feel almost like a date.

It wasn't a date.

Was it?

Maybe it was something about how some of my oldest memories felt like a beautiful echo of yesteryear, the rush of familiar emotions creating that sense of déjà vu. I never imagined that I would once again fall under the spell of the girl who had stolen my heart back at the fourth-grade sock hop.

Or that I'd look forward to singing at the top of my lungs — deliberately off key, as a joke, because how much more ridiculous could things get? — every time she needed to use the toilet.

Our bathroom routine was much faster now. Not exactly a science, but at least we seemed practiced.

With an ease that should not have been possible with only a day of being bound together, Olivia held the tooth-paste while I uncapped it, then she squeezed it onto my brush, followed by her own.

We danced in harmony around the sink, managing to give each other space as we rinsed and spat.

When it came to our more personally embarrassing matters, we leaned into a silent understanding and did our best to make the deeply uncomfortable feel almost ordinary despite the cuffs.

Once finished, we went into the other room for our sit-down with Maggie.

"Let's get to it," I said.

And then Maggie got going. "Good news first: I got the studio to agree to move the premiere."

"Wow. I mean, I knew you would, but how did you manage that?" I asked.

"People will do what you tell them to do if you don't give them a choice." She shrugged. "I sold it to them on the basis that it would help them rehab the image of the movie's shoot. I'm sure it's not a surprise to anyone in this room that Ryan's video has caused some serious damage to his previous image as a prestigious A-lister."

"I don't see how—"

"But the rumors of how bad things actually were on the *Cold Fury* set keep getting worse." Maggie firmed her voice as she cut me off. "Those rumors are starting to impact most of the buzz surrounding this film. Olivia's idea really was, or is, PR gold. It should distract the media."

"Wait," I interjected again. "Are you saying that the situation with the press is getting worse? I keep up with the headlines. If anything, the negative commentary seems to be dying down."

"There are rumors that things on set were even worse than originally reported and that there are more videos of you out there. It feels like the fire has been simmering, and the pot on this story is about to boil over."

"But that's a lie!" I insisted. "There aren't any more videos out there because it only happened one time."

"According to reports, you and André were constantly at each other's throats."

"That's because the guy was—"

"It doesn't matter. What happened, happened. This is our chance to fix it. You know this country loves a comeback story better than anyone else in the world. Do this, and we're golden."

"Great. So what's the catch?" I asked.

"It's not really a catch," Maggie said. "Just one little problem."

"How is that not a catch?"

"Let's call it a hiccup, or an additional responsibility."

"Please just get to it, Maggie."

She nodded. "You're going to have to do a bunch of the legwork."

"What kind of legwork?" I asked.

"Arranging hotel accommodations, the catering, booking the menu—"

"Why aren't your admins or assistants handling all this?" I interrupted. "That's literally their job."

"Normally, yes, they would. But this whole thing was last minute, and everyone's swamped. Moreover, having you personally take charge of these details is a good PR move It sends a message to the media and your fans that you're committed, involved, and humbled enough to take on responsibilities you wouldn't normally have to."

Ryan exhaled heavily. "So now I'm an event planner?"

Maggie smiled softly. "It's for the good of the movie and your image, Ryan. Besides, Olivia's here to help." She cast a pointed glance at Olivia.

"I'm happy to show the movie star how things are done in the real world."

"That's great to hear." Maggie nodded in approval. "The studio also wants to go hard on the romance angle for Ryan. So I'm going to need the two of you to play that budding romance up, even more than you already were."

"Wait." I shook my head. "We're not—"

"The studio agreed to move the premiere here because they like the story of Ryan trying to help his hometown and doing everything he can to get attention on Lydia's work rehabbing a hundred-year-old theater."

"It's eighty-five years old," Olivia corrected.

"Rounding up makes it sound more impressive. The point is, while Ryan was here doing his hometown hero work, he reconnected with his old sweetheart."

Olivia shook her head. "We were never sweethearts."

"Right," Maggie nodded. "That's been well established. And the way the two of you go at each other, I don't question it. But you should keep the banter. Lean into what works, just make sure you stay playful."

"Maggie—"

"I need you two to sell that. Got it?" Maggie asked.

But it was not like she waited.

"We fail to sell that specific story, then we fail with everything else. Do you understand?"

Olivia obviously understood but clearly didn't like it.

And I wasn't sure which of us hated the idea more. I was an actor, so I never minded playing a role. But there were feelings involved here.

I was hesitant, nervous, and excited. Could all of those things be true?

As with any role, I needed to find the reality in the emotions to unearth my best possible performance.

Yes, I was hesitant, because I didn't like manipulating the press. Olivia was right when she said that it was one thing to trick a ticket buyer and another thing to manipulate somebody reading an article.

I didn't like that part, but I could get over it. Especially because Maggie believed in the idea.

And was I nervous?

Definitely.

But why?

This role as a man who reconnected with an old flame would be an easy one to play. And maybe that was the issue, because it led right into the third emotion.

I was absolutely excited, and not by the duty Maggie was giving me. My looking forward to whatever this might be was about who I would be doing my duty with.

Olivia.

The girl from the sock hop.

"So can you both play up the romance angle or not?" Maggie asked.

"I'm good with it," I replied.

"Me too," Olivia said, in what sounded a little too close to a monotone. At least there were no feelings on her end.

"Great." Maggie nodded again. "Then we're almost done here."

"What else is there?" I asked.

"The studio also wants to see you two volunteering as chaperones at a sock hop where you attended fourth grade."

"When are they finally going to retire those dances?" I asked.

"Of course," Olivia said.

I blinked. "Wait! Don't I get a say in this? Because I absolutely do not want to go back there."

"Why?" Olivia asked.

"No, Ryan," Maggie said. "You don't get a choice on this one. You are being volun-told. It's part of the deal."

"And I'm sure that it's a part of the deal you can get out of. Why would anybody care about where I went to school 14 years ago?"

"Because it's great press." Maggie kept beating that drum. "PR gold, as they like to say. In this case, 'they' means 'I.'"

Going back to my old school was the last place that I wanted to be. Today, tomorrow, or at any point in my future. The reason my memory of that sock hop stood out so strongly even after all of these years was because it had hosted a rare and happy moment amid what was mostly an ocean of misery for me growing up.

My crippling shyness made the world itself claustrophobic.

Olivia somehow got me to open up.

So I was grateful that she would be with me for my return to the school. But I didn't want to go back to that place at all.

"One last thing," Maggie said.

"You already did the one last thing," I argued.

But Maggie continued. "The studio doesn't want anything about the handcuffs to be leaked. It's too risqué."

"I thought the studio loved risqué."

"I would have thought the same thing," Olivia added.

"Risqué works in the right places. But rehabilitating your presently divisive image is not on the list."

"That makes sense," Olivia said.

"I got a hotel room here at the Fisherman's Finest, and I'll help out however I can. But I do have a lot of calls I'll be needing to take while I'm up here, so this is mostly up to the two of you."

"Ninety-four things to do," Olivia clarified with a smile.

Maggie smiled back at her. But she was still all business. "You wanted the premiere here. I agreed it was a good idea, then made it happen with the studio. Now you two will need to do the work and make it happen on the ground."

NINETEEN

Olivia

WE GOT RIGHT TO WORK, heeding what Maggie had told us and starting to make our plans for a successful Hollywood premiere right here in Ocean Springs.

Ryan and I made for an awkward couple at first, with him overly tentative when it came to all of the party planning stuff, and a bit reluctant to follow my admittedly almost aggressive lead.

I wasn't trying to be bossy at all, but I respected the mission that Maggie had given to us and wanted to prove that I could be the star of this show too.

One of our first major tasks was convincing the haughty manager of Fisherman's Finest — a local who, despite his roots, seemed to wear an air of perpetual condescension — to accommodate our last-minute reservations. It was genuinely baffling; one would assume any hotelier of repute would leap at the opportunity for unexpected bookings.

Yet, it was in that moment when Ryan truly shone, taking the reins of that conversation and seamlessly turning it around. With finesse, he lavished the manager with a series of sincere compliments while skillfully high-lighting the immense potential for publicity the premiere would bring.

Ryan painted a vivid picture: a red-carpet event, the buzz of a Hollywood star — particularly one so keen on staying at Fisherman's Finest, his most cherished hotel along the scenic Californian coast, situated perfectly with an ocean view in the very town where he had fond memories of his childhood.

The hotel manager seemed invigorated by the challenge ahead. With a newfound enthusiasm, he assumed the role of our unofficial coordinator for Ocean Springs' accommodations. Under his meticulous and discerning gaze, he not only endeavored to organize rooms within his establishment but also extended his reach, liaising with other reputable hotels in and around the town. His intention was clear: to ensure that the press corps was comfortably grouped together, fostering a collaborative atmosphere, while similarly providing a cohesive lodging experience for the cast and crew.

Ryan had taken him from skeptic to advocate like a pro.

"Well done," I said.

"Years in this business teach you a thing or two. Like it's always about the narrative."

We called Ashleigh next and asked her if The Family Table was willing to handle our rather substantial order of last-minute appetizers. Unlike with the hotel, I could easily see how such a large and unexpected order might prove to be a supreme inconvenience, if not a downright impossi-bility for her, but Ashleigh said she would be honored to have the chance.

"I can totally give you guys a deal," she offered.

But Ryan shook his head so Ashleigh could see him on the FaceTime video. "Definitely don't do that."

"Why?" Ashleigh asked. "They won't want a discount?"

"Sure, they might want a discount, but I imagine that no matter how much business The Family Table might do while the premiere is in town, I'm sure that can use the money a lot more than the studios can. How about you take your regular prices and add 20%?"

"You mean for a tip?" Ashleigh asked.

"Nope. I mean that because Hollywood will always be wasteful with their money, I am hoping to redirect some of that waste your way. So maybe you can think of that extra 20% as an 'awesome charge.'"

Ashleigh laughed. "I can add an awesome charge."

"The only thing you should be thinking about before agreeing to add the extra percentage is whether it should be twenty percent, or something closer to thirty."

Ashleigh laughed again and then they got to talking appetizers. We ended up with an impressive selection of *Cold Fury* comfort classics in less than twenty minutes of brainstorming.

Frosty Meatball Poppers (bite-sized meatballs with a hint of mint); Blizzard Mac Bites (creamy mac and cheese balls, breaded and deep-fried to a crispy golden brown, and then dusted with a snowy parmesan layer); Chilly Chili Cups (mini cornbread muffin cups filled with a dollop of hearty chili and topped with a swirl of sour cream): Snow-Capped Potato Skins (crispy potato skins loaded with melted cheese, bits of bacon, and green onions, topped with a dollop of cool sour cream); and Tundra Tuna Melt Sliders (mini sliders made of toasted bread, a blend of tuna salad, and melted cheese).

"Sorry that all of our appetizers clash with your

Brooding Hollywood Heartthrob Diet, but we like to eat here in Ocean Springs," I teased Ryan after we hung up with Ashleigh.

"Guess I'll be enjoying some saturated fats."

"Your nutritionist will be appalled."

"But my mouth will be thrilled."

Ryan laughed as he made our next call, FaceTiming Lydia and giving her the news about the premiere, after we assured her that worrying particulars like accommodations and food were being taken care of.

"Just make sure that the theater is booked and the staff is organized."

"Done!" Lydia exclaimed. "I'm already on it."

Then she FaceTimed us back less than five minutes later and confirmed that the theater would be able to provide a screen as long as the studio was bringing the digital projector.

Following a quick call from Maggie, we were good on that front as well.

"This is actually kind of fun," I chirped, for some reason really wanting (needing?) for Ryan to agree with me.

"It is kind of fun," he said.

And I felt like someone (Ryan) had lit me from the inside out.

We called Brooklyn to ask her if she could take the lead on organizing the sock hop, which like Ashleigh she felt "honored to do," then there was a lull in our duties as we waited for vendors and invested parties to return our calls.

But the energy between Ryan and I was a lot warmer than usual and had been so for a much longer period of time. I wanted to keep the good vibes going for as long as possible, so I tried for some simple conversation, properly positioning myself to pitch an idea that I had been thinking about starting late that morning but hadn't been able to get out of my mind ever since, even though by then we were running into early afternoon.

"Why is the movie called *Cold Fury*?"

"The movie is set in the Arctic," Ryan explained.

"But how can fury be cold?" I kept teasing, enjoying how the corners of his mouth wrinkled in as he tried to determine if I was just messing with him.

"You don't need to get it," he finally said, though his tone was kindly explanatory rather than mean or in any way mocking. "It's simple marketing. Who knows? The movie could have even been born title first. Why are you nitpicking movie titles?"

"I have an idea, but I don't know if you'll like it. "

"There's only one way to find out. Give it to me straight."

"You know how we're doing all the Cold Fury themed appetizers?" I asked.

"You mean from the FaceTime call a half hour ago? Yes, I can sort of recall that."

"What if we served ice cream?"

"Why wouldn't I like that idea?" Ryan asked. "I love that idea. Ice cream isn't on the Brooding Hollywood Heartthrob Diet, but it is on my short list of things I never say no to."

And I suddenly realized that I wanted to be on that list too.

Except, of course, I didn't. I was just being a stupid little girl staring at her movie posters in bed again.

"I was actually thinking about making the ice cream." Then I swallowed and said what I actually meant. "I want to make ice cream for the premiere."

"You want to make the ice cream?" Ryan repeated, like I had been speaking Russian or something before. "With someone handcuffed to you? Isn't that an awful lot of work?"

"It sure is," I agreed with a nod. "But it's the kind of work I love, and I would be, like Ashleigh and Brooklyn both said, honored to play my part with pulling off this premiere. We could make the ice cream at my mom's house and freeze it. I'll make something different than what people are typically used to, and by different I actually mean better. I promise that it will be great."

"I have no doubt that it will be great. It just seems like maybe something we shouldn't be doing tonight. Maybe—"

Ryan got cut off by the sound of his phone ringing, with more of his magical movie timing cutting into our moment again.

"It's Maggie," Ryan reported after looking down at his phone.

"Answer it. Ask her what she thinks."

So he did, and Maggie said, "That's a great idea. It's—"

"PR gold!" Ryan and I finished her sentence in unison.

Even though he was obviously not the biggest fan of what was now a semi-regular two against one with Maggie and I teaming up against him, Ryan kept playing the game like a great sport.

We checked in with Brooklyn to make sure that everything was still going great with the sock hop planning, then went back to my house so we could borrow my mother's car.

Everything had been mostly agreeable between us for an almost unfathomable several hours in a row when our streak of conflict-free time together suddenly ground to a halt, and we found ourselves going back and forth about who would be driving.

I hadn't thought about that earlier because my driving had never been in question. I had a sort of phobia about sitting in the passenger seat while someone else was driving. Backseat of a taxi or a cab? No problem. Mom didn't love that I always sat in back when we went places because it made her feel like a chauffeur, but I really couldn't help it.

Still, after several minutes of escalating arguments that rose in both volume and passion, I realized that this was not a quarrel I could win when Ryan spoke in his most patient voice.

"Look, I have to drive. Because I'm to your left. Unless you want to sit on my lap."

I felt heat creeping into my cheeks as my stomach butterflies suddenly decided to swarm.

Only after Ryan said it did I realize how much I actually did want to sit on his lap.

But that was the last thing in the world that I was about to admit.

So instead, I climbed into the car and crawled over the driver's seat and onto the passenger side.

Then Ryan drove us to the grocery store where we could buy our supplies to make my homemade gourmet ice cream, starting with enough milk to flood a cereal factory, and almost as much heavy cream.

I had some solid ideas around different flavors for coffee and tea-based ice creams that could help to elevate it above the typical vanilla, chocolate, strawberry palette. With 1,500 seats in the theater, we had a lot of ice cream to make, but that didn't mean I was willing to skimp on my shot at developing a red-carpet flavor.

"Are you sure about this?" Ryan asked while clearly trying not to judge my ingredients, yet failing to keep the dubious expression off of his face. "Do we have time for all of this?"

"We'll make time. Just because it's a large gathering doesn't mean the choices should only be chocolate or vanilla. What if every time you turned on the TV you could only see another version of *CSI*?"

Ryan shrugged. "I would just assume that I was watching CBS."

We didn't notice any paparazzi when we pulled into the grocery store parking lot or when we went inside. I made fun of Ryan after he thought he spotted one of the more nefarious citizens of the "Vulture Press," as Ryan was fond of calling them.

I also made fun of him the second time, but the third time he thought he spotted someone, I saw him too. A man with wiry salt-and-pepper hair, wearing sunglasses indoors. Even from the dark lenses, I could feel his gaze boring into me with unnerving precision.

Fortunately for Ryan and me, the staff of the grocery store was overly friendly and beyond accommodating to the townie and her movie star shopping partner. Ryan managed to convince one star-struck store employee to go and get the manager, who came out just moments later and happily agreed to take Ryan's credit card number and charge everything later, after helping them slip out back through the loading dock post-haste.

But that didn't really work out for us, because the moment we stepped outside with our shopping cart full of ingredients, several members of the paparazzi were there to ambush us, or perhaps it was just the press.

In truth, the gathering of people seemed a lot more legitimate than the shifty guy in sunglasses I had seen inside, and there was even a news van parked on the far side of the lot, with its antenna raised.

But as Ryan had said earlier, when people are looking for dirt on you, it's fair to consider all of the press as paparazzi. And that was what it felt like as all of those cameras flashed in our faces and a growing crowd shouted out questions like rounds from a rubber band gun, slapping at our attention and making it impossible for us to just simply slip away like we deserved to.

"Who is she?" several members of the press shouted out.

Clearly, I was the most interesting part of this developing story.

I could feel Ryan's posture straightening beside me as he cleared his throat and prepared to play the most recent role that Maggie had given to him. He pulled me closer to him, our hands and cuffs still obscured by that scarf dangling between us.

"This is Olivia Bloom, a former girlfriend of mine."

"Or current girlfriend," I corrected him, then surprised myself by leaning over and giving him a kiss on his cheek.

Ryan blushed, and the crowd burst into *ooohs* and *woots* and all those grade-school sounds that everyone who had a boyfriend back then was subjected to. Then they started yelling questions:

"Since when?"

"How did you meet?"

"Was the auction rigged?"

"Does April know?"

That last one was a reasonable question, but I still felt a twinge of annoyance that they'd assume I'd date Ryan if he hadn't already broken up with his last girlfriend.

And maybe a twinge of jealousy.

Ryan held up his free hand to quiet them. Amazingly, they actually went quiet.

"We'll be happy to answer all your questions at the

premiere. But right now, we're in the middle of something."

They immediately started yelling questions again.

"I think it's better if we keep going," Ryan said.

So we gripped the shopping cart together and pushed it around the loading dock, then through the parking lot and over to my mother's car.

We loaded the groceries into the trunk and then into the back seat, all while still being studied like animals in an exhibit.

How were we going to get into the car without anyone seeing the awkward dance it took for us to both get seated?

But then Ryan solved the problem. "If you all don't mind, I would appreciate a moment with my girlfriend in privacy. She really isn't used to this yet." He laughed. "Believe me, she will be."

The press laughed along with him.

Then I did too, though my laugh sounded different.

"I'm not so sure about that." My chuckle died, then one of the more forward members of the press stepped forward.

"Just one last question, then we'll all get out of your hair."

"Ask away," I said.

The reporter pointed. "What is that scarf around your wrists?"

I had no idea how to answer that question. I had been afraid that someone in the press would ask about the hand-cuffs, but not about the scarf around them.

"It's a love ribbon," I replied without thinking.

And apparently that gave the press something else to love. They drifted away in a herd, then Ryan and I scrambled awkwardly into our seats and closed the car doors.

"Love ribbon," Ryan repeated with a laugh.

"It was the only thing I could think of," I defended myself.

Then there was a long silence as we drove back to my mother's house until Ryan finally broke it.

"Love ribbon," he said, laughing again.

TWENTY

Olivia

WE WENT BACK to my mom's house and made ice cream, and as embarrassed as I was to both admit it and feel it, there was something almost fairy tale feeling about the two of us making ice cream in my kitchen together.

We got a pretty good system going relatively fast, with the two of us moving in a surprisingly elegant rhythm through the kitchen, almost as if our handcuffs didn't exist.

With awkward laughter that turned into frequent giggling, we assisted each other with everything from measuring to mixing to flavor testing.

"This is the most delicious ice cream I've ever had," Ryan said.

I loved the look on his face.

"I highly doubt that. A rich and famous movie star like you has surely tasted some of the world's best ice creams."

"Yes, I have had some of the world's best ice creams," he admitted with a laugh, "but that doesn't mean that they tasted any better than this."

He made an *mmm* sound as he returned the spoon to his mouth.

And the little noise made me want to melt like a dollop of whipped cream atop a steaming mug of cocoa.

"What flavor is this again?" Ryan asked.

"It's a spicy chai." And then I recited the description I had been writing in my head. "It's a harmonious blend of aromatic black tea infused with warming spices like cardamom, cinnamon, and cloves. The subtle kick from ginger marries well with the creaminess of the ice cream, and a hint of honey adds a touch of sweetness."

"Wow." Another dip of the spoon into the spicy chai ice cream before it went into his mouth.

Mmm...

And I was chocolate in a fondue pot.

"You're really serious about this stuff, aren't you?" Ryan asked.

"I sure am." And then I blurted too much about making ice cream all at once. "I really wish that the art and craft of making ice cream had a specific, singular term like 'oenology' for wine or 'culinary arts' for cooking. But making ice cream for me is like painting on a blank canvas; every ingredient is a color, and every flavor combination tells a unique story. It's a delicate dance of science and art, where I get to be precise yet wildly imaginative. I love all of the experimentation, discovering unexpected harmonies between ingredients that aren't traditionally paired together. Every scoop is another opportunity to evoke a memory, a feeling, or even transport someone to a different place. Pushing the boundaries of flavor profiles isn't just about creating a dessert, but crafting an experience for the palate."

He stared at me with his spoon halfway to his mouth, like he'd forgotten he was going to take a bite.

I blushed, remembering now why I never talked to Taylor about anything I was passionate about. He would immediately either mansplain it to me or explain why whatever it was I was thinking of doing was stupid and doomed to failure.

If I'd known back then that he was planning to steal the ideas that he was criticizing me for having, I would never have agreed to marry him.

"Sorry for rambling," I said. "Sometimes I forget that—"

"That ice cream is amazing, and that you're amazing at making it?"

I blushed so hard I might've been in danger of dying from heat stroke. I shoved an enormous spoonful in my mouth, and pain stabbed up through the roof of my mouth into my brain.

Ice cream headache.

But somehow, it did nothing to cool off the heat wave happening in my cheeks.

So I quickly changed the subject.

"What was it like living in LA as a famous actor?"

"That was an abrupt segue," Ryan observed.

"It was time." I laughed.

He appeared to waffle between asking me a follow-up question about making ice cream and respecting my wishes and refraining from casting me into any further embarrassment.

I made it easier for him: "So, what's it like?"

"Probably an awful lot like living there as any other person, except that I couldn't ever go anywhere without people following me and taking pictures."

"You have to love it, though. What actor doesn't love all the attention?"

"This actor." Ryan jabbed a thumb at his chest. "I've always resented that part of the job. I hated it when photographers wanted to snap a picture of me emptying my trash can, or ambush me while I was trying to decide between my avocados at the grocery store, or—"

"You do your own shopping?"

"—get caught mid-bite into a sloppy burrito — of course I do my own shopping." He shook his head. "You really have the wrong idea about me."

Maybe I did.

"And I really hated it when, after the video went viral, the 'press' went from trying to catch me doing just about anything, to specifically wanting to catch me in the act of doing something nefarious."

"Like what?" I asked.

"It's not like they ever caught me doing anything, it's that they were always there. Like camped outside of my gym, where they got a full spread of me struggling through a difficult yoga position."

I'd seen the memes. Not that I was going to tell him that.

"Once I got chased down a hiking trail. I tripped and fell hard, scraping my knees and smashing my elbows. Nobody helped, just kept snapping away, immortalizing my fall."

"Oh, that sounds terrible."

"It's not the best." He laughed.

"But there are lots of awesome things about being famous, right?"

"Of course. Getting to work with some of the most talented people in the industry. Being part of projects that genuinely inspire and touch people. Access to unique experiences."

"Like what?"

"Private music sessions, dinner in world-renowned restaurants, sometimes before they've even officially opened. And no, none of them served ice cream that tasted better than yours." Ryan smiled.

And I smiled back. "Good. Then I have nothing to be jealous about."

Then he continued. "I also love all the learning I get to do, whether that means reading up for a role and understanding the history around the time and place of the story to give me ultimate context, or learning to ride a horse, shoot an arrow, fly a plane — whatever. I'm always down for the learning."

"What about all the freebies?"

Ryan laughed. "The freebies are great. A shallow perk, but a perk nonetheless. I usually give mine away."

"Can I have your next gift bag?"

"You can have all of my gift bags," Ryan replied.

And again I felt a stirring that I refused to acknowledge.

"Did you have a girlfriend in LA?"

Now why the hell did I ask him that?

(Like you don't know why.)

"Nope." Ryan shook his head. "We broke up."

"When did that happen?"

"When do you think?" Ryan laughed again, but this time the sound was grim.

"When the video came out?"

"Exactly." It came out slightly bitter. "She was an actress and couldn't handle the negative PR fallout for her career."

"That sucks."

"I got it then and I get it now." He shrugged again. "April's manager thought it was best that we break up, and she had a hard time disagreeing."

"April Fisher?" I asked. "You were dating April Fisher?"

"For a few months, yeah. Almost a year, I guess. We both wanted to keep the relationship a secret."

I didn't want to feel jealous, but envy was suddenly slithering through my bloodstream. The green-eyed monster barely ever reared its head around me, but the thought of Ryan (my Ryan, even though he was anything but) being with someone as glamorous and sought after as April Fisher twisted my stomach into knots.

I needed to stop being stupid.

"Do you ever still think about her?"

After he answered that question.

He seemed to consider it seriously before landing on his reply.

"No, not really. I mean, it's hard to forget about her entirely when she's on billboards and in magazines and playing Sophie Lion on one of my favorite shows."

"You love *Sophie Knows It* too?"

"It might just be my guiltiest pleasure," Ryan admitted with an embarrassed sounding laugh. He seemed like he might be about to explain his addiction to me when his phone rang.

"Hey, what's up?" Ryan answered, listening for a few beats before responding. "Yeah ... okay ... sure. I'll do it right now."

He hung up the phone and turned to me. "Maggie said we should check out CelebBuzz Daily."

"Did she say why?"

"Nope, just that we should check it out right now. The top story."

"Oh, great," I replied with a roll of my eyes, feeling suddenly uncertain.

But it wasn't a big deal when Ryan clicked on the article. I expected something scandalous, but instead, there were photos of me and Ryan at the grocery store. The paparazzi had captured us, which we already knew. So the only surprise was how fast the pictures had made it online, which really shouldn't have been a surprise at all.

Under the photos, there was a fashion segment with the caption, *Love Ribbons, They're All The Rage In Hollywood*, then a closeup on our hands.

Fortunately, the picture failed to capture the handcuffs. But we already knew that too, so if this was just about the love ribbon, then I thought that was funny.

So that's why I was laughing.

But Ryan didn't find it amusing.

"You don't think there's anything funny about that at all?" I asked.

"I think it's about as funny as an audit on my birthday."

We went back to making ice cream, this time in silence.

And in that quiet, I tried to consider his perspective, wondering what it must be like for someone to live under such incessant scrutiny.

I imagined how it might feel if every day when I left the house, there were people potentially hiding in the bushes waiting to take pictures of me, actively wanting to catch me in the act of doing something wrong.

Would I ever trust that the people in my life weren't all tattletales?

The phone rang again, but this time it was mine, and I knew without looking at the screen who it was because the Bad Blood ringtone loudly announced it was Taylor.

I didn't even take the phone out of my pocket.

Ryan glanced over, eyeing me curiously but not saying anything.

A few seconds later, my phone rang again. That time, I took out my phone and rejected the call before tucking it back down into my pocket.

I didn't want to talk to Taylor, and I really didn't want Ryan to ask me about the rejected call. Like a good man, he didn't.

Instead, he sensed my discomfort and said, "Can I help you with that?"

Ryan pointed to the large pieces of chocolate I was crushing into smaller ones, but before I could tell him that I had it, my phone buzzed with a text.

And then another, followed by another one just a second after that.

I grabbed my phone again, only to block Taylor so that he could never (ever) text me again, but I couldn't help glancing at the screen on my way to blocking him.

Three messages, all saying the same thing:

I jst wanna tlk
Can we chat? Pls?
U free?

No, I wasn't free, and I refused to give Taylor even a minute of my time.

Ryan noticed the slight downturn of my lips as I put my phone away. Taking a scoop of freshly churned ice cream with his finger, he placed a dollop on the tip of my nose.

I looked at him in shock.

"Got your nose," he grinned.

I exploded with laughter, taking a scoop of my own and retaliated by smearing some of it across his cheek.

Then it was as if the touch was too much.

As if our closeness was too much.

The weight of our moment began to dissolve as Ryan wiped his face, then grabbed a scoop of freshly churned ice cream and playfully held it near my mouth.

"Taste test?"

I leaned in, letting the cold sweetness brush my lips,

giggling at the absurdity of sharing a spoon while handcuffed.

"Have you ever thought about starting a business?" Ryan asked. "It wouldn't have to be an ice cream business or anything like that, but you're obviously very talented."

"Thank you," I said, embarrassed.

"You're welcome, but that doesn't answer the question."

"Sure, I've thought about opening a business."

"Then why haven't you? I bet you would be great at it."

"I actually had a business. Or at least I almost did," I found myself admitting, not sure if I wanted to be having this conversation at all, despite already being two long strides inside it.

"Oh yeah, what kind of business?"

"It was a coffee shop."

"Really? Where was it?"

"In Los Angeles," I told him.

"Keep on saying things that surprise me." Ryan laughed.

"It was my dream business. Not really exactly a coffee shop, but like a library where you could get smaller packets of coffee."

"Instead of buying an entire pound of something you don't know if you'll like?"

"Exactly!" I exclaimed. "It was called Bean and Book. Or still is, I guess. Taylor stole my idea."

"That's your ex-boyfriend?" Ryan asked, though thanks to my mom going on and on (and on) last night, of course he already knew.

"Yes, but I prefer to think of him as the man who stole three years of my life."

"So that brat at the restaurant was Taylor's sister?"

"Yep."

"On the bright side, you'll never have to be her in-law."

I laughed. "It came close to happening."

"You guys were engaged?"

"Up until he slept with my maid of honor, stole my idea, and opened the coffee shop for himself."

"Oh yeah. I heard that at The Family Table. I'm really sorry about all of it. I can see why your mom had so many opinions about your relationship with him."

"She always hated Taylor."

"Really? It doesn't seem like your mom hates anyone."

"Well, 'hate' is a strong word, but she did say that he had the personality of a damp napkin one time, before we moved to LA, and once when she visited us she said that if brains were dynamite, Taylor wouldn't have enough to blow his nose. And she might actually hate Stephanie."

"Well, that makes sense. Everybody should hate Stephanie."

We laughed.

Then Ryan said, "I'm really sorry that all of that happened to you."

"I would have thought that Taylor sleeping with Rachel was the worst thing that could have ever possibly happened to me. But after he cheated on me, I mostly felt grateful that the two of those miserable people would end up together. I got saved from a divorce a few years early."

"So what was worse than that?" Ryan asked.

"That they stole my business." Then I took out my phone and showed Ryan the Bean and Book Instagram account, with the feed full of trendy coffee and pastries.

The aesthetic boasted a warm blend of mahogany and sepia tones, evoking a comforting, vintage atmosphere that reminded one of cozy afternoons with a beloved book: a neatly arranged flat lay of artisanal coffee beans alongside classic novels, with delicate flowers placed intermittently; a steaming cup of cappuccino set on a worn wooden table; a particularly stunning shot of a dimly lit corner, with plush leather armchairs, a golden reading lamp, and scattered paperbacks; and the most recent image depicting an overhead shot of a gleaming counter, adorned with an assortment of pastries, with flaky crusts and rich fillings a beautiful contrast to the dark roast coffee beside them.

"It's kind of whatever." Ryan shrugged.

And I wondered if he had any idea how much he had just insulted me.

"What do you mean by that?" I asked.

"I mean, it looks cool enough, I guess, but Southern California is full of places like that, and I don't really see what sets that coffee shop apart."

"You can order coffee in smaller packets," I protested.

Ryan had just said that he got it a minute ago!

"Yes." He laughed, "I get the concept, and it's cute. It really is. But again, specialty coffee shops are a dime a dozen, and there really isn't anything special about what your ex-boyfriend and your maid of honor are doing here. Jennifer? Was that her name?"

His dismissal hurt a lot more than I wanted to admit.

"What is it?" he asked.

Ryan either saw a shift in my expression or a deflating of my posture, so I tried to shake it off, not wanting him to know that he had upset me.

"It's nothing," I said.

"It's something."

"I happen to like what they're doing at the Book and Bean, even if I can't stand them."

"I get that." Ryan nodded. "You're attached to the idea and you should be."

"Even if it's not a good idea? Because that's what you're saying, right? That my idea is generic and has been done at least as good, if not better, all across Southern California."

"That's not what I said." He gave me a patient little shake of his head. "I just think that you are so wonderfully creative, and you could have easily come up with something better than what I'm seeing in those pictures. Who knows? If you were the one running the place, I bet I'd be a lot more impressed with the photos on the coffee shop's Instagram feed."

"I really doubt that," I snapped, feeling slightly better about his earlier insult, but not exactly enjoying the feeling of him patronizing me.

"I'm not patronizing you," Ryan said, as if reading my mind.

"Then don't lie to me to save my feelings."

"Why do you think I'm lying?"

"Because you're an actor. You lie for a living."

"Your logic is absurd."

And now he was gaslighting me too?

"You just told me that my idea was basic, and now you're backpedaling because you know it was mean and maybe hurt my feelings. But that doesn't change what you actually think."

"I can assure you that I know exactly what I think," Ryan snapped. "I shouldn't have to convince you that I think you're more creative than—"

"How am I more creative?" I raised my hands in exasperation, exhausted by this movie star who felt like he had to humor me.

"Because," Ryan started, his voice soft and patient and thoughtful and so, so sexy. "You're the one who thought of moving the premiere to Ocean Springs."

He stared into my eyes with an intense gaze that felt soaked in appreciation. I dared to believe that he wasn't humoring me at all.

"All of those appetizers were your idea. Ashleigh was just prompting you." He kept staring, as if needing me to feel his acknowledgment. "And you thought of making the ice cream, both because it would go with the *Cold Fury* theme, and because you are good at it."

He finally broke eye contact to shake his head. "I would have never thought of that."

"Oh," I said.

And in the ensuing silence, our eyes told a story that our words could not.

I felt surprised and flattered … plus some other things that would have embarrassed me to mention.

TWENTY-ONE

Ryan

I took a seat on the bench outside of the shower, wishing I could stop thinking about Olivia, standing in there with warm droplets cascading down her skin.

Every time I thought I'd figured her out, Olivia presented a new mystery to unravel. From her mesmerizing eyes to the cadence of her laughter, she was like a song I couldn't get out of my head. As I waited for her to finish the shower, the humidity in the room crept up, warming my skin and making me hyper-aware of every breath I took.

The light scent of her shampoo wafted in the air. Something floral, but not too sweet, and now a scent I would probably associate with her forever.

Why was she having such an effect on me? Was it the handcuffs, or was there something more between us?

I clenched my fists and try to push away all thoughts of her, reaching for my phone as I heard the faint sound of Olivia singing. I distracted myself from her melody by texting a message to Lucas.

How is the location scouting going?

I loved seeing how inspired Lucas was over his next project and hoped he could make it big. I was genuinely curious about how things were going.

I have a few more small towns to check out, but they're all blending together. I'm looking for a place that really stands out.

You'll find it, I texted him.

How are things with Olivia? U2 still in cuffs?

Yeah. She's taking a shower right now.

SERIOUSLY? Lucas texted, then: *Dude ...*

What?

There's a hot girl that you like showering right next to you and you can't do anything about it? That's a punishment worthy of a Greek myth.

I never said I liked her, I texted.

But it didn't matter what I kept telling myself. Deep down, of course, I knew that I liked Olivia.

What did you guys do handcuffed together all day?

Besides having a good time? I didn't wait for him to answer before I texted again, my thumb dancing across the screen to get as many of my thoughts to Lucas as I could before the water stopped running. *We made ice cream today and it tasted like freedom.*

See. You totally like her.

I wrote three different versions of my reply before settling on *Maybe.*

Then the faucet squeaked off and Olivia's lovely voice lilted into the bathroom. "Could you please hand me a towel?"

"Of course."

I handed Olivia a towel, then closed my exchange with Lucas. *Gotta go. Talk to you later.*

Olivia was toweling herself off, while I kept trying not to look at the misty silhouette, wanting to prove myself as the gentleman I was, even though every impulse inside me was screaming to let me be anything but.

"Are you ready?" Olivia asked.

"Ready for what?" She couldn't possibly mean what I was suddenly dreaming about.

"The sock hop," she said.

I nodded. "Ready as I'll ever be."

TWENTY-TWO

Olivia

THE MOOD between us was many varieties of strange by nightfall.

Ryan and I entered the sock hop together, and it was like walking into another fairy tale, this one even more enchanted than the one where I had been making dream ice cream in the kitchen where I learned to cook with my very first crush.

I could never have imagined anything like this happening to me back when I was little fourth-grade Olivia Bloom dancing with the version of Ryan Jones that was still three years from anyone outside Ocean Springs knowing his name, and seven before the world would start hearing it.

In my wildest imagination, I never would have believed that he would grow up to be one of the biggest movie stars in the world, or that I would be handcuffed to him after a dinner I never asked for that ended up with what felt suspiciously like a date less two days later.

A real date.

And then today, acting like a couple in front of the

press, then engaging in one of my favorite activities by making all of that ice cream, churning the cream and sharing spoons of the dessert along with hours and hours of laughter and giggles.

Now here I was, wearing a floral sundress with a vintage print. A delicate dance of pastel hues, swirling patterns of soft pinks, blues, and yellows on a cream backdrop. The bodice hugged me just right, giving way to a skirt that flowed effortlessly down to my knees, moving with a whimsical flutter with every step I took. Delicate lace trims lined the hem, adding a touch of vintage charm that made me feel both nostalgic and timeless.

Ryan stood tall beside me, the custom-tailored shirt clinging perfectly to his well-defined torso, its crispness accentuating his broad shoulders and tapered waist. The jacket was testimony to my mother's skill as a seamstress, with every stitch and seam perfectly aligned, looking like he was wearing a bespoke garment instead of practically being sewn into the thing.

Brooklyn was a wizard with fabric and had worked her magic to accommodate the handcuffs. Ryan's shirt had a hidden seam on one side, seamlessly blending with the pattern and allowing him to slip into the shirt with ease, without any visible disruption in its design. Brooklyn had even added some quick-release clasps, an ingenious solution ensuring that he could get out of the shirt just as easily as he got into it.

She made my dress strapless, the tube top bodice wrapping snugly around my chest. And to ensure I could get into it without any hitches, the back was designed with stretchy smocking. This detail not only facilitated easy wearing but added an extra vintage flair to the ensemble. I simply had to step into it and pull it up. Velcro seams on the sides were camouflaged amid the vibrant patterns.

Mom also swapped out our love ribbon for one of her favorite paisley scarves, with intricate teardrops in swirling patterns; deep shades of burgundy and teal to give the scarf a timeless, bohemian elegance. She insisted it wasn't a sacrifice, but I knew that scarf was her favorite.

We got out of the car to a full battalion of paparazzi shooting pictures of us and shouting their questions. This time, Ryan took it all in stride.

"It's easier when you know where they're going to be and what you can expect from them," he told me. "Some actors even have great relationships with the paparazzi."

"You're just not one of them."

Ryan laughed. "Nope, I'm definitely not one of them."

But we kept holding hands even after our pictures were taken and after a battery of questions were answered. The mood was even more surreal inside the school, so I found myself standing even closer to Ryan.

The kids seemed a bit weirded out by the last-minute sock hop. Ryan was right that the tradition was overdue for retirement — the school had moved on to holding an 80s-themed extravaganza each year.

But the kids also seemed weirded out that me and Ryan were both there, considering we didn't have any kids of our own and he was the star of *Battlefield Now*, a movie most kids had seen at least once.

After a lot of awkward standing around that included Ryan and I both draining two glasses of punch before realizing that would only lead to more bathroom shenanigans, he leaned over to me and said, "Aren't any of these kids going to dance?"

"You remember what it's like. Everyone is too embarrassed to make the first move."

"So maybe it's up to us."

"You want to go out there and dance?"

"Maggie did say we have a lot of work to do to pull this off, right? And she also said that the studio was very interested in our chaperoning this dance. Seems to me like we would just be doing a good job."

"Well, in that case, after you."

Ryan gestured down at our handcuffs with a knowing smile. "I think we have to go together. Everywhere."

I felt a surprising flush of mourning knowing that soon he would be leaving Ocean Springs again and this would all be over.

We started to dance, awkwardly contorting ourselves to the beat while trying not to yank each other's arms.

Everyone watched us, some amused, others standoffish.

Then a couple of the kids got the right idea and ran out onto the dance floor to join us. And soon the majority of us were hopping and bopping to "The Twist" and other tunes from that bygone era before the music died.

And then everyone except for a few stragglers was shaking their body and having a blast.

I wanted to get lost in the moment and feel like a little kid again, just like all the scads of children so giddily dancing around us. But I felt acutely aware of all the photographers in the corners of the gymnasium, intermittently snapping photos and making me feel like Ryan and I were on total display.

We were like animals at the zoo, scrutinized and photographed from every angle. I realized how much of his life was spent either anticipating this kind of exposure, living through it, or even occasionally nursing the trauma that followed that kind of constant exposure like a shadow.

Maybe I really had seen that viral video out of context, and it had just been one of those days where Ryan finally had to blow his top.

Except that he had blown up at someone who was simply trying to do their best job.

I stopped thinking about that, because whatever happened in that video was none of my business, and I really needed to focus on the sock hop and all the happily dancing children.

I was surprised when the first group of shy kids gathered around us and mustered enough courage to request autographs.

There was Georgia, a bashful blonde with pigtails and glasses, clutching a spiral notebook. Tommy had fiery red hair, boundless energy, and no filter when it came to asking a movie star questions (like how many times a day he needed to use the restroom, which was an answer that I also happened to know). Taylor was a sweet girl with ebony braids and a gapped tooth smile; it wasn't her fault that she shared her name with the monster in my closet.

It wasn't surprising that the children wanted autographs, but I never expected them to want one from me, too. It made me feel silly but also kind of delighted, and I made large and exaggerated loops in my cursive lettering as I wrote out "Olivia Bloom" to look as fancy as I possibly could.

"There you go," I said, handing the notebook back to Georgia.

Another three waves of autograph seekers came until there was a small line forming. Ryan and I dutifully scribbled our names over and over, bringing joy to a short line of starry-eyed children.

Once the line had cleared, Brooklyn came over and took mercy on us.

"It looks like you guys need a break. Would you like to take fifteen minutes?"

Ryan and I traded a look, both of us smiling and

knowing how much the other one would love a few minutes outside the chaotic gym.

"That would be wonderful," Ryan said. "Thank you."

"I'm not a movie star, but I'll do my best to keep everyone distracted with quality entertainment until you get back." Brooklyn laughed.

"You're the best!" I shouted, already dragging Ryan toward the exit.

We walked the campus, and surely he was falling as deeply into the remembrance as I was. The school grounds were dotted with towering oaks, and we strolled down a winding path blanketed in a crunchy carpet of leave until we found ourselves standing in front of Room 18, our old fourth grade classroom.

The exterior entrance was littered with fallen leaves, which we both apparently felt a need to shuffle around with our feet at the very same time.

"Do you think it's open?" Ryan looked at the door.

I shook my head. "No way."

But then he put his hand on the knob and turned it and the door swung right open.

"After you," he said.

We entered the classroom, which looked surprisingly similar to the way it did all those years ago when it was still Lydia in front of the whiteboard. The floor was the same speckled tile, but the whiteboard was now a smartboard.

Even the reading area with its rainbow rug and plush pillows was unchanged, drawing me back through the years.

"Do you remember all those bean bags?" I asked, pointing to the corner.

"Of course I do. My reading room at home has bean bags in it because of those."

"Except I'm sure your bean bags cost like a million dollars."

"They didn't cost a million dollars," Ryan replied, sounding exhausted by all the times he'd had to defend his wealth in the last couple of days.

"Were they more than a thousand dollars?"

"I doubt it."

"You don't know?"

"No. I'm sorry. I don't remember."

"How rich do you have to be that you can't even remember whether or not you spent more than a thousand dollars on a bean bag?"

"There are six in the room and I bought them years ago. My decorator handled it." He laughed lightly.

"I suppose when money ceases to be an object, the details get fuzzy."

We shared a laugh, the tension diffusing.

Then Ryan told a funny story about getting in trouble for getting glue all over his hands in art class.

"…and then I thought it would be hilarious to sprinkle them with glitter. I got called Sparkle Hands for the entire rest of second grade."

When I was able to breathe again, he asked, "Now tell me your glue-based reminiscence."

"I ate paste once in kindergarten."

"Why?"

"I thought it was frosting."

Our giggles echoed off the empty halls.

And then our silence sounded so loud.

"Thank you for being easy to talk to."

It was an odd thing for Ryan to say.

"My pleasure. You too." I smiled, and my heart began to beat faster.

Ryan grew pensive. "I was actually really shy growing up."

I didn't respond, and wasn't sure that he wanted me to.

"Painfully so," he finished.

"Really?" I asked. "Madison said that she thought you were shy a couple of days ago, but I never really saw you that way."

"That's because you saw me in a different way completely."

We shared another one of those unsettling yet beautiful lulls of honest quiet between us, a silence that was almost an ache before Ryan started talking again, picking right up where he had left off.

"I was painfully shy, so when you asked me to dance at the sock hop, I was thrilled."

"I had no idea." And I wasn't sure how I felt about knowing it now, either. Did it matter if he'd been excited to dance with me all those years ago? Or was it just another piece of trivia for us to laugh over?

I decided to focus on the easier part of his confession. "I mean, I didn't know that you were such an introvert."

"Oh yeah. Most people have a hard time believing that an actor could be an introvert."

"Guilty." I raised my hand. "Honestly, I love knowing it, though. That was a real lightbulb moment for me just now. I suddenly understand you a lot better than I did just a couple of minutes ago."

"I'm happy to hear that."

"But how is it that a serious introvert can also be such a great actor? Doesn't acting inherently require a lot of attention always being paid to you?"

"Well, sure, but it's different, because it's like I'm putting on a character, and that's actually easy. I get to disappear inside the role and express emotions that I wouldn't necessarily ever be able to articulate otherwise."

He thought for a moment, grasping for the right words.

"It's like I get to take off one mask and put on another. The role becomes my armor, my sword and shield. Acting allows me to connect with the world in a way I can't do as myself. I've always felt things deeply, but never really had the right outlet to express myself because of my crippling social anxiety. Acting gives me a space to channel all those pent-up thoughts and feelings into a character. It sets them free."

"How did you know that you wanted to be an actor?"

"It's so dumb, but do you remember our Chicken Little play?"

"THE SKY IS FALLING!" I exclaimed, surprised by how loudly it echoed, and embarrassed enough to start laughing again.

"Exactly." Ryan smiled. "That was what did it for me. After that play, I knew I wanted to be an actor."

"Well, you were the lead. And quite dramatic as Chicken Little."

"Do you really remember my performance?"

"I only remember that we had the play. But I'm sure you were the best Chicken Little in history."

"Zach Braff was pretty good in the Disney version."

"Then he was the only thing good in that movie," I said.

Ryan made a face. "Not their best work. Maybe—"

"Wait, do you hear that?"

Ryan stopped talking, listening as notes of music from the gym floated into our old classroom.

"It's 'Earth Angel,'" he said, "from *Back to the Future*. Do you remember this scene?"

"Of course I remember this scene." I didn't know what

else to say with my heart pounding against my ribcage. "Everyone remembers this scene."

He looked deep into my eyes. "Shall we?"

"I thought you'd never ask."

I took his hand and the cuffs jingled melodically between us.

As we swayed to the music, the tension between us intensified.

Our faces drew closer...

And closer...

Until—

TWENTY-THREE

Ryan

"Excuse me…"

My heart plunged as a moment I hadn't even realized I'd been eagerly anticipating was abruptly snatched away.

One of the parent chaperones peered into the classroom, her sudden presence jarringly halting Olivia and me just as our lips had been on the cusp of meeting in a kiss.

I was torn between relief at the interruption and feeling crestfallen that the moment had been ripped away from us.

"Terribly sorry to interrupt." The woman apologized with a kind smile, faint creases forming at the corners of her sympathetic eyes. "Miss Brooklyn sent me to fetch you two lovebirds. It's pure chaos in there, and the kiddos are clamoring for the return of their guest of honor Hollywood heartthrob."

Olivia and I shared an awkward laugh, twin blushes burning our cheeks at having been caught in such an intimate moment. The atmosphere had been undeniably altered between us.

With the near-kiss now hovering above us like a raincloud, we dutifully returned to the lively sock hop, hands still linked since we were already tethered — an intimate posture the public seemed to relish.

I felt hyperaware of Olivia's nearness as we swayed and twisted on the dance floor, our charged moment replaying through my mind on an endless loop. Each time our gazes met, my pulse sped up again.

At last, the festive sock hop wound to a close. Yet the undercurrent of anticipatory tension continued flowing between Olivia and me as the photographers' flashes popped incessantly around us.

Behind our plastered-on smiles, that potent almost-kiss still crackled in the scant space separating us.

The cacophony of camera shutters and chatter continued to envelop us, but it was as if we were in a bubble of our own, still reeling from the almost-kiss.

Once safely ensconced in the plush leather backseat of the now familiar black Audi, a profound silence blanketed us. Muffled sounds of the streets outside provided a soft background, but the words we both longed to say remained locked behind our lips.

The Fisherman's Finest loomed ahead, its elegant facade illuminated against the darkening sky. As the car pulled up to the entrance, the weight of our unsaid feelings pressed heavier with each passing moment.

The lavish lobby went by in a blur, and the elevator's muted music seemed to amplify our tension rather than alleviate it.

I felt the soft press of her arm against mine, sending tiny electric jolts through me. Was she steeped in the same bubbling stew of emotions?

We got off of the elevator and walked the long hallway to Maggie's room, right next to ours.

Still quiet as we turned the corner, we made it the few

final strides in a lingering silence that almost made my limbs hurt with how heavy it seemed between us, until we were standing in front of Maggie's door.

I knocked, and we looked at each other as the door opened. There was so much I wanted to say to Olivia, and I was sure she had plenty to tell me. But for now, Maggie's Q&A would be the star of the show.

Her commanding voice punctured our reverie. "So, how did things go?"

"Great," Olivia and I exclaimed together.

We traded another look, but of course it was still perfectly awkward between us. And why? Because the relationship had suddenly changed.

I knew the story just fine. I had seen it play out countless times, both on the screen and in real life. If this was a movie, there would be no mystery as to what would have to happen next.

But this was real life, not a screenplay, and there was no denying that our almost kiss had shifted the temperature between us. Raised it or lowered it, I wasn't really sure. Things were no doubt different now, and I kept wrestling with the uncomfortable question of whether that was a good thing or not.

"Aren't either one of you going to give me any more specifics than that?" Maggie turned to Olivia. "I'm used to the sealed envelope from this joker, but surely you can give me something better than 'it was great'."

Maggie was right. Our silence after the single adjective had lingered for too long. I should have spoken up and saved Olivia the burden of having to manufacture an answer to make Maggie happy.

"Everything was wonderful," Olivia replied. "The sock hop was great. And the press seemed a lot more respectful than what I was expecting."

"Just wait!" Maggie scoffed.

"What do you mean by that?" Olivia looked at me instead of Maggie.

I said, "Tell Olivia what she doesn't want to know."

"What don't I want to know?"

"I've arranged a press junket for you tomorrow."

"Of course you did," I replied, not surprised in the least.

Olivia said, "I've heard the term, of course, and I guess I get the idea. A press junket is just a bunch of reporters all in one place at one time to ask us a bunch of questions, right?"

"Exactly," Maggie nodded.

"So isn't that a little bit like what happened at the grocery store when we were buying ingredients to make the ice cream?"

"A little bit, but not exactly."

"How is it different?" Olivia asked Maggie.

"It's different because they caught you off guard the first time, but then you caught them by surprise right back. That was the first time there was any hint of a relationship. That's a big deal for Ryan here. One of my biggest jobs as his manager has been to keep Ryan's relationships quiet. He has always expressed that privacy is important to him. There were a lot of rumors around his last relationship, so dodging those questions and redirecting the press's attention was practically a full-time job there for a while."

"You mean April Fisher?" Olivia asked.

Maggie looked at me in surprise. "You told her?"

"Yep," Olivia said first.

"He told you?" That time Maggie said it to herself even as she looked at Olivia, tasting the words as if trying to make them make sense.

"So I get that this round with the press won't be a

surprise," Olivia said, "but what makes it different? What will Ryan and I need to do differently?"

"You'll have to dodge a bunch of questions about your relationship."

"Okay." She didn't sound concerned, despite Maggie wanting her to.

"I think we should practice."

"Tonight?" Olivia seemed almost shocked by Maggie's suggestion.

"Yes, tonight."

"Please no," Olivia begged with her eyes. "I'm so tired and I just really, really want to go to bed. Please? If we have to practice, then can we practice in the morning?"

"Okay, dear." Maggie offered Olivia a half smile, obviously not liking it but willing to let it go in lieu of an argument that might sour the good vibes she was feeling toward a client who needed all the positive press he could get right now.

Maggie excused us for the night, then a few minutes later back in my room, we were proceeding through our pre-bedtime routine, more fluidly than ever.

I would even guess that if it hadn't been for our mutual exhaustion, the rituals might have been fun.

But that was the routine.

When it came to the mood between us, things still could not have been more awkward.

We got into bed, then tossed and turned for ten long minutes.

The next ten felt like they took twice as long to fall off of the clock.

I was painfully restless and could only imagine what Olivia must be thinking right now, what she must be feeling, what she must be wondering about me and whether or not I would say anything.

But it didn't matter how awkward it felt in the room or in the bed right then. The shyness inside my body and mind forbade me to talk, erecting a tall concrete wall in front of me that it felt impossible to climb over.

Olivia was more courageous, and after another couple of minutes of that unbearably leaden quiet, she said, "It's awkward because we almost kissed."

I froze in indecision, with no idea what I should say in light of her confession. But after less than a moment of thought, I echoed her sentiment.

"That's exactly what I was thinking."

And then we burst out laughing.

For a long while, right when it seemed like we might finally stop, our laughter got even louder.

"Can you believe this stupid situation we're in?"

"Not at all." Olivia shook her head. "I'm sure that movie stars get into catastrophes with handcuffs all the time, but this is definitely new territory for me."

"Why would movie stars get into catastrophes with handcuffs?" I asked. "Do you just need to make fun of me about being rich and famous so much that you'll say anything, even if it doesn't make any sense?"

"Oh, it makes sense," Olivia said, even though her retort didn't make any sense at all, but it was silly enough to get me laughing again, or maybe I just couldn't help it because she was still laughing.

It felt liberating, our heaving chuckles chasing away the thick tension that had been consuming us ever since our departure from Miss Lydia's old fourth grade classroom.

Everything felt funny now.

"Did you ever imagine yourself in a situation like this?" Olivia pondered aloud, her fingers playing idly with the chain connecting our wrists. "If we ever have grandkids, imagine the story we'd tell them."

She seemed embarrassed to have said that.

So I made her feel better. "Once upon a time, your grandma and I were handcuffed to each other for five days! Don't ask us how we went to the bathroom."

"They would want proof."

"Of us going to the bathroom?"

"No." She laughed. "Of the handcuffs."

Olivia raised our wrists to show me.

So we started taking goofy pictures, an entire series, all featuring me in bed with Olivia and our hands clearly cuffed.

But the wall between us and Maggie failed to contain our bubbling glee.

"Would you two keep it down in there?" Maggie yelled through the wall.

"We're trying!" Olivia shouted. "It's just so hard to keep quiet when you're handcuffed to a movie star!"

I exploded in laughter.

"So, you're too tired for a practice session but not for your standup routine?" Maggie snapped back.

We stifled our laughter by diving under the covers, trying our best to mute the next round of giggles. The soft jingle of the handcuff chain seemed to be mocking us.

When the boisterous laughter finally settled into a comfortable quiet between us, Olivia said, "So we almost kissed."

"Yes," I repeated, "we almost kissed."

"But it was just because of all the nostalgia."

"Exactly," I agreed.

"Nostalgia, and the fact that we were having such a great time."

"But it didn't mean anything."

"Of course it didn't."

"It couldn't mean anything."

"Right. Even if we came from the same world, we live in two different places now."

"Yep." Olivia nodded, then stated the obvious. "I live here in Ocean Springs, and you live in Hollywood."

"Santa Monica, but yeah. Same thing. It would never work."

That was a hard note to end the night on, but it still felt right for both of us.

So we settled back into our silence, and we both tried for sleep.

But neither of us got far in the endeavor, and soon I could feel Olivia shifting in bed again.

That sent me spiraling back to my earlier thoughts, not necessarily wondering what Olivia was thinking anymore, because now that the air had cleared between us, I had a better than decent idea.

But she was probably thinking about what we had just discussed. Our incompatibility. And I realized while trying to find sleep that neither one of us had mentioned anything having to do with our personalities.

Our collective objections to the pitfalls of our potential relationship had to do with location and proximity. Perhaps lifestyle was implied, but also maybe not.

Twenty minutes later, I realized that Olivia was just as awake as I still was, despite the earlier fatigue that I had felt like heat waves off of concrete.

She was shifting in bed. But maybe it wasn't just a lot of errant thoughts like it was for me. Olivia got warm at night.

"Hey," I whispered into the dark. "Are you awake?"

"Of course I am."

"Do you want to switch sides? That way you can be closer to the open window. Maybe that will help you fall asleep. It won't be as hot over there."

"Yes, thank you." Olivia laughed.

"Why are you laughing?"

"Because I was just going to offer you the extra pillow. I figured that might help you to finally fall asleep. So, do you want my pillow?"

"Yes, thank you," I replied.

But I also wanted so much more than that.

I hugged the pillow close to me as Olivia lay flat on her back.

"Would you like to meditate with me?" I asked after several minutes of silence.

"Please," Olivia replied.

And then we did, until we were finally sleeping together.

TWENTY-FOUR

Olivia

MAYBE I WAS BECOMING a movie star-like prima donna, thanks to my (handcuffed) relationship with Mr. Ryan Jones, but we both needed our beauty sleep the next morning.

After a long day and night, filled with too much tossing and turning before sleep finally found us, Ryan was insistent that we got to rest until the last minute, after Maggie knocked on the door at what felt like the crack of dawn (almost eleven a.m.), wanting to practice with me and Ryan before the junket.

"We can do it on the way, or right before it gets started," Ryan told her.

Maggie clearly didn't care for the plan, but like last night, she was still clearly choosing her battles and deciding it wasn't worth the argument.

Sure, we could practice right before the junket started.

But it was a madhouse when we arrived, and I was surprised yet again by all of the attention the world seemed to give about something so seemingly small.

I used to buy *Us Weekly* and *Entertainment Weekly* and

People, and I still sometimes read my mom's copies, but the spotlight given to the everyday activities of movie stars seemed so disproportionate to what those topics actually deserved.

Who really cared about any of this?

I kept asking myself that as we entered the bustling area surrounding the hotel conference room packed with reporters and camera crews. At the end of the day, Ryan and I were just two regular people. Me more so than him, but he was a lot more down to earth than I had given him credit for, and now I was realizing that all of the nonsense surrounding his art might have been responsible for ungrounding him.

Same was true for Maggie, who was finding it difficult to make herself heard over all of the boisterous activity around us. The junket was already a cacophony of over-lapping voices, with reporters jostling for position.

"How did you two meet?" Maggie shouted as we stood outside the conference room.

"I think she's asking you," Ryan said, nudging me.

"We met in fourth grade. We were in the same class."

"When did you know he was the one?" Maggie fired off another question.

"When we danced at the fourth-grade sock hop."

"No, no, no!" Maggie shook her head. "You didn't know he was the one in fourth grade. That story doesn't track. Try again."

"Ryan and I were great friends back in fourth grade and had a super awesome time dancing at the sock hop…" I paused my faux answer, then added, "I feel the need to mention our sock hop since you had us chaperone it."

Then I continued with my reply.

"But when he came back last week to help Miss Lydia out with the theater fundraiser and I saw him again…" I made an exaggerated swooning sound. "It was love at first sight, or second sight, I suppose." I giggled dramatically.

"If you tone it down a bit, you have the right idea." Maggie turned to Ryan." I wish she was more concerned."

"I am concerned," I said.

Maggie kept talking to Ryan. "Then I wish she was more serious."

I leaned in and smiled wide like the Joker, lowered my voice to a husky rasp, and said to Maggie, "Why so serious?"

Ryan burst into laughter, but Maggie just eyed me with irritation.

We only had 10 minutes left before the junket started, and Ryan insisted that we spend them in quiet meditation.

But once we were alone, he said, "I don't really want to meditate. I just needed to be away from Maggie. And I figured you needed an escape even more than me."

I laughed.

But then the mood did get meditative between us as we stood there in silence, waiting for the time to tick down, or for the junket to detonate with an explosive command for our attention.

Ryan took my hand and I squeezed it back, even though there were no reporters around.

As soon as we entered the conference room and sat, the junket got started, with urgent questions colliding in the air amid an unrelenting hum of curiosity. Intermittent bursts from camera shutters added to the discord, punctuating the buzz with rhythmic clicks.

I handled the questions like a pro, at first feeling like I was outperforming what even Maggie had wanted me to do. And the press seemed to love it.

I didn't like any of the nonsense, but I was better at pretending than I expected, appearing to laugh it up until the situation began to upset me and the questions went from prime to downright invasive.

The junket started with the same kinds of questions that Maggie had prepared me for, like:

"How did you meet?"

"When did you know he was the one?"

"How did it feel to reconnect with your childhood sweetheart after all this time, especially now that he's a rich and famous movie star?"

Even the press had to point out that Ryan Jones was rich.

"How does this Hollywood lifestyle fit with your small-town life?"

The question itself didn't surprise me, but the under-lying insinuation did, making it feel less like genuine interest and more like a baited hook.

"Ryan is from Ocean Springs," I declared, not just to the reporter who asked me the question but to any and all doubters who might hear my answer later. "Our bond is rooted deep."

While that may have been a long yawn away from the truth, many of our responses flowed with genuine ease. Like when I told a reporter that I just loved how Ryan meditated every night before bed and that I had started doing the same thing myself and it had been helping me to sleep. Admittedly, I had only joined him in this practice for a single night, but it already felt like a transformative habit taking root within me.

"I admire her deep well of creativity," Ryan crowed, when that same reporter redirected their interrogation onto him. "It's not just that Olivia gets one good idea every once in a while, it's that she has more than I can count, starting from when I first see her in the morning until bedtime."

That question ended with what the paparazzi might have considered a bit of innuendo, because the questions got hotter from there. More invasive, more intrusive, more like shoving me down the stairs instead of allowing me the grace to take one step at a time.

"How is the sex life?"

"Do you two want kids?"

"Does Ryan buy you expensive gifts?"

"How does it feel to be exploring the power dynamic between the two of you?"

"How has your family reacted to this whirlwind romance?"

"Is it true you're moving to Hollywood to be closer to Ryan?"

"Have you two discussed a prenup?"

"There are rumors of a secret engagement, any truth to that?"

"Have there been disagreements or jealous moments given Ryan's past?"

"Is there any truth to the rumors of you having a fallout with your close friends after meeting Ryan?"

I did my best to keep up with the answers, blurting the first thing that came to mind that stuck to Maggie's script.

Until Rusty stepped forward — the creepy paparazzo whose camera Lydia had broken when he stalked us after the auction.

He shouted, "Are you in this relationship with Ryan Jones just for his money?"

"What kind of a question is that?" I snapped, his question landing on me like poison dropped onto crops from a plane.

"I think that will be enough questions for now," Ryan announced to the reporters, managing to maintain his Hollywood smile, and that cool, effortless charm in his voice, a knowingness that seemed to suggest the movie star knew how to float above it all in a way that us mere mortals could only dream about.

But this time instead of feeling resentful or bothered by his bearing, I was only grateful as he gave the reporters a final wave that made it easier for me to find one last smile to flash as he ushered me away from the buzzing crowd and back into the dark corner, where we took our meditative breaths ahead of the junket.

"I'm so sorry for losing my composure," I apologized, standing straight and sounding strong even though I wanted to cry.

Not because I felt like I had fallen short on my job. I am human, after all, and that had been a lot, but I felt like I was letting Ryan and Maggie down.

Though I could have gotten over coming up short for Maggie a lot easier than for my movie star crush.

"Please, don't apologize. I'm just sorry that you had to go through that."

"Is it like that all the time?" I asked him.

He laughed, but it was a sweet and gentle sound.

"It is what I've been trying to tell you. That actually wasn't too bad, honestly." Ryan shrugged. "I guess at this point I'm mostly used to it, even if I spend a lot of my time trying to avoid dealing with it."

"You sure handle it well. I wouldn't wish that on my worst enemy."

"How about Taylor?" Ryan asked with a sly grin. "We can wish it on him, can't we? And Jennifer?"

"No." I laughed. "Taylor can't have the paparazzi, and neither can Jennifer, because they would both just love the attention."

"So I see." Ryan nodded. "Would you like to go back to my room?"

"Yes please," I nodded back, not wanting to admit that I was wishing he had meant that last question differently than the way I'm sure he intended it.

"I hope you never have to meet Taylor," I said on our way to the elevator.

Shockingly, onlookers gave us a wide berth as we entered alone and then exited the elevator back onto our floor, still talking about how I would be living in a best-case scenario world if I never ran into Taylor again, and Ryan saying he would like to meet the guy so he could punch him in the stomach.

"You wouldn't really punch him in the stomach."

"I think I just might." Ryan laughed.

Then we came face to face with the unrelenting reality that Ryan either lived in a world with Hollywood timing and had dragged me into it, or fate had a sick sense of humor.

"It looks like we have a guest," Maggie said, looking over at the man standing to her right, the man I swore I would never set eyes on again just seconds ago. "He was rather insistent that we wait inside your room, but I told him that out here in the hallway would be fine."

You must be Taylor, I could feel Ryan thinking right next to me.

Of course, I couldn't really know what he was thinking, but I also imagined that Ryan wanted to hold my hand and squeeze it.

"What do you want, Taylor?" I managed to keep the curl from my lip and the snarl out of my voice.

"I want to talk."

"I'm not interested in talking to you."

"Somewhere private," Taylor insisted.

"If you have something to say to me, then you can say it in front of my friends. Ryan isn't going anywhere."

"Why?" Taylor asked.

"Because we're bound by my love ribbon!" I yelled.

I could tell that Ryan was stifling a giggle.

Taylor didn't think it was nearly so funny.

"I can wear the noise cancelling headphones," Ryan offered.

"They're noise cancelling, not eliminating," Taylor opined as Maggie went inside the room to get them.

Ryan glanced over at me, and the corners of his mouth twitched in a smile.

"It'll have to do," I said.

"Fine," Taylor grumbled.

Maggie returned, and Ryan donned the headphones.

Then we entered our room — Ryan's room — and Maggie went into hers, leaving the three of us alone. Whatever was about to happen, it would be best not to have it happen in the hallway. For both mine and Ryan's sake.

I was ready (as I was going to be) for the conversation once we were on the other side of the door, but I noticed that Ryan had not turned his headphones on.

"I'm so sorry," Taylor started blubbering almost immediately.

"You should be," I said.

"I made a mistake."

"I know you did."

"I never should have betrayed you like that."

"Truer words have never been spoken."

"I want you back."

"I imagine you would right about now. I'm guessing things fell apart with Jennifer?"

"Something like that…" Taylor looked down at the carpet.

"Something like what? What happened between you and Jennifer?"

"She cheated on me."

"Ouch." I made a sympathetic face, but twisted it in a way where it was obvious how hard I was making fun of him. "Sucks, doesn't it?"

"I'm really sorry that I hurt you, Olivia. I know how it feels now."

"It'll probably hurt even more over the next several months as you realize that the one person you were willing to betray me for has now betrayed you, and that you have nothing left and no chance whatsoever of ever getting me back. Did she steal your business too?"

Taylor swallowed. "The business isn't going so well."

"Well, there are an awful lot of coffee shops in Los Angeles. They're like, a dime a dozen."

"I definitely didn't think it would be this difficult to get things going." Taylor made the mistake of thinking I felt so much as a molecule of sympathy for him.

"Is that all you have to say?" I let him know I was done with my posture and tone.

"I was hoping we could talk about this."

"You talked, I listened, and now I'm done with you. I would appreciate it if you left my hotel room now."

"I thought it was his hotel room." Taylor glanced at Ryan.

"It's our room. Now please go."

Taylor opened his mouth to beg me again.

So I shouted, "I need you to leave now!"

Then Maggie appeared in the room.

"Figures," Taylor said.

"What figures?" I asked, because, as usual with Taylor, he turned me into a stupid person who was dumb enough to take his idiotic bait.

"You're only dating him for the money," Taylor scoffed, "the same exact reason that you always dated me. You knew I had money, so you leached onto me and—"

"Okay, that's it, buddy." Ryan yanked the headphones off of his head and hurled them across the room.

Then he started shoving Taylor toward the door.

"Hey, get your hands off me!"

But Ryan ignored him, giving a heroic performance by getting the villain out of my scene.

"You're in our room. I can do whatever I want."

Maggie opened the door and Ryan shoved him into the hallway — a bit too hard, sending our love scarf falling off of the cuffs and drifting down to the floor, like a fluttering leaf falling from a branch.

"Hey, wait a minute," Taylor started as he spotted the handcuffs.

But that's all he got before Ryan slammed the door in his face.

I didn't know what to say or think or even feel right then.

Except grateful for Ryan stepping in and trying to save me.

But I also felt quiet, questioning my ability to know or judge people at all.

Because I had certainly been wrong about Taylor, who was a complete and total jerk. And my so-called friend Jennifer, who I had chosen as my maid of honor over Madison. Even Ryan, because I thought he was stuck up when he wasn't like that at all.

"I never really knew who Taylor was," I whispered to myself.

But of course Ryan heard me. "Sometimes people hide their true selves, even when those closest to them are looking."

"I don't." I shook my head. "I'm always who I am."

He hugged me. "And that's what makes you special."

I hugged him back.

Then we got ready for bed, got on top of the mattress, and tried to sleep.

But I thought about Ryan all night, counting down the minutes until it would finally be time for our red-carpet premiere.

TWENTY-FIVE

Ryan

I'VE NEVER BEEN able to sleep the night before a press conference, even when I'm *not* handcuffed to a beautiful woman who keeps stealing the sheets.

I tried yanking them back, but she'd somehow managed to wind them around her as she rolled back and forth in her sleep.

"Olivia," I whispered. "Are you awake?"

She let out a snort that could've been the beginning of a snore and rolled back toward me again, somehow stealing the few inches of sheet that still covered me.

I found it adorable, which was a pretty good sign that the ordeal of the last few days was driving me mad.

So I grabbed my phone and texted the sanest person I know. Lucas.

How's the location treating you?

Lucas texted back a handcuff emoji and a question mark.

Still there, I texted back.

Laughing emoji, skull emoji.

Thank you so much for your support.

Do you really want to hear about the location? Or is this about Olivia?

I think the paparazzi are going to call her a gold digger. And I'm pretty sure her ex saw the handcuffs.

Those both sound like Maggie problems.

Lucas wasn't wrong — if Olivia were an actress, like April and all the other starlets I'd dated since leaving Ocean Springs, I'd ask Maggie to take care of it, no big deal. An actress would be used to the pressure of public opinion, and they'd have their own manager to help negotiate the fallout until everyone forgot.

But Olivia had no idea the storm of attention that would descend on her. She was used to a kind of privacy that I'd forfeited years ago when I'd had my first success, and she would hate it.

Still there? Lucas nudged.

I just don't know if I can protect her from all the Hollywood sharks.

She's put up with you 24/7. She can clearly handle anything.

I couldn't help smiling. Lucas and his sense of humor had kept me sane through most of my career crises.

I texted: *I'm serious, what if it's too much for her?*

Then leave town as soon as you get the cuffs off. The sooner her fifteen minutes are over, the sooner you can both move on.

Eminently practical advice. But after I thanked Lucas and wished him happy scouting, I felt even more restless.

Because I wasn't sure I wanted to leave town. Not without Olivia.

Was this a Stockholm Syndrome thing? After being handcuffed to the only girl who danced with me in grade school, was I developing some sort of unhealthy attachment?

After things had gone sour with April, I'd wanted to take a break from relationships for a while. Not that she'd wrecked me — the opposite. Our time together had been fun, but as soon as it was inconvenient for her career to be dating me, April had ended it.

I'd been a little relieved not to have to juggle two pairs of press junkets and location shoots anymore, which was exhausting enough to outweigh the fun we'd have when we finally managed to squeeze in a date.

How could I let April go so easily after more than a year together in the public eye, but want to keep Olivia all to myself in private?

Maybe it would be easier for her if we told the truth about the handcuffs and let Maggie spin it, and make Olivia look like the hero for protecting my reputation by pretending to be my girlfriend.

She'd still get mobbed by the press and the paps, but it would be over as soon as they realized there was no more story to tell beyond a small-town fundraiser gone awry.

Then she could go back to her life, and I could go back to mine. I would be protecting her from the worst of it.

It was clearly the right thing to do.

So why didn't I want to do it?

TWENTY-SIX

Olivia

MORNING LIGHT FILTERED into our hotel room through the curtains and cast us in a warmly wonderful glow.

An overwhelming surge of exhilaration coursed through me, like the unbridled joy a child feels when waking up on Christmas.

And yes, that was about the most cliché thing a girl could say about feeling excited, unless she was making it even bigger and going straight for the comparison to her wedding day.

But really, that was how I felt.

Today was the premiere. The anticipation had been building, coupled with a gnawing fear. Soon, I would be stepping onto a genuine red carpet, even if we were an hour away by plane from the glitz and glamour of Hollywood.

Camera flashes would blind and dazzle, reporters would shout and scramble. Even after just a few days of this, the scene was all too easy to imagine. A small voice inside questioned if I was ready, if I would say the wrong thing, if I would embarrass Ryan and jeopardize his career.

This newly instilled fear made me understand, on a visceral level, why Ryan seemed so wary of the media spotlight.

The sudden limelight had given me a firsthand experience of Ryan's reality and, surprisingly, a pang of sympathy.

I realized that it wasn't just about attention or fame. It was about constantly feeling judged, analyzed, and exposed. Every step watched, every word magnified.

Ryan wasn't just wary or cautious, or paranoid. Ryan was traumatized.

So I had been wrong about him, and that meant that I had been wrong about the borders around my feelings.

It meant I was wrong about how much I had been lying to myself.

Our relationship had evolved into something complex. Since our almost-kiss, an undeniable tension lingered in the air between us. That newfound electricity was both thrilling and disconcerting, keeping me adrift in a sea of writhing emotions.

The thought of avoiding Ryan had lost its appeal. Instead, there was a budding desire to seek solace in his presence. Perhaps in a dimly lit space, just the two of us, maybe embracing the intimacy we'd only briefly brushed up against.

Self-doubt kept gnawing at me.

Deep within, I yearned to lose myself in all of the feelings I longed to feel rushing through me, but skepticism held me back.

I couldn't help but wonder if Ryan felt the same whirlwind of emotions. He was no stranger to the spotlight, living in the glamour of a movie star life for all of his adult years, while I was still a small-town girl who had struggled to find her footing in his world and was unable to make it in LA.

Being on the brink of a kiss was something for sure, but definitely far from the promise of an actual relationship. Each of us would probably be telling the story of our handcuffed misadventure for the rest of our lives, but the tale would sound different from each of our mouths.

For me, it would always be about the time I was hooked to Hollywood with the famous Ryan Jones. Yet when he recalled this episode at some point in the future, either before or after he finally landed that so far elusive Academy Award, he would surely be reminiscing about that time he returned to his humble hometown of Ocean Springs and got unexpectedly (and rather unfortunately) tethered to a clingy townie who had been obsessed with him since the fourth grade.

I kept telling myself that all of those thoughts were ridiculous and nothing better than poison inside me. And I started looking forward to the red carpet again, like I had last night as I lulled myself to sleep.

But the more I tried to push those thoughts away, the heavier they weighed on me.

The idea of facing a sea of cameras, their cold lenses capturing every flaw, every misstep, became overwhelming. How did Ryan do this time and time again?

Maybe because he got paid millions of dollars.

Then I thought of my ice cream, and I felt a bit better.

Ashleigh would be picking up the hand-crafted ice cream to serve, so all Ryan and I had to do was get ready for the event. We went through our morning routine, still quiet, but now like a harmonious ballet.

Things were peaceful between us until Maggie barged into the hotel room and blurted, "Have you seen the papers?"

"No," we replied in unison while trading an uneasy glance.

"What's in the papers?" Ryan asked.

"Well, I guess it's not in the papers yet, but it is on CelebBuzz, which means that the pictures will be everywhere soon, and starting right now."

"What pictures?" I felt a wash of cold dread rippling through me.

Maggie pulled out her phone and showed us the pictures I had taken of Ryan and me the night before last while we were losing ourselves to endless fits of giggles in bed.

Now those photos were online. With him bare chested and me in pajamas, the pair of handcuffs linking our wrists clearly visible.

"What the hell?" Ryan exclaimed at the phone before turning his gaze my way. "Why would you do that to me?"

"Do what to you?"

But then I realized, because the answer was so obvious. Those pictures, after all, had come from my phone.

"You think I did this?"

He was quiet for a moment, jaw working like he was chewing on what he wanted to say instead of spitting it out.

"Ryan, you have to believe me, I have no idea how those pictures got uploaded."

"I want to believe you," he said slowly.

"But you don't." Of course he didn't. He barely knew me, and he lived in a world where people regularly took advantage of people like him. "We've been handcuffed together this whole time. How would I have uploaded them without you seeing me do it?"

"I don't know." He looked even glummer. "Maybe while I was singing 'Twinkle, Twinkle, Little Star'?"

I couldn't stop the eye roll, but I fought to keep the pleading out of my voice. "Think about it. Why would I embarrass both of us like that?"

His lips pressed into a tighter line, but he did actually seem to be thinking about it.

"Maybe you needed the money." It sounded like he was trying to talk himself into the idea. "The papers would probably pay you thousands."

That hurt. "That's the kind of a person you think I am."

"The kind that's saving for her business, and who 'needs each and every tip,' and 'can't even afford to miss out on a single shift.'"

"That's not fair. I didn't want to let Ashleigh down, but that doesn't mean I would sell private photos of us."

"Okay, Olivia."

"Don't okay me." And now I was pissed. "I didn't sell those pictures, Ryan. And if I was going to, I definitely wouldn't have done it while I was still handcuffed to you, because I'm not an id—"

I stopped, unable to remember the last time I saw my phone.

"Where is your phone, dear?" Maggie asked, either reading my expression or drawing the same conclusion in tandem with me.

"I don't know." I shook my head, even more upset than I had been a few moments ago, because even if this wasn't my fault, it was still obviously (and totally) my fault. "Someone must have stolen my phone, or maybe I lost it."

I turned to Ryan, desperate.

"Do you remember where—"

"I don't know where your phone is, Olivia."

And I could tell by his eyes that he didn't care. He was already shutting me out. Mercifully, Maggie cared, so thanks to her encouragement, the three of us tore the room apart in search of my missing phone.

The atmosphere was tense as we scoured every inch of the suite. Lavish curtains were pulled back, revealing nothing but sunlight streaming in. Plush cushions on opulent couches were turned over.

I sifted through the ornate drawers of a mahogany desk I had never opened before, just in case I had somehow deposited the phone into the drawer as I slept, but I found only an array of hotel stationeries.

Ryan checked the mini bar area with a clenched jaw, moving wine glasses and bottles with deliberate care.

Maggie methodically examined the en suite bathroom, pulling back shower curtains and checking behind the pristine towels.

"Maybe I lost it outside of the room." I didn't want to surrender the search in Ryan's room (it was definitely his now, the way he was looking at me), but there was nowhere else to look. "Or again, maybe someone stole my phone."

"Maybe," Ryan repeated.

"You don't believe me."

"Wouldn't that person need your password before they could access the photos? You took the pictures. And now they're online. It's no big deal."

But Ryan's face said the opposite. I had never seen a person look more disappointed.

And I was the person who had disappointed him. Or at least I couldn't prove that I wasn't.

Maggie watched our back and forth, poised for her interjection.

"It's not like the first time this has ever happened to me. It's fine. I'm not even mad. I'm already over it." He sighed. "We'll be done with each other for good in just another couple of days."

"Ryan—"

"It's fine, Olivia."

His words were like nails in the coffin of everything that probably never could have been between us in the first place.

And that was killing me. Because even if I never saw him again once the cuffs came off, I couldn't stand that he thought that I would use him like that.

When he'd come back to town, I'd thought *he* was the jerk. But for him to leave forever, thinking that I was the kind of person who'd use his bad luck to humiliate him in front of the entire world?

That I would try to destroy the reputation he'd been working so hard to fix?

"I've gone to ridiculous lengths to protect your privacy ever since we met," I tried, but I could tell that he was no longer listening. He'd withdrawn to protect himself. From me. And that withdrawal scared me so much, I lashed out. "If you really believe that all I care about is money, then you're exactly the kind of arrogant jerk I thought you were."

"What's done is done," Maggie said. "I will deal with this handcuff situation, but can you please not give me any more disasters to juggle before the premiere is over?"

"How are you planning to deal with it?" Ryan sounded suspicious.

"I'll just say that the two of you were playing around." Maggie shrugged. "But for the love of God, please stop taking photos of yourselves in bed."

Our fairy tale morning had turned grim, making it

another long and awkward day before it was finally time for the premiere.

We barely spoke until we needed to get dressed for our walk down the red carpet. And then only because we had to.

TWENTY-SEVEN

Ryan
_____

MY PHONE BUZZED at 2 a.m., but I wasn't sleeping anyway, despite the fact that I had barely slept last night. Good thing the premiere tomorrow was here in Ocean Springs instead of LA — the only people who'd see the circles under my eyes close up would be Olivia and her friends. And I didn't care what they thought of me.

That's what I told myself as the phone buzzed again. I glanced over at Olivia, who was snoring softly on the other side of the bed, as far away from me as the handcuffs allowed.

I thought about that first night, when I'd moved to the floor to avoid her attempts to sleep-snuggle me.

I wished now that I'd stayed and enjoyed it, because she was never going to snuggle me again.

My phone buzzed again.

A text from Maggie, a list of details for tomorrow. I shouldn't have been surprised that she was up working.

I tapped back with a thumbs up, and a second later, got: *GO TO SLEEP*.

But that wasn't happening. So instead, I texted Lucas: *Am I an idiot?*

I had no idea what time zone he was in, but apparently he was up, because he replied immediately with: *You'll have to be more specific.*

Did you see the photos?

Handcuff emoji, camera emoji, fire emoji. Then: *I'm surprised you leaked them.*

That surprised me — Lucas should know me better than that. My thumbs over the screen as I told him that I didn't, Olivia did.

Are you sure? he asked.

She says she lost her phone.

And you believe her, right?

It had surprised me how much I'd wanted to believe her, despite how unlikely it was that she was innocent. Maybe she'd lost her phone — or maybe she'd left it somewhere for one of her friends to retrieve and upload the photos.

For all he knew, that had been the goal all along when Madison had bid on him at the auction. He couldn't see Lydia being involved, but he'd didn't know the rest of them well enough to be sure about anyone else.

My phone buzzed again.

AND YOU BELIEVE HER, RIGHT???

Hard to say, I texted back. *How well can you know anyone after a few days?*

The three dots blinked a few times before the text came through, and I imagined Lucas frowning and typing furiously while Roman tried to distract him. Finally:

After being handcuffed to someone for three days, you know everything that matters.

That's what I'd thought, right up until I'd seen those pics of us snuggling together in bed, giggling like lovers doing something naughty, posted for everyone in the world to see. I had never felt so violated, not even after the video with André went viral.

She says she didn't do it, I texted Lucas. *I don't know what to do.*

His reply: *You have to decide. Do you trust her?*

I didn't know if I was going to trust anyone ever again.

TWENTY-EIGHT

Olivia

MAGGIE KEPT TRYING to improve the mood between us, but neither Ryan nor I wanted anything to do with an improved mood. Even after she replaced our stupid, idiotic love ribbon (what had I been thinking with something so childish and dumb in the first place?) with one more aligned with our red-carpet attire.

I was wearing a sapphire blue gown, courtesy of Maggie. It hugged my figure, shimmering with delicate sequins and a tasteful slit running up my right leg. Ryan was a dashing counterpart in his tailored tuxedo, his crisp black and white sheen interrupted only by a deep blue velvet bow tie that subtly echoed the color of my dress.

Mom came over and sewed Ryan into his shirt and jacket again.

She tried her best to lighten the mood between us, but it was like trying to turn a box office flop into a summer blockbuster overnight.

"If it's not the ending, then it's just a plot twist, right?" my mother tried.

"This isn't a movie," Ryan replied, sounding terse with her for the first time.

He and I sniped at each other until we were sitting in the backseat again. Not an Audi this time, but a limo that had been Maggie's lone contribution to arranging something special for the event. She wanted us to arrive in style, but not in the standard limousine found at the typical red carpet Hollywood premiere. Instead, she went vintage, with a 1967 Rolls Royce Phantom V once owned by Clive Murphy, a British rock legend in the '70s.

Seated in the back of that Rolls Royce, mere inches from Ryan Jones, felt more like an agonizing irony than any sort of dream come true. A vacuum of space yawned between us, despite the surrounding luxury.

Did I have no compass for other humans at all?

Just after thinking that I had been wrong about Mr. Movie Star all along, after a few days that felt like years, it turned out I was totally right.

Because if Ryan thought that I would be so low as to manipulate him into laughing along with me while I took pictures of us that I had every intention of selling, then he was not the man I thought he was.

The very sight of him — on screen or off — threatened to become a scar, a painful reminder of the gulf between appearances and reality.

I yearned for the day when this charade would finally end and this whole stupid thing was forever behind us.

And Ryan Jones was just a movie star I used to know.

The Rolls pulled up to the theater, and Ryan opened the door to shouting and flashing cameras and all the rest of it erupting into my world all at once.

We stepped onto the red carpet together, looking as united for the world as we could, even though I had never felt more divided inside.

I'm sure Ryan was having a much easier time, considering he was an actor who knew how to bottle his emotions, or even crush them into powder if that's what he needed to get through the moment.

So, really, didn't that make him a little bit like a robot? Weren't actors basically nothing more than puppets who moved around according to other people's directions and served as mouthpieces for writers?

Without storytellers telling him what to do, directors making sure he did it right, and producers putting the whole thing together, Ryan Jones was just a giant faker who probably wasn't even qualified to stand on the corner in front of a furniture store twirling a sign announcing a fire sale where everything was 60 percent off.

Or maybe that was just me being mean because I was so upset about the situation and had to smile through all of it, not just down the red carpet but through each and every introduction to a studio person that either Maggie or Ryan dragged me over to meet.

André was a no show, which was probably a surprise to absolutely no one.

"Oh my goodness, this is all so wonderful!" Lydia exclaimed, practically skipping over to Ryan and Maggie. I had never seen her more delighted. "We have more than enough money to cover all of our debts now, plus do some rehab on the theater. This was such a great idea. Olivia, thank you so much. Ryan, the two of you saved this theater."

Lydia somehow managed to look even prouder, even more excited by this red-carpet premiere in her theater, one featuring a big movie star who happened to be a former student of hers, starring in the film and bringing another former student along to the premiere as his date. But then her face seemed to fall as she sensed the air of disquiet between us. "Is everything okay between you two?"

"It's fine," Ryan replied, in what might have been the worst performance of his life.

"Come on, Chicken Little," Lydia said. "What's wrong?"

But Ryan just stared at her, like he couldn't even process the question, let alone answer it.

Maybe I couldn't do anything about the pictures, but at least I could take some of the burden of this conversation while he mentally prepared for the premiere itself, and all the people he'd have to smile at afterward. "We're just two people who should have never spent more than a few minutes together," I said. "One dinner at most, but not this long, and certainly not in handcuffs…"

I shook my head, not quite sure where to take my next sentence.

Lydia seemed to wither inward, looking even more crestfallen than she had before. "I'm so sorry. I feel like this is all my fault."

Neither of us said anything.

But Ryan and I traded one last glance that indicated unfinished business for both of us before we circulated the lobby for another fifteen minutes, smiling and waiting while making intermittent small talk before the lights flickered and Lydia came on the speaker to announce that the movie would be starting in less than ten minutes, and it was time for everyone to start finding their seats.

Normally, at least judging by the last couple of days, this would have been the time where Ryan turned to me and asked if I was ready. But he didn't, and I was too angry and heartbroken to say anything. I'd given up trying to prove that I hadn't posted those photos, but I still couldn't accept that he'd believe I'd do something so low.

We slipped down the row and into our assigned seats, with me sitting next to Ryan's costar, Adele Harmon, an actress I loved. On screen, she exuded a timeless elegance, reminiscent of silver screen sirens from classic cinema. Her porcelain complexion was the perfect canvas for the blush that highlighted her cheekbones. Delicate wisps of strawberry blonde hair cascaded in soft waves down her shoulders. Her dress was a silky champagne number, draped effortlessly around her and catching the light just so, making her appear to glow from within. Truly a vision, and every inch the A-lister, yet warm, approachable, and disarmingly genuine as she greeted me, leaning over from her seat to pull me into a hug.

"I'm Adele. And I have been dying to meet you!"

"To meet me? Why?"

"Because you're Ryan's new girlfriend, and I just adore Ryan." She sighed as if love-stricken. "Maybe more than anyone I've ever worked with before."

"Really?" I was shocked.

Not that I didn't think Ryan could be pleasant, but Adele was a professional actress who played his older sister in the movie, and she had been in the game for an awfully long time for her to make a statement like that.

"Have the two of you ever dated?"

"Nope." Adele shook her head. "I've been married for 15 years."

"Oh," I said, cycling through a series of questions that I wanted to ask but not knowing whether they were appropriate or if I even cared.

Although, of course, I cared. It's not like I was a light switch that could just turn off my feelings about Ryan just because he had hurt me more than I had been hurt in months, ever since my flight from Los Angeles.

"Do you mind if I ask you a question?" I whispered to Adele.

We didn't have long before the movie started, but also knowing that I would never have a chance to ask this question again, whether or not I even had the right to ask it.

"Of course," she said.

I had to get over my fear that I was being intrusive. Not only was Adele used to it, thanks to being in the same profession as Ryan, but if she really adored Ryan as much as she just said that she did, I imagine she would be interested in helping me to understand the truth about him.

"What was the set like on *Cold Fury*, if you don't mind my asking? Was it as difficult as all of the rumors reported?"

Adele nodded. "I would say it was even worse."

"Oh," I said in surprise, not really seeing how two and two could possibly equal four in this situation: if things were even worse than reported, then how could things have been great working with Ryan?

"What is it?" Adele asked. "You look upset.

"In that video when Ryan is yelling at André, it just seemed a little, his behavior just seemed a bit, I don't know, toxic?"

"Ryan didn't tell you?"

I looked over at Ryan, engaged in conversation with the producer, Eddie, sitting to his left. His jaw was firm, and I realized right then that I could see through his acting. Ryan was pretending to be engaged in whatever he was saying to Eddie, but I knew he was stewing about what had simmered and exploded between us.

"Ryan hasn't seemed like he wants to talk about that video at all," I told Adele. "He bristles every time I bring it up."

"I don't blame him. That whole situation was so messed up."

"What do you mean?" I asked.

"André's behavior was insufferable for the entire month we filmed. Our director was a bully in general, but especially when it came to dealing with me. He would roll his eyes during my takes, constantly gossip about my private life, not that I have much of one with a husband and two kids. He even questioned my commitment to the role. In all that turmoil, Ryan was always my sanctuary. He kept wanting to intervene, and I kept staying his hand. But when André finally crossed a line by tearing up my script notes in front of everyone and starting to mock me, Ryan couldn't hold himself back any longer."

"Oh, my." My head was swimming in an ocean of conflicting thoughts, and waves of self-loathing for much of what I'd been thinking.

"Exactly," Adele agreed. "I wanted to tell the media the truth, but Ryan was adamant that he take the fall. He may be young, but he understands this industry inside-out, and intimately since he started so young. Ryan strongly felt that speaking up would brand me as 'difficult,' and that could be a death knell for my career. As for his own reputation, he felt he could navigate any fallout."

I sat there, speechless, when suddenly the lights dimmed slightly, signaling the beginning of the premiere.

Ryan had overheard me tell Madison what a horrible jerk he was because I'd seen the video of his tantrum without any sort of context. I'd believed the worst of him before he'd had a chance to tell his side of the story — and he'd obviously realized there was no point in explaining when my mind was already made up.

No wonder he'd refused to believe me when I said I

hadn't posted the photos of us in bed. Why would he, after I'd judged him so unfairly?

And if he thought I had so much contempt for him, why wouldn't he believe that I'd use him to make some easy money?

I had ruined everything. As miserable as I'd been since those photos got posted, I deserved it.

The film's producer, Eddie, stepped onto the stage, adjusting the microphone. "Good evening, everyone! I know you were all expecting André tonight, but our director is taking a much-needed 'creative break' and sends his regrets."

Eddie droned on while I imagined André drowning in a sea of rotten tomatoes. Now that I knew he was a monster, Ryan seemed like even more of a hero.

The theater buzzed with anticipation as Eddie left the stage.

I felt a tap on my shoulder and turned around to see Madison smirking in the seat behind me. But then she got a good look at me.

"Oh my. You look terrible."

"Thanks a lot. I appreciate the observation."

"Seriously. You look like a 'before' picture."

"Everything blew up with Ryan, and it's all my fault," I meant to whisper, though the confession left me in what sounded almost like a whimper. "I think he is actually a really good guy and I really blew it."

"Just apologize."

"I can't apologize right now. His big premiere is about to start."

"Then do it as soon as the movie is over. Everything will be fine."

"I don't think so." I shook my head. "I think the damage has been done."

"You'll fix this after the movie," Madison assured me. And everything will be fine. You can—"

But then the curtain rose and killed the rest of her thought.

The movie started, and for the next two hours, I felt seriously worried that things might never be okay with me again.

TWENTY-NINE

Ryan

As FAR AS the premiere of *Cold Fury* itself went, I wasn't sure that I'd ever had a more positive experience at the debut of a movie I was a part of.

I loved that we could walk a red carpet so far outside of Hollywood, away from the imposing movie studio lots and lavish theaters that always felt more congested than celebratory. Here, there was a welcoming warmth. I loved the amiable small-town atmosphere, the studio execs and producers mingling casually with locals as if they were old friends.

And of course, I loved seeing Adele, radiant as ever. Though it would have been nice to see her husband, Brandon. I really liked the guy — he was down to earth with an easygoing sense of humor. But with two rambunctious kids at home, I understood his absence. An hour flight from LA was still long enough to derail family plans if it came at the last minute like this one had.

It was great to see Lydia so buoyant and happy, beaming with pride for her theater, until Olivia and I came along and crashed her mood with our gloomy dispositions.

Just another take in the series of reshoots that was this entire messy situation.

But even the popcorn tasted better here somehow, warm and buttery, not mass-produced, just like everything in Ocean Springs felt more real, more richly textured.

That also meant my feelings were rawer and more exposed here. All the hurt and betrayal I felt at Olivia's willingness to exploit our relationship came flooding back. Then the movie started, and all of my old insecurities stirred, ghosts of the past rearing their heads.

I don't typically obsess about my performances — what's done is done. And I avoid reviews, knowing critics' slashes can metastasize into endless self-doubt if I let their words in.

But sitting in the darkened theater, I couldn't escape the nerves twisting my insides as my new film played out on the big screen. I was that little boy again, shy and unsure, waiting to be picked last for the kickball team. A celebrated actor still haunted by the rejected child within.

Of course, I want all critics and fans to love me. And after *Cold Fury* finished, they did, for what felt like an eternity through two minutes of standing ovation.

André was a terrible human, but his movie was beautiful. All about a betrayed spy making his way through a tense, intricate maze of deceit, with every alley chase, whispered secret, and covert meeting feeling so thrillingly real on the big screen. Adele, playing my sister, grounded my character.

I needed something to ground my character now.

The love scarf still dangled between Olivia's wrist and mine, but we were no longer holding hands, and we surely wouldn't be unless Maggie specifically requested it of us.

I couldn't imagine either Olivia or I wanting to hold the other's hand again, not after all the bitter accusations hurled between us. That tender trust we had been working to build now lay in shards.

Although, despite our clearly wanting distance from each other, Olivia still did a phenomenal job playing ball at the reception when the press put her through a series of questions about the movie.

"What did you think?" asked a gaunt-looking reporter with a big puff of bright red hair and a long slope to her nose. "Were you surprised to see how emotional the movie was at the end?"

"Not at all," Olivia answered, without a note in her voice that would betray the discord sounding off silently between us. "Ryan's strength has always been in his emotive characterization. You feel things just looking at him. I feel things just looking at him. We talked a lot about this film, and unfortunately, some of the negative buzz generated around that awful viral video from earlier this year cast a shadow on what might be the best performance of Ryan's career so far. And Adele was so wonderful in the film as well."

A near-perfect answer, even if Olivia was just playing nice for the cameras.

Then it was time for the reception, where drinks and refreshments were abundantly served. I had been craving some more of the spicy chai ice cream ever since we'd finished our batches at Olivia's house, or "her mom's house," as Olivia insisted on calling it.

But why didn't she think of it as her home? Olivia seemed so rooted here, so reluctant to leave, yet something seemed to be holding her back from fully embracing Ocean Springs.

I took a moment to breathe in the atmosphere, the giddy chatter of the crowd and the clinking of champagne glasses. All around, faces glowed, basking in the afterglow of the movie.

Yet despite the warmth of the room, I felt cold inside.

Olivia's blatant breach of trust was like a slap to my face, jolting me out of the rosy dream I had been weaving for myself.

She had never genuinely liked me.

I was just the ticket to a windfall for her, a way out of her little town, or financial relief from the weight of life.

Every smile and laugh were just Olivia biding her time, waiting for the opportune moment to cash in on our misfortune.

It hurt to think that way. Because deep down, the rejected little boy in me felt the sting of childhood all over again.

Perhaps Olivia was just playing the cards she had been dealt, and in her eyes, she might've felt justified.

Maybe she felt entrapped by this situation, a mere pawn in a game bigger than her. And selling those photos was her way of rebelling, of claiming some semblance of control in a situation where she had none.

I tried to rationalize her actions, to understand her perspective.

But every time I replayed the scenes in my head, the hurt was still raw, and my trust was just as broken. Every time I looked her way, I couldn't imagine leaving, but I couldn't imagine staying either.

We hadn't even been dating, so why did this feel like the worst breakup I'd ever gone through?

I longed for the detached playfulness I'd had with April. I would give anything to be able to walk away and never look back.

Olivia looked over at me as I scooped myself a third helping of the velvety ice cream, its light yet fragrant aroma instantly transporting me back to her cozy kitchen. Her face seemed to melt in several unreadable expressions.

I didn't know what to say to her. We were still hurt, still wary, both pin-balled between conversational partners throughout the premiere, so our few stilted interactions lacked the easy rapport we had grown used to during our moments alone.

I wanted to tell her that she made the best ice cream I had ever tasted in my life. I wanted to thank her for bringing such bold new flavors to my palate. But I was still so gutted by how much she had hurt me.

So those words and all the ones like it remained locked behind my lips as we traded brittle smiles, the space between us now so much wider than our tethered wrists.

Then I looked over and saw Taylor talking with a paparazzi and wondered something that it felt downright negligent to have never considered before.

Was it possible that Taylor had stolen Olivia's phone?

Had it been missing that long? Because Taylor was in my hotel room after those pictures were taken, and it was possible he knew — or had guessed — Olivia's password. I had learned it after just a few days because she didn't even try to hide when she typed it in. If she'd trusted him, she probably hadn't hidden it from him either. And if she never thought she'd see him again, why would she change it?

That's how I knew that her password was *icecream*.

If I knew it, then Taylor definitely knew it too.

And that made me feel like a fool for not considering the possibility sooner.

I waited for a lull between conversational partners, keeping my mouth full of that delicious ice cream and avoiding any new interactions until Olivia finally finished her long conversation with a short man boasting an impressive paunch.

"I need some privacy," I told her when there was no one else around us.

"Okay," Olivia replied, a hopeful note in her voice.

"To make a phone call," I clarified.

"Oh." Her face fell. "Maybe we should go to the projector room then."

I stationed myself on one side of the door while Olivia occupied the floor on the other side after putting in the noise-cancelling ear buds, same as we had back at her house while sitting on both sides of her bedroom door.

Then I called Lucas.

"What's up, man? Aren't you supposed to be at your big premiere?"

"That's where I am."

"Then why are you calling me? Are you dying to know how the location scouting is going up here? If so, the answer is 'killer.'" Lucas laughed.

"I would love to hear about it, but I only have a minute or two of privacy."

"Ha, you're still handcuffed to Olivia?"

"Yes. Exactly."

"Is that why you sound like someone ran over your puppy twice?"

"I don't have a puppy. But I did figure out who posted those pictures." The words left my mouth dragging the weight of shame behind them.

"It wasn't her."

"I think it was her ex."

"That's great!"

"No, it's terrible. Because it's too late to take back all the terrible things I said to her."

"That's what apologies are for."

"This is too big for an apology."

"Yes," Lucas said.

"Yes, what?"

"Yes, you are an idiot." He sighed. "Do you trust her?"

"Yes. Absolutely." My shoulders slumped. "Olivia has been loyal since this mess started. I was just quick to assume the worst of her."

"Then suck it up and apologize as many times as you have to. If you really like Olivia, then—"

"Wait a minute. I never told you that I liked her."

"Dude. Your feelings for Olivia could not be more obvious."

"How is it obvious? You mean because of the way we act for the press? You know that's just acting."

"Is this acting?" Lucas asked.

Then my phone buzzed with a series of texts, Lucas messaging me screenshots from a slew of pictures of me and Olivia that were all apparently online, captured by the paparazzi. I was candidly smiling at her in each and every one of them.

I didn't know what to say; the truth was too obvious.

"You want to tell me that's you acting, bro?"

"No. Of course it isn't."

The revelation from Lucas hit me like a ton of bricks. For someone who made a living diving into complex emotions on screen, I was remarkably dense about my own. But with a clarity that was sharp and unyielding, I finally accepted that I had feelings for Olivia. Deep feelings.

The weight of his words bore down on me, and for a moment, I felt truly vulnerable. I was an actor, known for my ability to navigate the intricate web of human emotion onscreen. Yet here I was, grappling with the profound realization of my own feelings for Olivia.

"I really like her," I confessed, both to Lucas and myself.

"That's about as surprising as a sunrise. Pro tip, bro: Stop whispering. Something tells me she'd like to hear this."

"I need a minute." And a lot more courage. "I'll call you tomorrow and tell you how it goes, then you can regale me with tales of perfect sunsets and cinematic vistas."

"Looking forward to it."

I hung up the phone and opened the projector room door, prepared to spill my heart for Olivia but was instead met with an overeager Eddie, who was now so pleased with the reception to *Cold Fury* that he was wasting no time in pushing a script into my hands.

"I have your next role, Ryan." He was already gushing, not giving me so much as a second to breathe. "You were born for this one. Picture a character layered like a winter forest, and…"

I stopped listening, because even though the producer was a freight train of enthusiasm, I had long ago learned that because enthusiasm was free; it was the number one currency spent in Hollywood.

Under normal circumstances, I would have engaged with the conversation, perhaps even been intrigued, even if I could never agree to my next project without talking to Maggie first. But I needed an exit from that conversation with Eddie. Every second he prattled on was one stolen from my time with Olivia.

Each new sentence from the producer felt like another brick in a wall being erected between Olivia and me. The weight of his compliments, the heady talk of multi-million-dollar deals, it all seemed so inappropriate given that Olivia had to stand a foot away, trying not to impatiently tap her feet as Eddie showered me with compliments and talked embarrassingly large numbers that I found humiliating considering Olivia was an inescapable audience.

I kept counting down the moments until we could finally flee the premiere, craving some quiet time with Olivia so I could open my heart and show her everything I had waiting inside.

Right now, I felt like every emotion inside me belonged to her.

By the time we were able to finally escape the premiere, Olivia looked like she had been dragged behind me instead of spending the night at my side.

And still we had to suffer through another round of fan photos and autographs. I smiled through all of it, and so did Olivia. She played her role as well as I had ever performed in anything, sticking to my side and supporting me, acting like the girlfriend she wasn't for no other reason than she was a person who kept her commitments.

An honorable woman — who I had accused of being the opposite.

Camera flashes constantly sought her, each snapshot echoing the crowd's adoration for Olivia. Though the camera loved her, the weight of the evening was clear in her tired eyes.

My own yearning was simple: to share a quiet moment with her, to untangle the mess of emotions and words welling up inside me.

We finally exited the theater, but the Rolls Royce had merely been a rental for our arrival at the event, leaving us a limousine packed with Adele, a still overly zealous Eddie, and a handful of studio executives.

Despite the full limo, at least there were no surprised faces when they saw that Olivia and I were still shackled together.

Everyone had something to say:

"Is this a new dating trend? Asking for a friend."

"Is that the ultimate 'clingy' relationship starter pack?"

"Who said chivalry was dead? He's literally attached to her!"

"You finally found a way to keep him from running off, huh?"

"That's one way to avoid the 'he's not really committed' conversation."

"Judging by your grin, I'm guessing that tonight was everything you wanted it to be?" I said to Maggie once the ribbing had finally died down.

"It exceeded every expectation," she said, beaming. "And it's not just about the premiere. Take a look at this."

Then she showed me a video: the missing part of my viral sensation from earlier this year, but instead of me screaming at André, it was the two minutes before the incident happened where he had been bellowing at Adele, reducing the poor woman to tears before I interfered.

"I finally managed to track it down," Maggie announced. "I've been working on it for months now."

"I don't know what to say." My heart was pounding for all the right reasons. "When can we release this?"

"It's already done." Maggie grinned. "So believe me, the handcuffs will be forgotten in no time."

The limousine pulled up to Fisherman's Finest.

We got out, and mercifully there were no paparazzi, but I still couldn't say what I needed to say with the crowds all around us, and onlookers in the lobby, three fellow passengers in the elevator going up to our floor.

I even had to stay silent in the hallway, seeing as we only had a few more steps until we reached our room, where privacy would finally be ours.

But then we opened the door.

THIRTY

Olivia

LYDIA STOOD HUNCHED in the middle of Ryan's hotel room, her slender shoulders slumped in defeat, her usual bright eyes dimmed with I thought looked an awful lot like remorse. She wrung her hands nervously, unable to meet our gazes, despite the reality that she had obviously been waiting for us.

"I'm so sorry," she said in a quivering voice. "I never meant for this foolish stunt to hurt you both so deeply."

She held out a small silver key, and with a trembling hand, she unlocked the cuffs binding us together.

The metallic click echoed sharply in the silent room.

Ryan slowly rotated his wrist, flexing his stiff fingers. An angry red welt circled his skin where the metal had chafed.

I gingerly rubbed my own tender wrist beside him, wincing at the rawness.

Our hands were now free, but a chasm yawned between them. The easy intimacy we had shared vanished along with the handcuffs. I ached at the loss, yearning to bridge the distance.

But the moment didn't feel right. The tender words I had been rehearsing were dead on my lips as the air hung heavy between us, laden with unspoken hurts.

"I hope someday you can forgive this foolish old woman for the pain I've caused." Lydia's eyes brimmed with tears.

And I still didn't quite understand what was happening as Ryan took her hand and gently squeezed it. "It's okay, Lydia. We know your heart was in the right place."

I nodded, managing a small smile. "You meant well."

Lydia blinked back her tears and straightened slightly as she left.

But Maggie was still in the room.

And that meant a gulf was still stretching between us.

A heavy, smothering silence blanketed the room.

Ryan cleared his throat, the sound painfully awkward. "I guess this is it. We're both free to go."

I nodded without meeting his eyes.

But neither of us made a move toward the door.

I still wanted (needed) to be alone with Ryan. We hadn't had a moment to ourselves since before we sat down for the movie.

Since before I met Adele.

Since before I learned the truth about who Ryan Jones really was and always would be, because that version of the movie star was the same as the little boy that I had danced with at the sock hop all of those years ago.

And now there was no reason for him to talk to me.

I had misjudged him, and this was the cost of me being so judgmental.

We just stood there, looking at each other.

"It was nice hanging out with you for the last three days," I said to Ryan.

"It was nice hanging out with you," he repeated.

Surely, he wanted to say more, but Maggie was still standing just a few feet away from us. He opened his mouth, and I could only hope it was to ask her if she could please give us a moment, when instead her phone rang. She raised a finger, asking *us* to give *her* a moment.

Maggie looked at her phone screen, then nodded to herself and turned to Ryan. "Johnston is downstairs in the lobby. He wants to talk."

"Uh oh." Ryan swallowed. "The studio head never wants to talk when it's something good."

"It's good this time. Apparently, you are going to be the lead in *Executioner* for a next summer release?"

"Not exactly." Ryan shook his head. "Eddie and I had a short discussion."

I tried to help. "It was actually a long discussion, but the producer just kept talking and talking and Ryan didn't agree to anything more than listening."

"Thank you, dear. I'm sure I'll be seeing you later," Maggie said to me before turning back to Ryan again. "We need to go."

"Thank you for everything," I said.

I wasn't sure why Maggie had said that she was sure she would be seeing me later, but I hoped that was true. When my gaze met Ryan's, any words of farewell got caught in my throat.

Since I couldn't make the words, I just jangled the handcuffs and said, "Do you mind if I take these as a souvenir?"

"Why would I mind?"

And again, I thought that his words were masking all of the many things that he wanted to say.

We walked down to the lobby together, then I climbed into that same black Audi that had been ferrying Ryan around since he landed in Ocean Springs, then rode home in a miserable blur, sinking deep into the buttery leather seats, resting my head against the window and watching the glowing streetlights slide by through a film of tears.

A sob lodged in my throat, choking me.

As the lights faded behind us, I sunk into despair.

Ryan was a world-famous actor now, far beyond my reach. We came from different worlds. I was just a small-town girl, and he belonged to the glittering realm of Hollywood.

What future could we possibly have?

Even if by some miracle he returned my feelings, a relationship between us could never work. His life was full of luxury hotels, red-carpet premieres, entourages and assistants. Mine was quiet mornings walking dogs along misty trails.

He would grow bored slumming it in my humble world. And I would surely wilt under the glare of the tabloids and paparazzi that hounded his every move.

It was hopeless. However hard it was, I had to let him go. Contacting him now would only reopen the wound. Ryan would be better off forgetting I existed. A clean break was kindest — for both of us.

Halfway home, I could no longer bear it.

"Stop here please," I choked out.

The driver pulled over without question.

I slipped off my glittering heels and stepped out onto the dark, deserted street. The pavement was cool under my bare feet. Above me, the night sky stretched endlessly as I began the walk home.

I moved quietly through the darkness, a shadow in my sweeping gala dress. With my freed hand, I dashed away the endless stream of tears that kept spilling down my cheeks.

I ached to turn back, to run into Ryan's arms and hear the words I had been too afraid to say.

I tiptoed upstairs once home, gently shutting my bedroom door behind me, not wanting Mom to know I was home or see what a mess I had become. Crumpling onto the bed, I buried my face in the pillow as sobs wracked my body.

The door creaked open. Mom rushed in and curled up behind me, cradling me against her. She stroked my hair, gently rocking me as I wept.

"It's heartbreak, honey. I know it hurts. But it will get better."

Her soothing voice was a small comfort, doing little to fill the Ryan-shaped hole carved out of my chest. I would carry this regret forever, like a bruise upon my soul.

Some pains run too deep to fully heal and can only scar over.

This for sure was one of those.

I cried until no more tears would come, until sheer exhaustion claimed me.

Mom held me close until I finally drifted off into a fitful sleep.

But even in slumber, I couldn't escape the aching loneliness for the man I had pushed away.

I WOKE up the next morning with what had to be a migraine. Though I had never had the misfortune of suffering through such a volcanic headache before, I had heard tales of woe from everyone ranging from my mother to Madison, who started getting them shortly after her second child was born.

I went pee (all by myself this time), drank a glass of

water (much easier with both of my hands), and managed to fall right back asleep (all alone in my bed), only waking who knows how long later to what seemed like afternoon sun streaming into my window and Madison sitting at the foot of my bed, petting my leg.

"So I'm guessing my mom called you," I mumbled.

"She did." Madison nodded. "You're still wearing last night's dress."

"So what?"

"So I'm not going through this with you again."

"Going through what?" I asked, as if I didn't know.

"Sweetie, you look even worse than you did after you broke up with Taylor."

"Technically, I didn't break up with Taylor. He broke up with me when he cheated on me."

"This isn't about Taylor," Madison redirected the conversation.

"And what is it about?" But I knew that one, too.

"It's about you liking Ryan," Madison said, in a voice that dared me to challenge her.

"So what? Of course I like Ryan. He's a famous movie star. He's charming and handsome and smart and emotional and kind and caring and considerate and funny and loving and—"

"I get it." Madison reached over and squeezed my hand.

"And I can't stand the thought of living without him," I finished.

"Then what's stopping you from making things right?"

"Maybe the fact that we're not right for each other. Like, at all."

"What makes you say that?"

"His life is back in Los Angeles, and my life is here."

"It doesn't have to be," Madison argued.

"Of course it does. This is where I was born and raised. It's the place I came back to after I left. It's where you live."

"Honey, I have a family. And while I will always love you no matter where you're living, you shouldn't choose your location around me."

"It still doesn't matter." I shook my head, adamant.

"And why not?"

"Because the two of us are obviously not good for each other."

"Are you nuts?" Madison started cackling. "Why on earth would you ever think that?"

"Because we were always going at each other."

"You two were practically strangers and were suddenly handcuffed together. Were you supposed to get along perfectly right from the first minute?"

I didn't answer.

Madison kept going. "You've just proven that the two of you are compatible. You spent days together in hand-cuffs. That's like years in regular dating."

It was a hard truth to confront, but as the words left Madison's mouth, I knew how much I had been lying to myself.

"I know you're right," I told her.

"So what are you going to do about it?"

"Can you take me to the hotel? Right now? So that I can tell Ryan?"

Madison grinned. "I'll race you downstairs."

I bounded out of bed and started toward the door, laughing, but then I stopped dead in my tracks.

"I realize that we should be in a rush here because we don't know when he's headed back to LA. And I can definitely wear the same dress as last night thing, but there's no way I'm leaving this house without brushing my teeth."

"Great idea." Madison nodded while fanning the air in front of her face. "And shame on me for not suggesting it first."

I laughed and dashed into the bathroom.

Two minutes later, I was sitting shotgun in Madison's car.

She raced through three yellow lights on our way to the Fisherman's Finest. It felt like I might pee myself with impatience while we sat through our only two reds.

She dropped me off front, and I ran to the front desk, clumping across the old concrete floor on my way.

"Are you here for Ryan?" the clerk asked, because of course I was.

"Yes!" I exclaimed proudly.

Because, yes, I was there at the Fisherman's Finest Hotel to meet the possible love of my life, famous movie star Ryan Jones.

"I'm so sorry, Ms. Bloom, but Mr. Jones just left for the airport."

"Oh." I was crestfallen. I stared at that polished concrete floor all the way out of the hotel and into the parking garage, where Madison was just getting out of her car to approach the hotel entrance.

"What happened?" she said when she saw me.

"It's nothing," I replied to keep from crying, because of course it was everything.

"What happened?" Madison asked again.

"Ryan already went back to LA."

"That doesn't mean anything."

"It means that he obviously doesn't like me the same way that I like him." I wiped a tear away. "And it means that I guess I'm glad he's gone, because at least he saved me from making a big-fat fool of myself."

That was it. I would spend the rest of my life without

him. Living in my childhood bedroom, sleeping on the bed where I'd apparently tried to snuggle him in my sleep. Showering in the same bathroom where I'd watched him bathe in silhouette and let my imagination run wild. Eating bacon and eggs in the same kitchen where he'd drooled while lecturing me about the evils of saturated fat and eating breakfast at breakfast time.

But at least I still had my full-size Ryan cardboard cut-out.

I burst into tears.

THIRTY-ONE

Ryan

I HAD NEVER FELT SO miserable.

This wasn't plain old sadness or even standard heart-break, which I was no stranger to after my first devastating split from Marsha in middle school. No, this was an ache that permeated every cell, a hollowness that left me gutted.

Even though it had only been a few days.

Maggie sat across from me in the car on our way to the airport, headphones on as she cycled through a series of rapid-fire calls and efficiently crossed items off her lengthy to-do list.

I was glad that my manager was currently too busy for me. All I could think about was Olivia and the wretched state I had left things between us.

I replayed our tense goodbye a thousand times, cursing myself through every one of them. She had every right to resent me after I accused her of betrayal. I should have trusted her, believed in the connection we shared. Instead I had lashed out, pushing Olivia away instead of pulling her closer, and right when I realized the depth of my feelings.

It wasn't just my shyness that stopped me, paralyzing as

it was. Olivia had made it (repeatedly) clear that she wanted nothing whatsoever to do with me.

Now any chance to make things right had slipped through my fingers.

Not that it mattered anymore. I had to forget Olivia, forget the hope of ever experiencing the intoxicating taste of her lips on mine. She clearly didn't reciprocate my feelings. And now I would have to live with that rejection slowly eating away at me like a disease.

For the rest of my life.

I glanced at Maggie, still engrossed in her work. I needed to talk to someone who knew me, who understood heartbreak.

Before I could second guess myself anymore, I pulled out my phone and dialed Lucas. He picked up on the second ring.

"Dude, you need to meet me in Washington. This location is epic."

"Tell me about it," I said.

"Whoa, you sound like somebody brought your puppy back to life just so they could run it over again. I bet that hearing all about my location scouting adventure is like the last thing that you want to do right now. What happened with Olivia at the premiere last night?"

"Nothing good."

"Don't tell me that the event was a bomb…"

"The premiere was amazing, but I never got a real moment alone with Olivia after the movie started. Between the crowds, applause, and after-party schmoozing, privacy was impossible. Even handcuffed together, it didn't matter — there were always people vying for our attention. And then Maggie kicked her out because Johnston flew in to talk to me."

I rubbed my temples as too many emotions swelled in

my chest. "I should have asked Maggie for just five minutes alone with Olivia so I could lay my heart bare, tell her how I really felt. How much I cared for her. But the moment slipped away, and now I'll have to live with that regret. Then again, I deserve to feel this way after what I did to her, but it's still killing me."

"What you did to her?" Lucas repeated. "Dude, don't be so hard on yourself. And start giving Olivia some benefit of the doubt. How do you know she wouldn't understand? Have you had this conversation with her?"

"I just told you that talking to her was impossible."

"Well then, why are you assuming that there's nothing for you guys to work out now? You like Olivia, right?"

"Of course I like her."

"Well maybe it's like Jurassic Park."

"How is my relationship with Olivia anything like Jurassic Park?"

"Instead of 65 million years in the making, it's been 20. But you've known her all your life."

"Maybe," I said, not really getting the analogy. "But her life is in Ocean Springs, and I live in Los Angeles."

"Dude, that is some seriously weak sauce that you're drizzling on this argument. You don't have to live in Los Angeles. In case you forgot, you're like stupid rich now. You can literally live anywhere in the world. And Ocean Springs is a one-hour flight away from Los Angeles anyway."

"Even so, I still don't think that we're good for one another."

"You don't think, or you don't know?" Lucas asked.

"I don't know. Mostly, I don't really think that she likes me in that way."

Lucas laughed. "Okay, dude, you're using a lot of words like 'think.' So I'm thinking that it really sounds like you need to give Olivia a call. If she survived being hand-cuffed to you for three months—"

"It wasn't three months, it was—"

Lucas ignored me. "Then surely she likes you."

"Maybe you're right," I said, but I was in far too much pain to pontificate any further. "Tell me all about your location scouting."

I tried to change the subject, but Lucas wasn't having it.

"No way, bro. I'll tell you all about it after you call me back and let me know how your next conversation with Olivia goes."

"Fair deal." I laughed, somehow shocked to realize that I felt just a little bit better already.

We ended the call, and my gaze drifted back to Maggie. Her concentration was unwavering, fingers moving deftly across her tablet with startling efficiency. But I was glad to see her so occupied. It meant I could think.

I still wasn't ready to call Olivia, despite cradling the phone in my hand and seriously considering dialing her number several times.

What if I apologized and she still hated me?

What if I had to live with the fact that Olivia Bloom loathed me?

For the rest of my life?

I considered what Lucas had said, because of course he was right; of course it was time to face my fears and doubts.

My thumb hovered over Olivia's name, and I was about to make the leap when the phone buzzed in my hand, six times in rapid succession as my messages filled with a half-dozen photos from Lucas that I had not seen before.

They were a lot like his last batch Lucas, except that in

this one, Olivia was smiling adoringly at me instead of the other way around, her gaze lingering on me with an unmistakable affection.

These weren't manufactured moments, no artful positioning of the camera or rehearsed smiles. Every frame was raw and unfiltered, and it yanked at my heartstrings.

I pulled the key to mine and Olivia's ill-fated handcuffs out of my pocket and held it between my fingers, studying the only artifact of our time together.

Olivia had taken the handcuffs as a souvenir, but I had claimed the key, knowing it was a memento that I would never get rid of, no matter what happened between us the next time we spoke.

I wondered if I could turn it into a piece of jewelry, maybe a necklace I could wear under my shirt to keep her close to my heart. Or—

I stopped, shocked by what I was seeing on the key. Surprised, but then delighted by what it might all mean.

"Stop the car!" I shouted to the driver.

Maggie finally looked over at me.

"I'm going to need a second," she said to whoever was on the other side of her call then turned back to me. "What's happening here?"

I showed her the key. "This."

"The handcuff key? I don't get it. What am I actually looking at?"

I tossed her the key. "I need to check on something. I'll join you back in LA."

The driver pulled over to the side of the road. "Is this good, Mr. Jones?"

"Perfect," I said, getting out of the car.

"Are you sure about this?" Maggie asked.

"I've never been more sure of anything in my life," I

replied, then slammed the Audi door and started on my long walk back to Ocean Springs.

I made it about a mile down the road before an old Dodge Caravan pulled over a few paces in front of me. Then the door slid open to family of four, with dad behind the wheel and mom sitting shotgun, a set of siblings sitting in the middle seat with the boy and girl both staring at me, just as gobsmacked as their parents that they were looking at Ryan Jones in the flesh, just walking down the street like a regular person.

"You headed back to Ocean Springs?" asked the dad.

"We'd be happy to take you," offered the mom.

"Do you really know how to fly a plane?" the boy wanted to know.

"Did you and Lucas Stone really use to live in a house together?" asked the girl.

I answered all of them, making eye contact with each one of the family members in turn as I addressed their individual questions.

"Yes, I'm headed back to Ocean Springs and I appreciate the offer for a ride." I climbed into the back seat. "I do know how to fly a plane, and I did live with Lucas Stone, who is still one of my best friends."

The brother and sister — Jeremy and Sydney — argued over who got to shut the door, both of them losing when Mom (Sheila) leaned back and closed it for them. Then Dad (Jackson) pulled back onto the road.

The ride back to Ocean Springs was full laughter. Jeremy and Sydney fired incessant rounds of questions at me, wanting to know all about my adventures making movies around the world while hanging on my every word. Jackson and Sheila kept apologizing for their overly inquisitive children while acting like they weren't just as curious.

But they were kind enough to not only let me a hitch a

ride back into Ocean Springs, they were patient with me while driving through Lydia's neighborhood in search of her house.

Not only had many years passed since my last visit to Lydia's, I was a child the last time, and so a labyrinth of time had clouded my memory. Once-familiar streets kept playing tricks on my mind, twisting and turning in unfamiliar patterns. I kept searching for a glimmer of recognition as Jackson kept weaving through (what had to be) Lydia's neighborhood, hoping to glimpse something familiar enough to trigger a cascade of memories.

After twenty minutes I began to feel foolish, even though no one in the almost obnoxiously friendly family seemed to be in any hurry whatsoever for me to find the place. But still, Lydia had a flare for drama and was sometimes a chameleon when it came to her fashion choices. So what were the odds that she had reinvented her home's facade in the last few years? A fresh coat of paint in a hue I wouldn't recognize, a revamped exterior?

Surely that was likely.

But I didn't want to call ahead of time or give her a heads up that I was coming. I needed to see Lydia's reaction and feel the truth as I looked her in the eyes and asked about the stunt she had so obviously pulled.

"That's it," I shouted when I finally recognized the house.

I didn't remember her home being at the end of a quiet cul-de-sac, or maybe I didn't even know what a cul-de-sac was, but there was no doubt that I had the right house once I saw it. Lydia's house still exuded that same artistic flair. Victorian-era architecture, with intricate woodwork and a wraparound porch, painted in a soft shade of lavender, with ivy creeping lovingly around the base and climbing up toward the dormer windows. The garden was a riot of colors, with blossoming flowers placed like audience members applauding Lydia on her walk to the front door, where wind chimes hung from the eaves to tickle the salty breeze.

"Thanks for the ride!" I gave the family a wave as I got out of the Caravan. "You guys were a lot of fun!"

Sheila: "Sorry the kids asked so many questions."

Jackson: "My number is in your phone. You ever need a ride while in Ocean Springs, I'll drive you anywhere you need to go."

Jeremy: "Can we make a TikTok real quick?"

"No, you can't make a TikTok!" Jackson and Sheila replied in unison.

"Tell Lucas I said hi!" Sydney cried out.

"I will!" I promised while closing the Caravan door.

Lydia's front door was open before I got there. She looked at me in surprise. "I thought you went home to LA."

"I was on the way, but then I realized something and needed to come back here to ask you."

"What did you want to ask me?"

But I could tell from the look in her eyes that she knew.

"You never lost the key to our handcuffs. That was all a ruse."

"A ruse?" Her face was unreadable. "Why do you think that?"

"That's not a denial, and I know you. Thinking back, I can see what a performance you were giving, the way you were pretending to look for the key. But I'm still embarrassed that I fell for it. I imagine you got everyone involved?"

Lydia said nothing.

"We weren't keeping the theater manager. She planned

to stay late that night while you pretended to frantically look, right?"

This time Lydia answered. "How did you know?"

"Your 'new' key had the same little groove in its side as the original."

"I'm sorry. Yes, you're right, I did have the key all along."

Lydia's gaze dropped, avoiding mine. "I've seen you two grow up, watched both of you dance around the feelings I always suspected you shared for each other. When I had the chance to create a situation where you two would be forced to spend time together, well … I took it."

"But using handcuffs? And deceiving us both?" My voice dithered between hurt and exasperation.

She sighed heavily, her shoulders drooping. "I know it sounds absurd, and perhaps even invasive. But Olivia's been struggling lately, feeling lost and out of place after coming back home. And seeing you, the boy who's always had a soft spot for her, successful and thriving, I thought maybe if I could bring you two together, that you would find some sort of solace in each other."

"So dramatic," I said, trying to lighten the moment. "You could have just told me, Lydia. Played matchmaker the old-fashioned way."

She met my gaze with a vulnerable glint in her eyes. "Would you have listened? Or would you have brushed it off?"

I would have brushed it off.

But I couldn't admit that out loud yet.

"I know it was wrong, but sometimes the heart makes us do crazy things. I just wanted to see you both happy. And I thought that happiness might be with each other."

A complicated broth of emotions bubbled within me, but at the forefront was a realization. Perhaps Lydia's methods were unorthodox, but her heart was in the right place. And even though I felt deceived, I couldn't overlook the undeniable connection I had rediscovered with Olivia during our forced time together.

Maybe Olivia didn't share the depths of my feelings, but there was an unmistakable spark in her eyes whenever our gazes met. Each stolen glance, each lingering touch was like an unspoken word, promising something deeper, and real.

But the weight of uncertainty, coupled with the potential embarrassment if I had misread the signs, made me hesitate every single time.

Now, after Lydia's unexpected intervention, the surge of emotions within me felt too intense for further restraint.

It didn't matter how much the shame and embarrassment, or my shyness, might threaten me.

I had no choice but to make my confession.

"It's okay," I said to Lydia, "I'm not mad. I really do like Olivia. A lot."

"Then tell her. Do you know how to get to her house from here?"

"I absolutely do."

"Then you should go and see about a girl."

I grinned as I turned around and started running.

"Call me later and tell me everything," Lydia called after me.

"I will!" I yelled back as I ran even faster.

I dashed toward Helen's house, my thoughts racing even faster than my feet, playing scenarios like scenes in my mind as I prepped my confessions.

I didn't stop running until I got there.

I knocked on the door three times before she answered.

"Ryan Jones," Helen said with a wide smile.

"Is Olivia home?" I smiled back.

"She's not." She shook her head. "And hate to tell you that I'm not sure where she is."

"I have an idea — I'll let you know if I find her!"

Then I turned around and ran toward where I suddenly felt sure that Olivia would be.

"Make this kiss a classic!" Helen yelled after me.

I pushed past the stitch in my side as the gentle lapping of waves held the promise of not just a confession but a shared future.

If I was right about the reason for the feeling of a rocket ship launching in my heart.

And even though my side was splitting, once I saw Olivia again, the pain would all be worth it.

THIRTY-TWO

Olivia

I SAT at my favorite spot on the beach, slowly savoring an ice cream cone that, while tasty, was lackluster compared to the delectable frozen treats I could have crafted myself.

With each lick, I found my thoughts drifting back to Ryan, reminiscing over our time together as I created those small batch delights we both enjoyed.

Before I'd ruined everything between us with my childish outbursts, judgmental attitude, and quickness to assume the worst of him.

Now Ryan was back in the glitz and glamour of Hollywood where he belonged, while I remained here, anchored to the familiar shores of Ocean Springs. My heart ached, heavy with regret, longing for what might have been if only I had opened both my eyes and heart a little wider.

But dwelling on could-have-beens served zero purpose. I needed to look forward, focusing on the bright spots waiting on the horizon. There was so much to feel hopeful about, so many promising opportunities in my future that had nothing to do with Ryan Jones.

I would move on and move forward.

Like the impossibly exciting prospect of turning my passion for crafting artisanal frozen treats into an actual business. Maybe awesome ice cream maker really could be my job.

Ashleigh had been so impressed with the small-batch ice creams I created for *Cold Fury*'s premiere event that she was eager to feature my wares on a regular basis at The Family Table.

I initially assumed her enthusiasm was an attempt to cheer me up in the aftermath of my disastrous non-relationship with Ryan. But Ashleigh was adamant that my unique frozen creations could be a real draw for her restaurant. She couldn't stop raving about the depth of flavors, the unexpected ingredient combinations, and the exceptionally smooth, creamy texture.

According to Ashleigh, my spicy chai ice cream had been the talk of the post-premiere reception. Her patrons were already begging to know when more of my distinctive frozen delights would be available.

I would start to formalize my flavors, play with branding ideas, and source my ingredients from local farms and purveyors.

Potential brimmed within me, sweet and cold as a scoop of my homemade gelato, clever name pending. My future was a blank page I could fill with flavor, no longer dependent on the movie star who slipped away.

"You have no idea how much of this ice cream I could sell," Ashleigh had gushed.

The more I contemplated her proposition, the more thrilled I became by the prospect of producing small batch ice creams to be featured on the menu at The Family Table.

Ryan was right — I was highly creative, constantly conjuring up new flavor combinations and innovations. Ice cream was the perfect medium for me to fully exercise my limitless imagination.

I could experiment with unexpected ingredients, layer textures, and blend flavors in endless permutations. The potential felt deliciously boundless.

Supplying Ashleigh would only be the beginning. My mind was already churning with grand possibilities for my future ice cream endeavors.

I had even landed on a name for my potential business venture: Tea-riffic Ice Cream. The playful moniker felt catchy yet classic, evoking a sense of nostalgia and summertime reverie.

I slowly finished the last bites of an utterly average cone from the aging ice cream shack down the road. The decades-old joint had been barely scraping by for years, just managing to stay afloat each season.

As I swallowed the last chalky mouthful, I found myself contemplating the precarious fate of the dilapidated shop. Perhaps after yet another lackluster summer, the weary owners would decide to shutter its doors permanently. Maybe I could make an offer to take over their lease and transform the space into a charming locale for Tea-riffic Ice Cream.

My modest savings could just cover the initial investment if I was thrifty.

Or maybe the current owners would consider taking on an enthusiastic new business partner, someone eager to breathe new life into the operation. I could overhaul the menu, spruce up the dated seaside decor, and give the place a much-needed facelift.

Lost in thought, I glanced up and noticed a vibrant

cerulean kite swooping gracefully overhead. It danced through the air, dipping and darting with the breeze. The vivid color was sharp in a crispy blue sky that looked like a piece of the ocean itself had taken flight.

The sight brought a wistful smile to my lips, reminding me of the blustery afternoon Ryan and I had spent together here, with the wind pulling wildly at our kite strings and fate pulling at our heart strings now that I was willing to admit it.

He had confessed it was his first time flying one, sharing how he'd always longed for a kite as a child after watching a little girl flying her own not far from here.

A little girl who just happened to be me, all those years ago.

Our shared memory from this very spot felt strangely fated.

If only I hadn't ruined everything with my rash judgment, petty outbursts, and failure to trust Ryan when it mattered most.

If only I had mustered the courage to apologize once I realized my mistake, before the damage was irreparable.

Perhaps we could have found our way back to each other. Talked through the misunderstandings and given that undeniable spark between us a real chance to grow.

But it was too late now. Whatever potential existed had crumbled in the aftermath of thoughtless words and false accusations.

Now Ryan was back in Hollywood, resuming his cushy, glamorous life I had been so quick to judge and so foolishly quick to discard.

I rose from my spot in the grass and ambled toward the swooping kite, curious to get a better look at the faceless figure maneuvering it in the distance. As I drew nearer, I realized with a jolt that the silhouette belonged to none other than Ryan Jones himself.

My heart stuttered in my chest.

What was he doing here?

Wasn't he supposed to be on a plane bound for LA by now?

"Ryan? Is that you?"

Of course it was.

My pulse pounded as I closed the remaining distance between us.

Ryan looked windswept but happy, his cheeks flushed from the sea breeze. He gave the kite strings a gentle tug to keep it dancing gracefully overhead.

"What are you doing here?" I called out, wanting to run but barely able to walk another love-stricken step. "Aren't you supposed to be in LA?"

Not that I was questioning fate.

"I can't go back to Los Angeles. Not yet."

"Why not?" I desperately hoped that I knew the answer to that one.

"Because I need to tell you something."

"What do you need to tell me?" I asked, daring to hope.

"I wanted to tell you about Lydia."

Lydia? "What about her? Is everything okay with the theater?"

"The theater has never been better." Ryan offered me his Hollywood smile and melted every part of me. "She never lost the key."

"Wait … what? She pretended to lose it on purpose?"

"She was trying to play matchmaker. She hoped that us being stuck together would … spark something."

I let out an incredulous laugh, shaking my head in

disbelief. Our former teacher's dramatic scheme seemed absurd yet oddly touching.

"I wanted you to know the truth before I left."

"Well … I appreciate you telling me."

An awkward silence swelled between us.

The kite dipped and swayed overhead, still a vivid spot of color against the empty blue.

My thoughts felt just as unmoored.

I stared down at my hands, lost for words as I drew a deep breath of the briny air.

"Is that the only reason you came back?"

"No." Ryan shook his head, his expression growing serious. "There was something else I wanted to tell you."

"What?" I smiled. "Are you waiting for a script?"

"No," Ryan laughed. "I would never want anyone to write this down for me." He took a step closer, his eyes never leaving mine. "I came back to tell you … that I think I'm … I want to apologize for ever making you feel—"

I placed a hand on his arm, stopping him. "You don't need to. I understand now why you did what you did. I'm sorry I didn't give you the benefit of the doubt. And I'm sorry that I said such terrible things."

But still there was something he needed to say.

I smiled, my vision blurred with tears. Happy tears, sad tears, I didn't know. Not yet. "You don't have to be shy with me, Ryan."

Relief flashed across his face.

Then he swallowed and said, "I think I'm falling in love with you, Olivia."

"You think?" I managed to whisper despite losing my breath.

"I know that I am completely, totally, head over heels in love with you. I've never felt this way about anyone before, Olivia."

His expression washed over me, warm and dizzying. Hardly daring to believe this was real, I searched his face for any hint of doubt or humor.

But his gaze was unwavering, brimming with affection.

"How do you know for sure?" I pressed, still struggling to accept that someone like Ryan could have genuine feelings for an ordinary girl like me.

"That's easy." His smile widened. "I have at least 101 reasons."

"101," I repeated. "Is that a specific answer?"

He somehow smiled even wider and shrugged again. "When you get as rich and famous as me, numbers sort of lose their meaning. I don't even know how much I pay for bean bags." He paused, then added, "And…"

"And what?" I asked, not sure what else could even be said.

"And I wanted to do this." Ryan leaned closer, the same way he had as when we were in the classroom, when we were so close to each other that we had almost kissed. I felt his fingertips on the small of my back.

My heart raced as he pulled me closer.

And then his lips met mine.

Every ounce of doubt, every moment of pain, was swept away by the heady rush of love and longing surging between us.

Until we finally pulled away.

I pulled out the cuffs from my pocket, slapped one onto Ryan's wrist, and the other one onto mine. Although this time I let him keep his right hand free.

"What did you do that for?" Ryan asked in shock.

"It's fine." I laughed. "You still have the key, right?"

"Nope." He shook his head, but he wasn't smiling so widely this time. "It's headed back to LA with Maggie."

We stared at each other for a long while after that.

Then I broke our silence yet again. "I guess this time I don't care at all."

"Me neither," he shrugged.

We kissed again.

And we didn't stop until nothing on the silver screen could rival our radiant glow.

THIRTY-THREE

Olivia

SEVERAL WEEKS HAD PASSED by in a blissful blur since Ryan and I had traded our mutual confessions of love on the windswept beach. Tea-riffic Ice Cream was now a cheerful fixture across from the sandy shore, thanks to a smart partnership with the tired owners. A newly fashioned sign beckoned tourists and locals alike with a retro logo I designed myself.

I leaned against the smooth counter, absently licking a spoonful of my latest experimental flavor — a sweet medley of vanilla custard swirled with shards of toffee and ribbons of salted caramel.

Ryan stood behind the counter, cheerfully scooping our signature earl grey and ginger ice cream for an eager young couple. His eyes crinkled happily as he handed them their waffle cones.

"Enjoy!"

My heart warmed as I watched him. Hard to believe this down-to-earth guy joyfully dishing up cones was the same brooding movie star I'd once dismissed as an egomaniac.

As the door chimed shut behind the couple, Ryan sauntered over to me, planting a frosty kiss on my lips.

"Mmmm, that's delicious! New flavor?"

I grinned. "Just a little something I'm calling Candy Cuffs."

Ryan threw his head back and laughed. "Two thumbs up."

Then his phone interrupted us.

"Let me guess," I said. "It's Lucas."

"Of course, it's Lucas."

"Dude." His face appeared on Ryan's phone. "You ever heard of a place called Canyon Springs?"

"Nope. Are you inviting me to a day spa?"

"I'm inviting you to come and check this place out with me. It's where we're for sure shooting my first movie."

"You've made a bunch of movies," I interrupted.

"Hi Olivia!" Lucas waved, then explained. "This is my first movie as a producer. You and Ryan should totally come and visit me here."

"It's a date!" I chirped. "Just text me the details and I'll make sure we're there."

"So I guess we'll see you at the day spa," Ryan said.

"Location of my first produced movie," Lucas corrected.

"I've gotta go. Olivia wants me to taste her candy cuffs."

"What—"

But Ryan hung up the phone.

And our lips met in a slowly blissful kiss.

No matter how many times we came together, that intoxicating rush remained.

Eventually we broke apart, faces flushed, pulses racing in tandem.

Ryan trailed kisses along my jawline, nipping gently at my earlobe.

"Ready for that taste test now?" he murmured.

My heart skipped a beat. "Always."

Twenty minutes later, we were closing up shop, then walking home together, hand in hand as the credits were rolling on this chapter, with our love story just getting started. It looked like I would be hooked on Hollywood forever.

The End

What to read next

About The Author

Mia Summers is a sucker for love. There's nothing she likes better than snuggling up in a soft fleecy blanket with a hot cup of cocoa and an even sweeter romance to read the night away. Especially if she's reading about Hollywood heartthrobs or hunky hockey players. But after telling her best friend one too many times how she would have written the most recent novel, her friend blurted out, "Well then, why don't you write your own romance novels?" And that is exactly what Mia did.

www.ingramcontent.com/pod-product-compliance
Lightning Source LLC
Chambersburg PA
CBHW010536100726
47903CB00011B/3025